THE GUNS OF PRESCOTT

THE CROCKETTS' WESTERN SAGA: 11

ROBERT VAUGHAN

Paperback Edition

This book is a work of fiction. Any references to historical events, real people or real places are used fictitiously. Other names, characters, places and events are products of the author's imagination, and any resemblance to actual events, places or persons, living or dead, is entirely coincidental.

Published in the United States by Wolfpack Publishing, Las Vegas

Wolfpack Publishing
5130 S. Fort Apache Road 215-380
Las Vegas, NV 89148
wolfpackpublishing.com

Paperback ISBN 978-1-64734-764-2
eBook ISBN 978-1-64734-763-5

THE GUNS OF PRESCOTT

Chapter One

"Are you sure you have to go?" Sara Sue Sanders asked as she put a piece of hot apricot pie in front of Gid Crockett.

"You and your sister are making it hard to leave," Gid said, "but you know Will. Once he makes up his mind, there's no changing it."

"I thought both of us had decided we want to get out of Texas," Will said. He rubbed his shoulder, which was recovering from a recent gunshot wound.

"Look at my big brother," Gid said. "Do you see me complaining about my leg? I was hurt a lot worse than he was, but no, it's Will who said we need to go to California. To just be lazy for a while."

"I think it will be good for both of you," Millie Jean Sanders said as she sat down at the table beside Will. "The folks in Tilden will be grateful to you two from now on. Cleaning out the Felton gang was something that needed to be done."

"I'm glad we were able to help, but in all the scrapes we've been in over the years, I think that was the first time both of us got shot," Gid said as he took a bite of his pie. "I guess I want to see the ocean, too, so it's not all Will's doing."

"I wish I was going with you," Sara Sue said as she put her hand on Gid's shoulder.

"Oh, no you don't," Millie Jean said. "Will and Gid made it possible for us to leave our old life behind, and now we have to make this store the best pie shop in Cotulla."

"I think you've already done that," Gid said. "What else have you got?" He put his fork down and looked toward the pie safe.

"Oh, no. Not another one," Will said. "The train should be here within an hour, and I want to make sure the horses are well fed and watered before we board them."

"Well, you're not leaving here without a hug," Millie Jean said as her eyes began to fill with tears.

"Now, none of that," Gid said as he pushed back from the table. "You know we'll be back."

"I know, but you both mean a lot to my sister and me," Millie Jean said as hugs were given and final goodbyes were spoken.

The brothers took their leave of the two young women,

then hurried down to the livery stable to get their horses.

"They seem to be doing very well," Gid said.

"Yes," Will replied. "I'm glad we could help them out, and I'm glad you had the idea."

Will and Gid had met Millie Jean and Sara Sue Sanders back in Tilden, Texas. Unlike most women who had grown hard by plying the trade of soiled doves, there was a softness and a sweetness about the sisters.

When Millie Jean learned that their stepfather had raped Sara Sue when she was only fourteen, Millie Jean took her little sister and ran away. She tried to provide for both of them by picking up one job and then another, but eventually as a last resort, she went on the line. She tried to protect Sara Sue from the same fate, but eventually Sara Sue became a prostitute as well. Will and Gid learned of their story and were moved to help the young women escape the world's oldest profession. The pie shop was the result of their donation.

Will and Gid changed trains in San Antonio, then started the long trip west. They were two days leaving Texas, and just before they left the state, a very pretty young woman boarded the train. She didn't look to be over eighteen or nineteen, and an older woman, who Gid presumed to be her mother, got on the train with her, but left the train before it departed the station. The young woman sat alone in the front seat of the car.

Their route took them through a corner of Indian Territory and Colorado, then crossed into New Mexico. At one stop, a young man boarded the train. He was wearing a low-crowned black hat with a silver hatband, a red shirt, and a string tie. His pistol hung low, and there was a look of arrogance about him.

When he saw the young woman sitting alone, the man sat beside her, even though there were other empty seats. Gid watched the interplay between them. It appeared that red shirt was making advances toward young woman, unwanted advances from the looks of her body language. After a few minutes she got up and changed seats, and she had no more than sat down, when red shirt moved to her seat, and again sat beside her.

They were too far away for Gid to be able to hear their conversation, but he did hear the girl say "no" a few times, each response more animated than the previous response.

Gid stood up.

"Are you sure you want to do this?" Will asked.

"You saw what happened," Gid said. "She's tried three times to get rid of that son of a bitch. What if it was our sister? Wouldn't you want to do something?"

"We don't have a sister."

"I know, but if we did."

Will chuckled. "Put on your shining armor, Gid."

Gid walked up the aisle until he reached the seat where the young girl was sitting.

"No, please, leave me alone," he heard the girl say.

"I'm not a' goin' nowhere 'till you give me a kiss," the man in the red shirt said.

Gid stepped up to them. "Leave my sister alone."

"What?"

"You heard me. This is my sister. Now, find another seat. Better yet, find another car."

"You've got no right to tell me to leave this car," the man in the red shirt said.

"Have you ever heard the expression might makes right?" Gid asked.

"No. What does that mean?"

"It means you either find another car, or I'll make you find another train."

"That's crazy. How are you going to make me find another train?"

"By throwing you off this one."

The man in the red shirt looked at Gid for a moment, and after taking measure of him, nodded.

"I didn't know she was your sister. I'll . . . uh, I'll find another car."

Gid watched the man leave, then looked down at the young woman.

"Are you all right, Miss?"

"Yes, sir," the young woman said. "Thanks to you. Do you mind if I sit across the aisle from you, and the man with you? I think I would feel safer."

"The man with me would be my brother."

"Then I guess as I'm your sister, he would be my brother too," she said with a broad smile.

Will looked up to see Gid and the young lady approaching.

"I see that the man in the red shirt left," Will said.

"He decided he would rather ride in a different car," Gid said

The girl laughed. "After a little persuasion," she said. "My name is Lucinda. Lucinda Boyd. But of course, you would already know that, seeing as how I'm your sister."

"What?" Will asked.

"Well, you might say it was a matter of expediency," Lucinda said.

"Don't ask," Gid said with a little laugh.

"Where are you headed, Lucinda?"

"I'm going to Albuquerque. My mother seems to think I need to go to a finishing school."

At the next stop, Will saw the man in the red shirt leave the train.

"I don't think you'll have to worry about your unwelcome seat companion anymore, Miss Boyd. He just got off the train," Will said.

"He's probably decided this was an easier way to change trains, than the way I suggested," Gid said.

Lucinda laughed out loud, then covered her mouth. "Oh, excuse me, that wasn't very lady-like of me."

"Well, that's why you're going to finishing school isn't it? To learn to be a lady?" Gid asked.

Lucinda laughed again.

Eight hours later, when Lucinda left the train in Albuquerque, she remained on the platform, waving to Will and Gid as the train pulled out of the station.

"Too bad we lost Miss Boyd," Gid said. "Her conversation made the time pass quickly."

Will laughed. "You do know we're going to be on this train for a few more days."

"Oh yes, now tell me again why we're going to California."

Several miles west, and somewhat south of the Atlantic and Pacific rail line, "Colonel" Jubal Sandos stood before eleven men known as the Prescott Defenders. Because they were wearing uniforms and standing at rigid attention in a platoon-sized formation, one might assume that this was an element of the US Army from near-by Fort Whipple, but that would be an incorrect assumption. The Prescott Defenders were a vigilante group that had been formed in the capital city of the Arizona Territory.

It was Sandos' idea that the men would wear military uniforms and be as structured as an army unit. Sandos had appointed himself to the rank of colonel, a rank he had once legitimately held with the U.S. Army. The vigilante group was not associated in any way with the local sheriff's department, with whom they were at odds, but drew their authority as deputies of the court appointed by Judge Andrew Briggs. That authority included the right to sustain their economic base by assessing and collecting taxes from the various entities in and around Prescott.

"Gentlemen, I want Cokeberry and Vestal to make the rounds on Montezuma Street, Snow and Coates—you take Granite Street, and if I hear of you two stepping into even one crib, I'll withhold your pay for a month, do you hear me?"

"You don't have to worry about us, Colonel," Ike Snow said. "We like the women at the Palace. Them's high class whores."

"I'm just saying, that's all. Dawes, you and Newman take Gurley, and Evans and Crawford—you go down Goodwin."

"What about me?" Amos Chapman asked.

"I want you to ride out and hit all the mines. Are there any questions?"

"No sir," all eleven men answered in unison.

"Then go collect the taxes," Jubal Sandos said as he

abruptly turned to enter the building behind him.

After giving his orders, Sandos stepped back into the building occupied by the Prescott Defenders. The building, which Sandos referred to as the "headquarters" was on the corner of Gurley and Cortez Streets right across the street from the courthouse. On the wall inside the headquarters building was a detailed map of Prescott, with every business establishment annotated with the owners' names, as well as the names of all of their employees.

As Sandos sat behind his desk, he heard the men out front, detailing how they would divide up their assigned routes to collect the taxes.

"Vestal," Jonas Cokeberry called out to Roy Vestal. "We got Whiskey Row. If we don't get a move on, we won't be but half done by nightfall."

"I'm ready," Vestal replied with a broad grin.

Whiskey Row referred to the forty saloons that stood side-by-side on Montezuma Street.

The others of the platoon separated to go on their own missions, which had been assigned by Sandos.

The first business Jonas and Roy entered was the Plaza Bit Saloon. Stepping up to the bar, Roy ordered whiskey.

"You'd better make that a beer," Jonas said. "We should hit at least fifteen or twenty of these today 'n if you drink a whiskey at ever' one o' 'em, you're goin' to be drunk as a skunk before noon."

"Yeah," Roy replied with a smile. "I want a beer," he said to the bartender. Then as his smile broadened, he added, "a *free* beer."

"I know, I know," the bartender said. "First drink of the day is free to anyone belongin' to the Prescott Defenders."

"You got your tax ready?" Jonas asked.

"Ten dollars," the bartender said, handing Jonas the money. "Listen, you need to talk to Sandos. My boss says ten dollars a week is too much."

"We quit chargin' you a dollar a day extra for each girl you've got," Jonas said. "Anyhow, you get a lot of the money back when we come visit the ladies. You should just be thankful we don't ask for a free poke."

As the men of the Prescott Defenders were making their calls on the businesses in town, Ed Bower, Sheriff of Yavapai County, and who had his office in Prescott, was visiting with Judge Andrew Briggs.

"Judge, I know you've deputized all the Prescott Defenders, but they are little more than hoodlums themselves. I think you should un-deputize them."

"Ed, you've only got one deputy and there's no way you and Jimmie Burns can police the entire county by yourselves. You've got to admit, the Defenders provide a big service to Prescott and this whole county. They've brought in cattle rustlers, horse thieves, and even murderers. You just ask the big mine owners what they would do without them. How many times have they gone along beside an ore wagon when it had to get to Ash Fork or Maricopa to meet the train?"

"I'll agree, sometimes they do some good things," Ed said.

"I'd think you'd be thankful for them, especially since you don't have to pay them one penny for what they do."

"Maybe they aren't taking anything from my budget, but they are bleeding the town dry," Sheriff Bower said, "and you know it."

"I've not heard one complaint from any business in the whole county."

"No, and you aren't likely to hear anything, because Jubal Sandos has everybody too scared to complain."

"If lawlessness were to suddenly break out in the county, I mean more than you and Burns could handle, and we didn't have the Prescott Defenders, we both would be receiving lots of complaints. I think we are in position where we have to take the bad with the good."

Chapter Two

Kurt Beaumont stood out in front of the Axis Mine holding his hands on his hips, looking at the work that had kept him busy all day. He picked up one more board and with a charred stick marked the words, keep out. Then he nailed it to the barrier he had placed over the entrance to his mine.

Looking down the gulch, he saw several makeshift shelters belonging to those men who had chosen the placer route along Lynx Creek. In hindsight, Kurt should have stuck with placer mining, but he thought he could find a vein where the gold had come from originally. Within an easy ride from this spot were the Accidental, the Pointer, the Box Elder, the Big Gun, and the Jersey Lily, all lode mines that were taking out good color every week. Nobody had hit a real bonanza, but it had been several months since the Axis had shown anything.

But now, Kurt had run out of capital. He tried to find a partner that would go in with him, but no one in Prescott had confidence that the Axis was a promising mine. It was a hard decision, but he had decided to go back home to New Orleans to see his ma and pa, find a job to pick up a little operating capital, and in six months to a year, he would return and show the naysayers that the Axis had more to give.

Kurt climbed down the mountain to a flat area where Woman had helped him erect a shelter for himself, and a corral for his burro. He looked to the left where almost hidden in the pine trees, he saw her wickiup. For a moment, he felt guilty leaving her alone in this place, but she could take care of herself. He wished that he knew her name, but he did not.

Woman was a Yavapai Indian who had refused to go to the Apache Reservation at San Carlos when her tribe had been ordered to leave. Even though Prescott was less than ten miles away, Kurt didn't think she had ever gone to the community. She subsisted mainly on game and wild plants, but Kurt had introduced her to some of the pleasures available to civilized societies. He gathered up the last of his dried fruit and a tin of honey to take to her. In addition, he had some horehound candy that he would give her.

Picking up a gutta-percha bag that contained the few

traces of gold he had found in the past year, he pulled the skin door back and left his home. He hoped he could convert the gold into enough money to get him all the way to New Orleans.

"Woman," Kurt called out when he approached the skin-covered wickiup.

A wizened old lady of indeterminate age, stepped through the opening. She smiled when she saw him, but she made no sound.

"I've brought you some vittles," he said. At one time he had tried to teach her some English, and now he was sorry he hadn't spent more time with her. "I'm going to be leaving for a while," he continued. He made motions with his fingers indicating that he would be going down the mountain. "You watch my place." He cupped his hands around his eyes, looking toward the mine. "I'll be back."

Woman nodded her head, but she didn't make a sound.

Kurt turned to go, leading his burro as he made his way to the trail that went down the mountain. When he was about a hundred yards away, he looked back to see that Woman was following him. He waved, and she waved back.

On the way down the mountain as he walked along Lynx Creek, there were calls from the other miners, wishing him good luck, and hoping that he would be back before too long. He went out of his way to stop by to see Jake Carmichael at the charcoal kiln.

"Are you leaving for good?" Jake asked.

"I hope not," Kurt said. "I boarded 'er up, and I don't think anybody'll cause any mischief up at the Axis till I get back."

"Nothin' will happen. Everybody on the creek will watch out for you, and don't forget—you got a good watchdog in Woman."

"That's why I stopped by," Kurt said. "Will you take her a bushel of charcoal now and then? And maybe take her some hard candy if you think about it."

"We'll take care of her, if she'll let us," Jake said.

"I'll be beholden to you, but I'd better be getting' on to town."

"You're a good man, Kurt Beaumont."

Kurt nodded his head and leading his burro, headed for Prescott.

When Kurt reached town, he looked around at the frenzy of building that was going on. There was a new two-story building going up that had an inside wall made of bricks. He thought that was smart, after all the fires that had occurred over the last several years. For a long time, the Quartz Rock had been his favorite saloon, but it had burned several years ago. Now as he walked down

Montezuma Street, he passed a pantheon of saloons with names like the Cabinet, the Parlor, the Bit, the Nifty, Kearney's, Diana, and Jackson & Tompkins, among some two dozen more. But he kept going until he reached his favorite saloon, The Beatrice. Looping the reins of the burro around the hitching rail in front, he went inside.

"Well, if it isn't Kurt Beaumont," the bartender greeted. "You've not been in here in a month of Sundays."

"Hello Ki." Kurt's response was dispirited.

"What's wrong? You seem down," Ki said.

"I guess you could say that I am," Kurt said.

"Oh, dear, has something bad happened?"

Kurt chuckled. "I guess you could say that, if you think runnin' completely out of money counts as somethin' bad."

"Everybody's been there," Ki said. "Just get you some more beans and head on back up the mountain." He drew a beer and set it in front of Kurt.

"It's more than that. I haven't seen one hint of color in that hole in the mountain for at least six months," Beaumont said.

"You think the Axis has played out?"

"No, and that's the problem. I know there's gold in that mine, Ki, I just feel it in my bones. The thing is, it's me that's played out. I'm just plain tuckered." He drained his mug.

"What are you going to do?" Ki refilled his beer.

"I'm goin' back to New Orleans and work with my pa for a month or two. As soon as I get rested up and earn enough money to stake me for a while, I'll be back."

"Are you worried about leaving your mine untended?"

"Naw, the placer men will know if anybody goes up there that ain't supposed to be there, and of course there's Woman who's nearby."

"Is that old woman still hangin' on?"

"She is," Kurt said. "I don't know how I inherited her—it's like an alley cat wandered in and she's mine now."

At that moment a peal of laughter came from outside, followed by two men who pushed through the batwing doors. The two men were wearing the dark blue uniforms with a Prescott Defender patch on their chest.

"Ki," one of them greeted as he stepped up to the bar. "I bet you're happy to see us."

Ki took a deep breath. "Weren't you just here?"

"Last week. Now it's time to pay up again."

Ki opened the cash draw, pulled out a five-dollar coin and handed it to Jonas Cokeberry.

"Well now, would you lookie here, Jonas?" Vestal said, pointing to Beaumont. "Looks to me like we got us a miner to collect from. Twenty-dollar gold tax, mister," Vestal said, holding out his hand.

"That's funny," Kurt said, as he took another swallow

of beer.

"What's so damn funny?"

"You're wantin' to collect gold tax, when I don't have no gold."

"You tellin' me there ain't no gold in your mine?"

"I'm tellin' you I can't find it."

"Then it's either twenty dollars or sign over your mine."

"You got no right to take my mine," Kurt said.

"Yeah, we do," Cokeberry said. "It's called . . . what did the colonel say it's called, Vestal?"

"Confiscation for not payin' taxes. Confiscation means takin' it from you," Vestal replied authoritatively.

Beaumont shook his head. "You're not takin' my mine."

"We'll just see what Jubal has to say about that," Cokeberry said.

"Wait." A slender, well-dressed man with a few streaks of gray in what was otherwise very dark hair stepped up to the bar then. "Ki, pay this man's tax."

"That's mighty big of you, Housewright. Wish we could stay and visit with you, but we've got other folks to call on," Cokeberry said as he and Vestal left.

"Mr. Housewright, you didn't have to do that," Kurt said, "but I thank you. I got a little gold dust with me, and as soon as I get it weighed up, I'll be back with your money."

"When Sandos' rapacious arseholes come in here for their extortion money, I'll do anything to get them out."

This was Nigel Housewright, the owner of The Beatrice. He was a British transplant, and his comment was spoken with a sophisticated British accent.

"None of us like the Defenders," Ki replied.

"Then why does the town let them do what they do?" Kurt asked.

"Apparently there are some citizens of our fair community, specifically people who don't own a business, who think there is more good than bad from them. And don't forget, Judge Briggs has deputized the lot of them."

"I can't get out of here soon enough," Beaumont said.

"You are abandoning your mine?" Housewright asked, surprised by Beaumont's comment.

"For the time being," Beaumont replied. "It hasn't been very productive of late, and I need to earn enough money to get back on my feet. The best way for me to do that, is to go back home."

"We will miss you, my friend," Housewright said.

"Right now, I'll head down to the bank and turn in my poke," Kurt said as he patted his vest. "Then I'll be back with your money."

"You don't have to do that," Nigel said. "You can pay me when you come back."

"That won't do," Kurt said as he put on his hat. "I pay my debts." He shook hands with Housewright and headed for the door.

Later that afternoon Sandos sat in his office counting his money. He set aside seventy dollars for Judge Briggs, and one hundred-fifty dollars for himself. That left thirty dollars apiece for each of his eleven men, which was much more than they would be making as a cowhand, or what they would make working in the mines, or even panning gold on their own. Because of that, none of his men questioned how much Sandos was making.

Sandos made an entry in his ledger, detailing the week's transactions.

Leaving the Prescott Defenders headquarters building, Sandos walked up the street to the county court-house.

"The judge in?" he asked the clerk.

"Yes, sir, go right on in."

The corpulent man sitting behind the desk was bald headed and wearing glasses that appeared to enlarge his eyes.

"Hello, Sandos. Here to do business again?"

"Yes, your cut of this week's take." Sandos counted out the money. "Seventy dollars."

"Uhmm . . . that's a little short this week isn't it?" Briggs said as he slid the money into the top drawer of his desk. "I've been thinking. I should get a flat fee of a hundred dollars a week no matter what you collect."

"And what makes you think you deserve that?"

"Well, look Jubal, you wouldn't get a damned penny from this taxing scheme, if I hadn't appointed all of you as deputies of the court."

"Don't get greedy, Briggs," Sandos replied, purposefully leaving out the honorific title of judge. "You wouldn't want somebody to just accidentally drop the word to Ben Weaver that our most respected judge is getting a share of the tax money, now would you?"

"No, no, none of the newspapers need to know that," Briggs said. "Whatever you can give me is fine. I don't want you to think I was making any kind of a demand—I was just commenting."

"Yeah, I thought that's what you meant."

"I don't know about you, Will, but my butt is getting sore from sitting in this train for so long," Gid said.

"It hasn't even been a week, yet," Will replied. "We'll be to San Francisco in less than a week for sure. If we were riding horses, we'd still have three weeks to go before getting out of Texas."

"I know this is a lot faster, but at least, on a horse you're outside, and you can stop anytime you want to."

Will chuckled. "Yeah, well now, you might have a good point there."

"I wonder if we could get in to see the horses. I think that would make me feel better."

"You know there's not a direct access to the stock car, but I suppose if you wanted to climb onto the top of the car, then down the side and see if you could slide open the door you might . . ."

"There's no way I'm going to do that, and you know it," Gid said.

"Then the best you can do is walk back to the rear end of the train and look at it," Will said.

"Then let's do that," Gid proposed.

Will chuckled. "All right, Little Brother, if it'll make you feel any better."

"At least we'll get to move around a little bit."

Will and Gid were in a Pullman car which was four cars up from the tail end of the train. The next two cars behind them were coach and they were quite crowded, sometimes with as many as three people to a seat. In most cases, however, one of those passengers would be a child.

"Mama, look at him, he's a *real* big man," a little girl said with an awe-struck voice, pointing at Gid as he and Will walked down the aisle.

"Oh, sir, I apologize for my daughter," an attractive young woman said.

Gid laughed. "No apology needed, Miss. Your daughter's not only a beautiful little girl, she is also very observant. I am rather over-sized."

"Mama, he said I was beautiful," the little girl said

with a proud smile.

"Shh," the little girl's mother said.

Will and Gid stepped out onto the back deck of the rear-most car, and here they could feel the wind whipping by, and hear, much more loudly than in the cars, the wheels passing over the rail joints. By looking through the slats of the stock car, Gid could see some, but not all of the horses. He recognized their horses because they were in the front two stalls.

"You think they're wondering what's happening to them?" Gid asked.

Will laughed. "No, I think they're thinking that they've come an awful long way since we put them on the train, and they're damn glad they're not walking."

Gid chuckled as well. "But, like me, I'll bet they're getting tired of riding on this train."

"Damn, Little Brother, you'd bitch if they hung you with a new rope."

"Well the next time we stop to take on water, let's get 'em out and exercise the poor things—even if it's just for a half-hour."

"We can do that I suppose," Will said, "but right now I could use a bite to eat."

"Is it going to be dinner or supper?" Gid asked.

"It depends upon where we are," Will said. "In Texas, it's supper, but on this train, it's dinner."

After supper, the two returned to their car and played a few games of cards until it was time to go to bed. Gid took the upper bunk, and Will lay in the lower, looking through the window. A full moon allowed him to look at the passing countryside in shades of black and silver. He could feel the gentle rocking of the car and hear the clacking of the wheels over the track joints. He couldn't help but look back on his life and think of all the events that had brought his brother and him to this point. They were headed for California. What would they find there? Riches? Probably not, and even if they did, it would take a lot to change their lifestyle.

Women? Well, there would always be women, but probably no one that would alter their lives.

Adventure? Yes, that he could count on, one hundred percent. Adventure, specifically, trouble, seemed to come to them. Or more accurately, they seemed drawn to trouble. Were they headed for it now?

Will drifted off to sleep and didn't wake up until Gid was shaking him the next morning.

"It's time for breakfast," Gid said.

"All right. I wonder where we are, now?"

"I was just talking to the conductor. He said we'd be in Ash Fork by nine o'clock."

"Ash Fork. There's a new place for us. Is it in New

Mexico or Arizona?"

"I think it's about half-way through Arizona, so we should get to California by tomorrow for sure," Gid said.

"I'm ready," Will said as he swung his legs off the cramped bed and stretched his arms.

* * *

When the telegraph key in the office at the railroad depot in Ash Fork, began to clatter, the telegrapher, who had been pouring himself a cup of coffee, set the cup down then hurried over to respond. After assuring the telegrapher at the other end of the line that he was ready to receive, the instrument began its series of dot and dash clicks.

"Oh, oh," the telegrapher said as he began recording the message. "Mr. Sinclair isn't going to like this."

After verifying that he had received the telegram, Boardman, the telegrapher, tore the message off the pad so he could take it to Amon Sinclair, the station manager.

Six passengers had bought tickets for the next westbound train, which was due within another hour, and they were all sitting in the waiting room, two men, two women, and two children. The men were reading, the women were in conversation, and the two little girls were sitting on the floor playing with dolls. Sinclair was annotating today's traffic in his record book.

"Boardman, what have you heard?" Sinclair asked. "Is the west-bound on time?"

"Yes, sir, should be here by eight thirty," Sinclair said.

"Good."

"But it won't be going any farther."

"What do you mean, it won't go any farther? What are you talking about?"

"I just got this message. There's a fire on the west side of the trestle over the Little Colorado, and some ties and supports have burned."

"It's up to the Southern Pacific branch line to fix it then, I suppose," Sinclair said. "And who knows when that will happen. They want everyone using the southern route so they won't be in any hurry to get the trestle repaired."

"Well, what do we do?" Boardman asked.

"First we'll have to tell the waiting passengers," Sinclair said. "The A & P will have to pay for their passage back to Maricopa Station if they still want to head on West."

"It seems to me like the Southern Pacific should have to pay for something," Boardman said. "They'll be getting the fares from these people. And now what about the incoming passengers?"

"We'll offer them the same option, but that would be a three-day trip on the stage," Sinclair said. "Send a telegraph to Flagstaff and see if we can get an engine down here to pull the train back to Albuquerque. Once the engine gets here, that would take less than a day to make a connection."

"No matter what we offer, we're going to have a bunch of disgruntled passengers," Boardman said, "and it's not our fault."

Chapter Three

Kurt Beaumont was in Ash Fork, having come up on the stage from Prescott. He had made arrangement to board his burro at the City Feed Yard. Normally, it would cost fifty cents a day to board an animal, but Clem Whitehair was a good man. He had said that since Jack would not have to be kept in the stable, he would only charge five dollars for a whole month. Kurt had paid fifteen dollars, hoping that he would be back by the end of the summer.

After paying Nigel Housewright for the "gold tax" for the Prescott Defenders, and boarding Jack, Kurt had just over sixty dollars left from converting his gold to cash. His train ticket cost thirty-five dollars, leaving him enough money to get him back to New Orleans, but not enough for him to live on his own once he got there. He knew his parents would put him up, but that wasn't the way he wanted to go home. He wanted to be self-supporting as he started working with his father.

Kurt decided to send a telegram to his pa thinking that would be better than coming home unannounced. After buying his train ticket, he wrote out a telegram and went back to the ticket counter.

"I'd like to send a telegram."

"I'm sorry, but this telegraph line is only for use by the Atlantic and Pacific," Boardman said. "If you want to send a letter, go to the post office and the mail will go out with the eastbound train." Boardman told Kurt the information, knowing full well that no mail would be going out today.

"Thank you," Kurt said as he wadded up his message and put it in his pocket.

Leaving the depot, Kurt crossed the street to the Sunset Saloon and Restaurant where he had ham and potatoes for breakfast. When he was finished, even though it was morning, he bought a beer. When he paid for his breakfast and the beer it came to almost a dollar. That left him only twenty-four dollars to get home.

Maybe, he could pick up a job here in Ash Fork. He had clerked in his father's store; surely some store here would be able to use him. But he knew that such a job would pay no more than thirty dollars a month, and he would have to find a place to live and buy his food. At that rate it would take him at least six months, and maybe longer, before he would have enough money to go back home. Besides, he had already bought his ticket.

Kurt's musing was interrupted by a loud call from a card game that even at this early hour of the day was in progress toward the back wall of the saloon.

"A straight flush? A straight flush? Who the hell gets a straight flush in a card game?"

"Only a lucky son of a bitch," another said.

"Which describes Webb. He's a lucky son of a bitch, so that's why he drew a straight flush," another said. The others around the table laughed.

"Boys, this next hand will be my last," Webb said. "I've got to get back home before my wife comes after me with a frying pan."

"Well, at least your last hand got you even, so you won't have to go back home dragging your tail between your legs because you lost too much money."

"Which is why my next hand will be my last."

Listening to the conversation of the card players gave Kurt an idea. Maybe he could win enough money playing cards, to replace the twenty dollars that he had been forced to give to the Prescott Defenders. Once he won the money, he would walk away, just as the man called Webb had said he would do.

Will and Gid had planned on leaving the train in Ash Fork to exercise their horses if possible, but shortly after they stopped, the conductor came walking through the car.

"Folks, I'm sorry to say that this is as far as we can go today. There's been a fire on a trestle ahead of us that has taken out some ties and supports. We'll be staying in Ash Fork until another engine can come and hook on to the back of the train and pull us out of here."

"And then where will we go?" a man said in a very loud voice.

"You'll be connecting with the Atchison, Topeka and Santa Fe in Albuquerque, and then the Southern Pacific on to California," the conductor said.

"And how long will that take?" the man continued.

"There is another alternative," the conductor said. "You can take the Gilmer and Salisbury Stage to Prescott, which is fifty-two miles, then take Wells Fargo on to where you can catch the Southern Pacific."

"And we all expect the Atlantic and Pacific to pay for this inconvenience."

"Yes, sir," the conductor said. "When you leave the train, see Mr. Sinclair and he will fix you right up."

As the passengers were leaving the train, there was a lot of complaining, but as far as Will and Gid were concerned, California was less of a specific destination than it was just another place. And as Ash Fork was just another place, it didn't particularly matter to them whether they got off the train here or continued on.

"What are we going to do?" Gid asked after getting their vouchers from the station manager. "Are we going back to Albuquerque or are we riding south?"

"Who is it that has been complaining about staying on the train so long?" Will asked.

"I guess that's my answer. We're riding south."

They unloaded their horses, and took their belongings, which consisted of a pair of saddle bags for each of them.

"Didn't the conductor say it was about fifty miles to Prescott?" Gid asked.

"I believe so," Will said. "How about staying here overnight and starting for Prescott tomorrow?"

They attempted to get a room at the Railroad Hotel, but the line from the passengers who had left the train was about twenty deep, and people were jockeying to see who would be roommates in the few rooms that remained to be let.

Will and Gid didn't bother trying to find a room. They took their horses to the Ash Fork Livery, and as they suspected would be true, they paid for a spot in the loft to store their saddle bags and to lay down their saddle blankets. This wouldn't be the most comfortable night they had ever spent, but as they planned to leave the next day, it would suffice.

"Now what?" Will asked.

"I don't know what you plan to do, but it looks to me like the Sunset is doing a fine business and I intend to stay there until nightfall," Gid said.

"Sounds like I'll be right there beside you, Little Brother."

Will and Gid played faro for a while until Will saw a seat open at a poker game, so he walked over to join the game. After about five hands, he determined that none of the other three players was a professional gambler, and it was a convivial game with winning and losing about evenly spaced, except for one player. That player, Kurt Beaumont, lost several hands in a row, until he announced he was out of money.

"Damn, I was going back to New Orleans, but I've gambled away all my traveling money," Beaumont said. "I, uh . . ." he reached into his inside vest pocket and pulled out an envelope.

"I need to raise some money. I don't plan on playing cards any longer, but, like I said, I need some traveling money, so I've got a proposition for anyone who's interested."

"What's the proposition?" Clemens, one of the other players asked.

"I've got a gold mine down in Prescott that I'm willing

to sell."

Clemens laughed. "Mister, do you have any idea how many people try to sell off bogus gold mines? Damn, I would've thought you'd know better than to come up with a scheme like that."

"No, no, it's a real gold mine," Kurt Beaumont insisted. "I've got the deed, and assay reports. For a while it was doing right good, but I admit it ain't paid out much in the last few months. But I know there's still gold there."

"Then why would you want to get rid of it?" Yates Erickson, one of the other poker players asked.

Beaumont took a deep breath. "Because I'm tired and I'm broke."

"They's lots of folks that get to where you're at," Erickson said.

"Let me see your paperwork," Will said as he reached for the envelope Beaumont had laid on the table.

"You can't be serious, Crockett—you ain't really going to fall for that old trick, are you?" Clemens asked.

Will looked over the deed and the assayer's report, both of which appeared to be legitimate.

"Mr. Beaumont, will you meet me at the telegraph office tomorrow morning at nine?" Will asked as he returned the documents to Beaumont.

"I could meet you there, but it won't do no good."

"Oh . . . and why not?"

"Cause the telegraph line is just for use by the railroad," Beaumont said.

"Then meet me at the livery. My brother and I may want to do business with you."

"Addie, would you like to ride up to Simmons with me?" Biff Reed asked his twenty-two-year-old daughter. Biff owned the Reed Hotel, believed by most, to be the finest hotel in Prescott.

"What are you going up there for?" Addie asked.

"D.C. is raffling off a fine pair of mares Saturday night at the Cabinet, and he hasn't sold enough tickets. I told him I'd take some up to Doc Thibodo and see if he could sell a few more chances so he doesn't have to take a loss."

"I'm sure Mr. Thorne could afford to take a loss on the animals, but I think you offered to go, just to get away from here for a little while," Addie said.

Biff smiled at his daughter. "You know me too well, but you didn't answer my question. Do you want to go with me?"

"I'd love to go with you, provided you'll take the buckboard," Addie said.

"And why don't you want to ride a horse?"

"Because there was a notice in the *Advocate* that said Hershel Cane has new potatoes already," Addie said. "Could we go on up and pick up two or three bushels to give away?"

"If that's what you want to do, we'll go see Hershel, too."

Addie smiled as she turned to go. "I'd better see if Mr. Shy will let me have off this afternoon."

"I'm sure Gerald can run the apothecary by himself for the rest of the day, but before you leave, run back to the kitchen and asked Doris to put something together for our lunch. I'll get the team hitched to the buckboard and bring it out front."

"Fried chicken, or ham sandwiches?" Addie asked.

"Now did you really have to ask that?"

"Fried chicken it is," Addie said with a chuckle as she hurried to the little café that was actually part of the hotel lobby.

"No, I don't mind at all," Gerald Shy said. "Go ahead, enjoy your ride with your dad. I can handle things here."

"Thanks, Mr. Shy," Addie said. From Shy's Apothecary, Addie walked down to the headquarters building of the Prescott Defenders. Jubal Sandos was alone in the building, sitting at his desk, writing in what Addie knew to be his ledger.

"Hello, pretty girl," Sandos said, greeting her with a smile. "What brings you by? Oh, wait, I know. We haven't seen each other since yesterday, and you just couldn't stand to be away from me any longer."

"That's not it at all, you arrogant thing," Addie replied, though she ameliorated her response with a broad smile. "I just thought I'd let you know that Papa and I are going to go up to Simmons this morning, and we won't be back until sometime late today."

"And you couldn't leave without a kiss goodbye," Sandos said.

"Maybe," Addie agreed, as she gave him a chaste kiss on his lips.

After going to breakfast at the Sunset where they each had a pickled egg and a ham biscuit, Will and Gid walked back to the livery stable.

"Are you serious about this?" Gid asked. "A gold mine—in Prescott, Arizona?"

"Why not?" Will asked. "Why were we going to California?"

"I don't know. We said something would turn up," Gid answered.

Will smiled. "Something has turned up, it just turned up before we got to California."

Kurt Beaumont was sitting on a bench in front of the livery stable, and he had the envelope Will had seen the night before.

"Good morning, gents," Beaumont said when he saw the two men approaching.

"I wasn't sure you'd be here," Will said.

"And where would I go?" Kurt asked. "You boys got most of my money last night, and I mean it—I don't have a red cent left to my name. If you don't buy my mine, I'll have to hide out on the next train going east, and I don't reckon I want a railroad detective puttin' me in jail, just so as I can see my ma and pa one more time."

"Then let me see your deed," Will said. "Maybe my brother and I can help get you home."

Will showed Gid the document.

"I've not looked at too many deeds for gold mines, but this looks like it's the real thing," Gid said.

"It is real," Beaumont insisted as Gid handed the paper back to him.

"Then you won't mind if I send a couple of telegrams, will you?" Will asked.

"I wouldn't mind, but like I said last night, the telegraph line here is only for the use of the railroad. You just have to take my word for it that I own the Axis Mine," Kurt said. "You can see by the date that I staked my claim in 1870, and Wilson Wells notarized it for me." He ran his finger over the raised stamp of the notary public. "If you go to Prescott right now and go into the office of Rush and Wells, they'll tell you this deed is authentic."

"How much gold have you taken out of your mine in nine years?" Gid asked.

"I'll be honest with you. I ain't come anywhere's near hittin' a bonanza, but I've kept myself in grub and supplies," Kurt said, "but not a stone's throw away from my mine, stands the Accidental. It hit pay dirt back in the sixties, and it's still payin' out, about sixteen hundred dollar a ton for first class ore and five hundred dollars for second class."

"That all sounds good," Will said, "but I still can't get over why you'd walk away from it."

Beaumont put his head down. "I told you I was tired, and that's true. It gets old being a one-blanket miner. I've been livin' in the hills for nine years, and I'm ready to get out. I want to go home to New Orleans, find me a nice little Cajun woman, and have me a passel of kids. You boys probably don't know what I'm a tellin' you, but that's how it is."

Gid put his hand on Kurt's shoulder. "Brother, you don't know how much I know what you're telling us."

"I think you've convinced my brother," Will said. "Let's talk money."

"All right, how does twenty-five hundred dollars sound to you," Kurt said.

"I'd say—it doesn't sound good at all," Will said. "Come on, Gid, we're wasting our time here."

"No, don't go," Kurt said. "What would you be willin' to give me?"

"Five hundred dollars," Will said, "and that's generous considering we've getting a pig in a poke. Like Clemons said last night, there's a lot of bogus paperwork around here when it comes to selling mining claims."

"I told you I own this mine," Kurt said.

"And I tend to believe you, but not for twenty-five hundred dollars."

Beaumont pulled out the assayer's report. "Look at this. Last year alone, I took out a thousand dollars from my mine. Surely it's worth more than five hundred dollars."

"It might be worth more, it might be worth nothing," Will said. "If it's worth more, you still have five hundred dollars. If it's worth nothing, I'm still out five hundred dollars."

Beaumont was quiet for a moment, then he nodded, and let out a sigh.

"You're right. I need money, and five hundred dollars is five hundred dollars more than I have now."

"Then let's find a notary here in Ash Fork, and if you sign this over to my brother and me, we'll give you the money."

"All right. And, I do hope this mine pays out for you boys. Oh, by the way, there's a cabin there."

"A cabin?"

"Well, it's not really a cabin, but it's where I been livin' while I was workin' the mine. You'll find some tools there, a couple of shovels, a couple o' pickaxes, a wheelbarrow, a sledge hammer, some spikes. 'N inside they's a iron stove, 'n it's good enough to heat up your coffee, do some cookin', 'n keep you warm when it's cold outside." Beaumont smiled. "I even left me a couple o' cans of peaches there, along with some coffee. I wish you two the best of luck in the mine. I know there's gold there, I just know it. Oh, and there's one more thing. Look up Clem Whitehair at the City Feed Yard in Prescott. I paid him to put Jack up 'til the end of summer."

"Jack?"

"Yeah, he's my burro," Kurt said. "And another thing—you got a neighbor that's old and crotchety sometimes, but all you got a do is keep horehound candy around, and ever' thing'll be fine."

"We'll remember that."

"And sometimes I get a bushel of charcoal and share that, too."

"We'll do our best to get along," Gid said.

Kurt nodded his head. "I know you will."

"We were told Prescott is about fifty miles from here," Will said, "so what do you say, Gid, let's get on our way. Is there a town between here and there that we might pass through?"

"Simmons ain't too far."

"Then that's where we're headed," Gid said. "Mr.

Beaumont, I hope you have a good trip, and I hope you find your little Cajun woman real soon."

"Thank you." Kurt smiled, and patted the carpet bag where he had put the five hundred dollars. "The trip's gonna be a lot better now, than what it would have been when I started out."

"I'm a poor one to be giving advice," Will said, "but if I were you, I wouldn't get into any more poker games between here and New Orleans."

"I hear ya," Kurt said as he turned to walk toward the Sunset Saloon.

Chapter Four

"Do you think Doc Thibodo will sell those tickets?" Addie asked as she and Biff were returning from Hershel Cane's place that was in the hills north of Simmons.

"If he doesn't, he'll probably buy them himself," Biff Reed said. "He could use a new pair of mares."

"Mr. Cane seemed interested in them, too, when you told him why we had come up here," Addie said. "Do you think he charged us too much for the potatoes?"

"He probably did, but I paid it gladly. You know Doris won't let you give these away," Biff said.

"What do you think will be on the menu tomorrow?"

I'll bet it'll be potato fritters," Biff said.

"If I can get her to fix onion and potato hash and then mix eggs in with it, why Jubal will be there in a minute," Addie said. "I do believe he could eat that at every meal."

"Honey . . ." Biff started.

"Papa, no," Addie said. "I know what you are going to say and I don't want to hear it. You know how I feel about him."

"I know," Biff said as he let out a long breath. "I wish you didn't feel that way about him, but you're a twenty-two-year-old woman, and I guess it's really none of my business. But that doesn't mean I'm not concerned."

"Papa, why do you hate Jubal so?"

"Sweetheart, it's not that I hate him, it's just that I don't think he's right for you. You know what most of the businessmen think about him and the Defenders, and how they extort such a heavy tax from everyone."

"Papa it's not extortion. The court has approved of those taxes."

"Yes, I know, but that doesn't make it right."

"I think the town should be beholding to Jubal for all that he does. Where would the town be without the Defenders? Sheriff Bower and Jimmie Burns certainly can't keep all the trouble makers in line."

"You're a sweet girl, Addie. I just hope your feelings for him aren't misplaced, and that you aren't hurt."

"Hey, boys, lookie what's comin'," Abe Connors said. Abe Connors, Nate Harper, and Pogue Dillard were on the Prescott to Ash Fork road. Abe was pointing out a buckboard on the road ahead of them that carried two people, a middle-aged man and a very pretty young woman.

"Now, how do you think an old fart like that, can get such a purty young thing to ride with him out in the middle of nowhere?" Abe asked.

"Hell, that's easy," Nate said. "He's prob'ly hit a big bonanza, 'n now he's givin' 'er money to be seen with 'im."

"You know what I'm a' thinkin'?" Pogue asked.

"What?"

"I'm thinking that purty one might just welcome some young blood, 'cause you know that old sum'bitch can't do nothin' for her."

"Or, what we could do, is see if he'll pay us enough money not to do nothin' to her," Nate suggested.

"A hunnert 'n fifty dollars," Abe said. "Fifty dollars apiece."

"Yeah," Pogue said. "But I'm almost hopin' he don't pay us. That's a good lookin' woman. I'd kind'a like to have me some o' that."

"Why don't we do both?" Nate suggested.

"What do you mean, both?" Pogue asked.

"Take the money from that old man, then have a good time with the girl."

"Yeah," Pogue said with a little laugh. "Yeah, that's a damn good idea."

Addie saw the three men riding toward them, and though there was nothing overt, there was something about them that triggered Addie's apprehension.

"Papa, those men," she said, quietly.

"They're just three men traveling," Biff said. "No different from anyone else we've seen on the road."

"I don't know, there's something about them that bothers me."

"It'll be all right, don't worry."

Addie couldn't shake her apprehension as the men drew closer, then when the three men drew their guns, her fears were justified.

"Old man, we're goin' to have us some fun with this purty young thing here. Why don't you watch, 'n we'll learn you what it takes to satisfy a woman."

"No, that's my daughter!" Biff called out.

"Then you can either watch your daughter get broke in or pay us a hunnert 'n fifty dollars to keep us from doin' it."

"I'll give you everything I have, but I don't have that much money. Please, leave her alone!"

It was mid-afternoon and, in the time since they had left Ash Fork, Will and Gid had met a stagecoach and two riders on the road. They were startled when they heard a loud shriek.

"Will, that sounds like a woman's scream."

"I think you're right, Little Brother."

Urging their horses into a gallop, they crested a hill where they saw an empty buckboard with two horses in harness. About fifty yards away in a gulch off the side of the road, they saw a woman, and four men. One of the men was holding a gun to the head of an older man, while the other two were attempting to get the fighting young woman on the ground.

No longer at a gallop, Will and Gid rode down the hill, unobserved by any of the five until they were much closer.

"Help! Help! Please help us!" the young woman called out when she saw Will and Gid approaching.

One of the two men with the woman turned toward Will and Gid.

"You better stop right there where you be, or we'll kill this old man and the girl," one of them said, he pulled his gun and pointed it toward the girl, who was now being held from behind.

"You know what, mister?" Will said, as he and Gid pointed their guns toward the three me. "You need to think this through. You aren't pointing your guns at us, but we're pointing our guns at you."

"Didn't you hear what I said? I said we're going to kill the woman and the old man."

"And we're going to kill you," Will replied.

For a long moment, there was a standoff.

"Look, we're not the law," Will said. "If you men put your guns back in your holsters and ride away from here, we can end this thing now. Otherwise, there's going to be some killing, and I guarantee that all three of you will die."

"What are we going to do, Abe?" the man who was holding a pistol to the older man's head, asked.

"Don't do nothin' yet. Let me think about this," Abe said.

The one who had been pointing his gun at the man, lowered his pistol. "I'll tell you what I'm going to do. I'm going to do like this here man said. I'm gettin' out of here."

"Pogue, you cowardly son of a bitch!" Abe called out as Pogue started toward his horse.

"I'm goin' too," Nate said.

"That leaves only you, Abe," Will said. "Like I told you, put your gun down and ride away from here like your two friends, and you might live another day. Otherwise, you're going to die, right here, and right now."

"No," Abe said, his voice dripping with fear. "No, now, there ain't no need for nothin' like that. We was just funnin' around a bit, is all. We wasn't really goin' to do nothin'."

Abe stepped away from the girl and held both hands up, the gun still in his hand. "See, I ain't pointin' the gun at her no more."

"Get out of here, all of you," Will said, waving his gun.

Abe, Pogue, and Nate mounted their horses, and rode

away at a gallop.

The young woman ran to the older man and they embraced.

The older man looked up. "I'm Biff Reed, and this is my daughter, Addie. I don't know who you gentlemen are, but I've never been happier to see anyone in my life."

"I'm glad we happened along at what seems to be just the right time. I'm Will Crockett, and this is my brother Gid."

"You certainly did, and we can't thank you enough," the young woman said as she began rearranging her clothing. She had long brown hair, blue eyes, and a spray of freckles across her nose.

"If it isn't too nosey of me, may I inquire what brought you two here at this most fortuitous time?" Biff Reed asked.

"We're going to Prescott," Gid said.

"We're from Prescott," Biff said. "Addie and I would be pleased to have you ride along beside us the rest of the way if you would consider it. I think you more than likely scared those ruffians away, but who knows if they would try to accost us again if they saw we were going on alone."

"Did you recognize any of those men?" Gid asked.

"No, but we heard their names. Abe, Nate, and Pogue," Addie said. "I'll tell Jubal and he'll send The Defenders out right away."

"The Defenders? Is that what the sheriff calls a posse

in these parts?" Will asked.

"No," Biff said. "The Defenders have nothing to do with the sheriff."

"But you do have a sheriff?" Gid asked.

"We do, and he's a very good man, but The Defenders—how can I tell you what they are?"

"Papa, I don't think you are the one to say anything. You see my father doesn't care for Mr. Sandos, so he can't say anything nice about what he and his men do. But I can say, Prescott would be a much more wicked place, if it weren't for Jubal and his men."

"Where will you be staying when you get to Prescott?" Reed asked, as he changed the subject.

"Initially, I guess we'll get a room at a hotel, but never having been to Prescott, we're open to recommendations."

"May I suggest the Reed Hotel?" Reed said with a smile. "And your first two weeks are free."

"The Reed Hotel? And you said your name was Biff Reed?"

"Yes, I own the hotel."

"We wouldn't want to impose on you."

Reed laughed. "Mr. Crockett, you and your brother just imposed on us, and a welcome imposition it was. Please, accept my invitation."

"Well, in that case, how can we refuse such a generous offer?"

Chapter Five

During the ride into town, they learned that Biff had lived around Prescott since 1867 when placer miners were everywhere and gold nuggets were there for the taking. "And you didn't stake a claim?" Gid asked.

"Oh, yes I did," Biff said, "but that was before the Yavapai and the Apache were put on the reservation, so Addie and her mother were still back in Ohio. But when Grace got sick, I wanted her and Addie with me, so I brought them both out to Arizona Territory. I knew I couldn't leave a child to take care of a sick woman. So, I sold my claim, and with the money opened the Reed Hotel."

"And you've been there ever since," Gid said.

"Not quite," Addie said. "We burned out in '71, right after Mama died, but then Papa built back a bigger and better hotel. And I say we've got the best business in Prescott."

"I wouldn't go so far as to say that," Biff said, "but I'm

proud of what we've acquired."

"So do you two run the whole thing by yourselves?" Will asked.

"No, Addie decided she didn't want to work for her old papa, so now she works at the apothecary. She's the best employee Gerald Shy has."

Addie laughed. "Papa, except for Mr. Shy, I'm the only one there."

"Then doesn't that make you the best he has?"

"Papa you are incorrigible."

"Where are our manners, Addie?" Biff asked. "Here we've been prattling on about ourselves, and we haven't even asked what brings the Crocketts to Prescott. Are you staying or just passing through?"

Will looked at Gid and they both laughed. "We thought we were on our way to California, but we sort of got sidetracked."

"California? Yes, I'd say you are going a little out of your way," Biff said.

"We bought a gold mine from a guy named Kurt Beaumont. Have you ever heard of him and does he really have a claim to sell?" Will asked.

"He does," Biff said. "I suspect he was a little upset just before he left town."

"And why was that?" Gid asked.

"He was assessed a rather stiff tax by the Prescott

Defenders."

"Papa, Mr. Beaumont was no different from anyone else who has to pay the tax," Addie defended. She addressed Will and Gid. "You say you bought his gold mine?"

"Yes. Are you suggesting that we shouldn't have?"

"No, it's a legitimate mine," Biff said. "From what I understand, it hasn't produced anything for a few months now, but Kurt's an honest man, so I'm sure he shared that information with you."

"He did," Will said.

"That's the hotel there," Addie pointed out as they rode into Prescott.

"That's a fine-looking establishment," Will said, "but first we need to find the City Feed Yard. It seems we bought a burro that's living there and we need to board our own horses as well."

"All right," Biff said. "The Feed Yard is on the road to Fort Whipple. You can't miss it, and I'll tell the desk clerk to hold a couple of rooms for you."

"Thank you, Mr. Reed, your offer is very much appreciated," Will said. "We might look over the town a bit before we check in."

Biff smiled. "The rooms will be there when you're ready for them, and, oh, if you should be interested in a small libation, my personal favorite is The Beatrice."

After leaving the Reeds at the hotel, Will and Gid

continued on down Gurley Street until it crossed Montezuma Street.

"Tell me, Gid, how would a beer sound to you about now?" Will asked

"Sounds like the best idea you've had in a long . . ." Gid started to say but he paused in mid-response, then asked a question.

"Wait a minute, Reed said The Beatrice. Are you sure he was talking about a saloon and not some ladies' dress shop?"

"There it is, and if it's a dress shop, it has swinging front doors, men going in and out, and it smells of spirits," Will replied with a slight chuckle as they wrapped the reins of their horses around the hitching rail out front.

When the two men went inside, the saloon was twice as long as it was wide. Two crystal chandeliers hung from the ceiling and several lanterns were mounted on the walls. There was a long, walnut bar than ran down the left side, with a well-polished, brass footrail. A gilt-edged mirror with an etching of a sailing ship was behind the bar. It was flanked by glass shelves upon which stood a myriad of colored bottles of liquor.

The bartender was a slender, bald-headed man, wearing garters on his sleeves. He moved down before the two brothers, then using a towel, wiped the counter, even as he spoke to them.

"What can I get for you gentlemen?" he asked.

"A beer," Will said.

"And I'll have the same," Gid added.

The bartender drew the beers and set the mugs before them. Will and Gid picked them up and took several swallows before setting the mugs back down.

"You boys must be thirsty."

"It's a long ride down from Ash Fork," Will said.

"That where you're from?"

"That's where we left the train. What's your name?"

"Malachi Hastings, though folks call me Ki."

"Ki, I'm curious—why The Beatrice? I've never heard of a saloon with a name like that," Gid asked.

"You'll have to ask Mr. Housewright. He owns the place. He's never given a reason for calling it The Beatrice, but there are those who say it's named after a girl he left behind back in England. That's him playing the piano."

Looking toward the piano they saw a slender, dark-haired man wearing, not the denims and flannel of most of the customers, but a dark blue jacket and gray trousers. The other thing they noticed was that he wasn't playing an upright piano that was the standard instrument of saloons but was playing a baby grand. Also, the music was unlike anything one would normally hear in a saloon.

"What's that he's playing?" Will asked.

Ki chuckled. "It's called *The Minute Waltz,* but Nigel

says it takes two minutes to play it."

"It's sort of catchy," Will said.

"Oh, you should hear him when he gets started. He plays all kinds of what he calls classical music, Beethoven, Vivaldi, Bach. That tune he's playing now is by Chopin. Only reason I know all this, is because he's told me over and over what he plays. Says he's trying to educate us."

At that moment, two uniformed men stepped into the bar.

"Damn," Ki said quietly. "This town has forty saloons. I wish those galoots would find another place to aggravate the customers."

"Soldiers?"

"Humph, I wish," Ki said. "They call themselves the Prescott Defenders—the keepers of the law, but there's nothing official about them."

"Prescott Defenders? Didn't Mr. Reed mention them?" Will asked.

"Yeah, but he didn't say they wore uniforms," Gid said. "I didn't get the impression they were so important."

"It's part of their arrogance," Ki said.

Stepping up to the bar, both Defenders ordered whiskey. Ki poured their drinks, set the bottle down on the bar, then held out his hand.

"Whatcha got yer hand out for?" one of them asked.

"You haven't paid for your drinks, Snow."

"You know the first drink for a Defender is free," Snow replied.

"Sounds like quite a racket you've got going there, cheating saloons out of drinks," Will said.

"We ain't cheatin' nobody, mister, we're the Prescott Defenders. Ever'body knows the rules," Snow said. "Just who are you anyways?" Snow looked to be in his late twenties or early thirties. He had a big nose, close-set eyes, and a sweeping moustache.

"The name's Crockett," Will said.

"And what about you?" Snow asked Gid.

"Crockett."

Snow looked confused. "Don't get smart with me, you two. Tell me your names or else I'll make you wish you had."

Will smiled. "You've never heard of two people with the same name?"

"So, your name's Crockett 'n your name's Crockett? What'd ya'll do just find someone else with your same name so now you're travelin' together?"

"It was something like that," Will replied.

Snow smiled. "Well, I'll be damned. Where ya'll from?"

"Around."

"Whatcha doin' here?"

"Right now, I'm drinking a beer," Will said.

"All right, but this town don' need no deadbeats

hangin' aroun'. You fellers just keep you noses clean, 'n you won't have no trouble from the Prescott Defenders."

"That's reassuring," Will said. His response was sarcastic, but Snow didn't understand sarcasm.

At the piano, Nigel Housewright finished *The Minute Waltz* and began another song.

"That one's *Moonlight Sonata,*" Ki told Will.

"Hey you, Housewright!" Snow shouted. "Quit playin' that high-falutin' music 'n play somethin' purty. Play *Marchin' through Georgia.*"

Housewright continued to play Beethoven.

Snow pulled his pistol.

"If you don't stop playin' that, I'm goin' to fill that pianny of yours full of holes."

Snow aimed at the piano, but before he could pull the trigger Will took the whiskey bottle from the bar and brought it smashing down over the man's head. Snow dropped his gun and fell to the floor.

"Why you son of a . . ." the other Prescott Defender said, as he started to draw his gun, but his comment and his draw was interrupted when he saw a pistol suddenly appear in Will's hand.

"Pick up your friend, and find another saloon," Will ordered.

A groggy Snow was helped onto his feet, then the two men left the saloon.

Will's action was applauded by Ki, the eight customers, and Penny and Elaina, the two percentage girls who were present.

Nigel Housewright, who had continued to play music throughout the excitement, now finished the piece with a flourish, to a light applause from the others. He stood up and made a slight bow.

"May I enquire as to whom I owe my appreciation for preserving peace in my establishment?" Housewright asked with a precise British accent.

"It was this gentleman here," Penny said, pointing to Will.

"I thank you, sir," Housewright said.

"No problem. My brother and I were enjoying the music and didn't appreciate that buffoon butting in like he did," Will said, with a gesture toward Gid.

"You gentlemen are most gracious, and if you will allow me, I would like to repay your kindness with more than words."

"No, now, that's not necessary," Will said, raising his hands. "I didn't do this for any money, and I sure don't plan on taking any from you."

"Oh, I have a better idea than that," Housewright said. "Suppose you join me for dinner tonight?"

"Uh, is that for both of us?" Gid asked.

"Indeed it is, sir," Housewright replied.

"Then where shall we meet?"

"How about The Gem? A couple of hard-working women have opened up a restaurant and dining room just north of the Raible Brewery," Housewright said. "And I can say from experience that the food is a cut above the usual fare in a frontier town."

"I heard their names spoken," Addie said. "One was Abe, one was Pogue, and one was Nate. I assume those were first names, I didn't hear any last names."

Addie was in the Prescott Defenders headquarters talking to Jubal Sandos.

"I know who they are," Jubal replied. "They are wanted for bank robbery and murder."

"Oh!" Addie said, putting her hand to her mouth.

"You were lucky nothing happened to you."

"It wasn't all luck," Addie said.

"What do you mean?"

"Two young men—Will and Gid Crockett, came to our rescue. You should have seen them, Jubal. They were brave and decisive. The three men who accosted papa and me left with their tails tucked between their legs.

It was actually quite funny, though I admit that some of the humor might have been the result of being relieved."

"I'm glad nothing worse happened to you, though I wish the two you speak of would have brought them in instead of letting them ride away. As I said, they are wanted for murder and robbery."

"But Will and Gid probably saved our lives. Especially if the three men who confronted us really are murderers."

"Oh, don't get me wrong, sweetheart," Jubal said, putting his hand lightly on her cheek. "I don't know what I would do if anything happened to you. We were going to go out after those three men anyway, but now I have even more incentive to bring them to justice."

"You told Sandos about our little adventure on the road, did you?" Biff asked.

"Yes. Papa, he said those men are wanted for murder."

"Then we are even luckier than we thought that Will and Gid came along just in time."

"Jubal said that the Defenders were going to go after them."

"If they knew about them, it's too bad they hadn't gone after them earlier," Biff said. "We didn't need that experience on the road."

"You can't give Jubal credit for anything, can you? He knew immediately who those men were," Addie said. "I know that you don't like him, Papa, you've made that quite clear."

"It's not that I dislike him, it's just that I wish you didn't like him as much as you do."

"He's a good man, Papa, you've seen what all he has done for the town," Addie said defensively.

"Not everyone shares your opinion."

"Papa, please try to like him. It's very important to me."

"I'll try and keep an open mind, Addie, but, please, give it more time before you make any, life-altering decisions."

"If you are talking about marrying, he hasn't asked me . . . yet."

"And if he does ask you?"

"I will say yes."

Chapter Six

The Gem was one of the nicer restaurants Will and Gid had been to recently. And the meal, which was Swiss steak, caramelized onions, and roasted potatoes, was outstanding.

"This is about the best thing I've eaten in a long time," Gid said as he carved through the tender beef.

"Mrs. Munds and Mrs. Wilson are trying their hardest to make a go of this place," Nigel said. "Their husbands were both killed in a mining accident, and the employment opportunities for single women are scarce in Prescott. By the way, if you gentlemen are looking for a place to stay, may I recommend the Reed Hotel? You'll find no finer accommodations anywhere in the whole town, and they are the only hotel with private loos in every room."

"Private loos? What's that?" Gid asked.

"A loo is what the English call a toilet," Will said.

"That is quite correct," Housewright said.

"Now how is it that you know that and I don't?" Gid asked. "We're brothers, and I know you've never been to England."

"Because, Little Brother, you may be the strong one, but everyone knows I'm the smart one," Will teased. Then to Housewright, Will said, "I'm glad you have such a good opinion of the Reed Hotel, because that's where we will be staying. We already have rooms there."

"You won't be disappointed."

Will started to tell Housewright the story as to why they would be staying at the Reed Hotel but decided to keep his own counsel.

"Oh, gentlemen, here comes Governor Fremont and the Honorable Tom Fitch," Housewright said. "I'll call them over and introduce you."

"Fremont? Do you mean John C. Fremont?"

"Yes, one and the same," Nigel said. "He's a gentleman with quite an accomplished and historic resume." Nigel hesitated. "Some say he owes everything to his wife, Jessie."

"We know about Jessie. Her father was a senator back in Missouri," Gid said.

"An accomplished woman," Nigel said, "but she couldn't have written all that she has without the exploits of Governor Fremont. As the territorial capital, Prescott is lucky to have both of them in residence."

"And who is Mr. Fitch?" Will asked as the two men came into The Gem.

"An accomplished lawyer who is now a representative to our territory legislature."

Housewright lifted his hand. "Governor?" he called, and the two men headed toward the table.

"Gentlemen, may I present His Excellency Governor John C. Fremont and The Honorable Thomas Fitch. These two men are Will and Gid Crockett."

"Gentlemen," Fremont said, extending his hand.

Fitch did the same and then excused himself to join another table.

"Sir, it is a pleasure," Will said, "but actually, we've met before."

Fremont got a confused look on his face. "Have we? I'm sorry, I don't seem to remember that occurrence."

Will smiled. "I can understand that, General. The set of circumstances made the meeting much more memorable to me, than it would have been to you."

"General? You met me during the war?"

"Yes, sir. It was just outside Forsyth, Missouri, in 1861."

"Ah, the Battle of Springfield," Fremont said with a smile. "You were one of my men?"

"No, sir, I was on the other side."

"You were with the Rebel Army, and we met?"

"We did indeed."

25 October, 1861

Before Will and Gid joined with Quantrill, they were Confederate soldiers under General Kurt Van Dorn. The Union army, under General Fremont, was camped on the Pomme de Terre River about fifty miles from Springfield. General Van Dorn had sent Will, then a lieutenant, on a reconnaissance mission to find out more information about the army that faced them.

The closest town to the encampment was Forsyth, and Will knew a farmer there, Bud Coleman, who had been a good friend of his father's.

"It hurt me somethin' awful to hear about Drury 'n Amanda," Coleman said.

Drury and Amanda had been Will's parents. They were killed and their house and barn burned by Jayhawkers who had come from Kansas to raid Missouri farms.

"Thank you, Mr. Coleman, I appreciate the kind words."

"What can I do for you, boy? I don't reckon you just dropped by for a friendly visit."

"Well, I do hope the visit is friendly enough, but since you brought it up, you can help me. I don't know if you are aware of it, but you've got the Yankee army camped just north of your farm."

"Oh, I know it all right, them sons of bitches stoled a cow. I went to see the head man, but he claimed he didn't know nothin' about it."

"I have to be honest with you, Mr. Coleman, I'm a lieutenant in the Confederate Army with General Van Dorn," Will said. "And I'm here to find out what I can about the Yankee Army. I need some reason to be poking around, so I'd like to borrow a mule and a plow so I could pretend to be working in the field."

Coleman chuckled. "Son, you've been away from farmin' too long. This time o' the year, there ain't nothin' to be plowed."

"Does water ever stand in that field?" He pointed to a plot of land north of the homestead.

Coleman smiled. "A slough, yes. You could be plowing a channel to drain that there slough."

Half an hour later, Will was in the field nearest the Yankee army encampment, walking behind a plow, being pulled by a mule. He had been studying the encampment, estimating the size of the army, counting artillery pieces, and observing anything and everything he thought might be good intelligence. Then, as he was about to turn around at the edge of the field, two soldiers came toward him.

"Mister, you want to come with us?" one of the soldiers, a sergeant, asked.

"What for?"

"We got some questions we want to ask you. We're

takin' you to see the general."

This would be even better, Will thought. Assuming he could talk himself out of this, he would be able to get an even closer look at the army.

As Will walked through the encampment under guard of the sergeant and the other soldier, he took in as much as he could, without being too obvious. When they reached the middle of the encampment, Will saw a bearded man in a general's uniform, sitting on a camp stool, drinking coffee. He looked up as Will and his escort approached.

"What do we have here, Sergeant?"

"General Fremont, this here feller was pokin' around where he don't have no business bein'."

"I wasn't poking around, I was plowing a field."

"Who you kiddin', Mister? It's too late 'n the year to be plowin' on anythin'," the sergeant said.

"Do you have an explanation for what you were doing?" General Fremont asked.

"I was opening up a channel so that water will drain into the river, rather than remain standing in the field," Will said.

General Fremont stroked his beard and thought for a moment, then he nodded.

"Let him go, Sergeant. We've got enough enemies without making any more."

"Thank you, General."

Prescott, Arizona

"I hope our meeting wasn't too unpleasant for you," Governor Fremont said, his comment bringing Will's thoughts back to the present.

"Governor, it wasn't unpleasant at all. You might say that you saved my life," Will said with a big smile.

Addie was talking to Jubal Sandos.

"The men who came to your rescue, I believe you said they called themselves Crockett?"

"Yes, as I said, they ran the three men off, then they escorted my father and me back home."

"Is one of them a big man?"

"Yes, that would be Gid."

Jubal scowled. "You know them well enough to call them by their first names?"

"Yes, Will and Gid Crockett. Like I told you, they rode with Papa and me almost all the way from Simmons to Prescott."

"Addie, I'd rather you not have anything to do with either one of those men."

"Why would you say that?"

"They intervened—rather violently I might add, with two of my men while they were in performance of their duty. As Ike Snow and Dan Coates were collecting tax at

The Beatrice, the smaller of the two Crockett brothers brought a whiskey bottle down on Snow's head, in a cowardly attack from behind. Then the Crockett brothers ran them out of the saloon at the point of a gun.

"It had been my intention to arrest them for interfering in the performance of duty of the Prescott Defenders. But as they were the ones who came to your rescue, I'll let it go, this time."

"My, that doesn't sound like them at all," Addie said. "That certainly isn't how they appeared to me."

"My dear, you are sweet and innocent, one might even say naive. Men such as the Crocketts are well able to play innocent to hide who they really are."

"I . . . I suppose that is possible."

"You know, it was for just such a reason that I formed the Prescott Defenders," Sandos said. "I want to protect people like you, and, especially you," he added with a seductive smile.

"I, uh, had better get back to work," Addie said, blushing slightly at the attention she was getting.

"Ike," Sandos called after Addie left.

"Yes, sir?" Snow replied, responding to Sandos' summons.

"Has Abe Connors paid us what he owes us yet?"

"Not yet."

"They held up that stagecoach two weeks ago, didn't they?"

"Yes, sir."

"I think it's time we took care of Mr. Connor, Mr. Dillard, and Mr. Harper."

"Take care of them?"

"Cut our ties with them," Sandos said. "They can't be trusted."

"Abe is the only who knows they're working for us."

"I want to take care of all of them."

Chapter Seven

When Will and Gid went downstairs to have their breakfast in the hotel coffee shop the next morning they saw Addie sitting at a table having a cup of coffee.

"Good morning, Addie," Will said. "Do you mind if my brother and I join you for breakfast?"

"I've had my breakfast, but I'll drink coffee with you, as you have yours."

"Thanks, that will be pleasant," Will said.

"May I ask you a question?" Addie asked.

"Yes, of course."

"Are you violent men?"

"Why would you ask such a question?"

"I've been told that you are violent men. Are you?"

Will paused for a moment before he answered. "I suppose you could say that we are, but with two caveats. We are living in a violent time, and we have only used violence when evil men have forced us to do so."

"You mean like yesterday, when you came to the defense of my father and me."

"Yes."

Addie looked down at her hands. "That was rude of me to question you. I'm sorry. Who knows what would have happened to me if you hadn't come along when you did?"

"I'm glad we could help you, but Miss Reed, have you thought about what you would have done if we hadn't come along?"

Addie shook her head.

"Do you own a gun?"

"Oh, no, that would be . . . ."

"I suppose you are going to say unladylike," Will said, "but having a gun may be the only way to save yourself from whatever a man may try to do to you."

"I suppose you are right. Maybe Mr. Sandos will have something that I could learn to use."

"Gid and I think you should have this." Will nodded at Gid, who pulled something from his vest pocket and held it out toward her.

"What's that?"

"It's a Derringer. A small gun that you can hide in the pocket of your dress. It would be a way for you to protect yourself if you ever needed it."

"Isn't that gun too small?"

"A gun this small is what killed President Lincoln," Gid said.

"Still, I can't accept that as a gift."

"Why not?" Will asked. "It didn't cost us anything. It belonged to a man . . . well, let me just say, we picked it up along the way somewhere."

"How does it work?"

"It's quite simple. You pull the hammer back, then pull the trigger."

Addie reached out for it, taking it from Gid, and lifting it for a closer look.

"Two days ago, I would've never considered carrying a gun, but after what happened yesterday, I will gladly accept your gift."

"Miss Reed, this gun makes a good defense weapon, only if nobody knows you are carrying it. Don't tell your father, don't tell your best friend. Don't tell anyone."

Addie's lips formed a wry smile. "You don't have to worry about that. Carrying a gun is not something I will be bragging about."

"Good."

"I have to get to work now, but thank you," Addie said, and taking the last swallow of her coffee, she stood and walked away.

"You think she'll carry it?" Gid asked after Addie left.

"I don't know," Will replied. "But I hope she will

recognize the advantage of having it."

"I think she will," Gid said.

"As soon as we finish breakfast, I think we should look up Wells and Rush and see what to do about our deed."

"Why? The deed we had notarized in Ash Fork is good here too, isn't it?"

"I suppose it is, but Beaumont told us to look up this place, and he said they would tell us if the deed is legitimate," Will said. "It's a small price to pay, just in case somebody contests our rightful ownership of the Axis."

Gid laughed. "Did anybody ever tell you, you try to borrow trouble, Big Brother?"

The building housing the office of Rush and Wells was less than a block from the Reed Hotel. Walking toward it, they saw a couple of men wearing what they now knew to be Prescott Defender uniforms. As the Prescott Defenders continued down the street there was an arrogance about them, manifested by the way they occupied the boardwalk, whereas the pedestrians they encountered did everything they could to get out of their way.

"Little Brother, something tells me we're going to have a run-in with these Prescott Defender bastards."

"I think you're right," Gid agreed. "I already don't like the sons of bitches and we haven't even been here two full days."

"There it is, just ahead of us," Will said, pointing to a squat, white-planked building.

The sign painted on the window read Rush and Wells, Courts of Record in Arizona Territory.

"Anybody here?" Will called as he and Gid stepped inside.

"I'll be right there," someone called. A rather rotund man with white chin-whiskers and bald, except for a band of white hair that circled above his ears, stepped out of a back room.

"I'm Will Crockett, this is my brother, Gid. Kurt Beaumont told us to look you up."

"John Rush," the man said extending his hand. "How is old Kurt? I've not seen him around for awhile."

"We met Mr. Beaumont in Ash Fork," Will said. "I believe he intends to relocate in New Orleans."

"New Orleans? That's hard to believe," Rush said. "He's had his claim on the Axis since almost the beginning."

"That's good to hear," Will said, pulling out the deed. "Then this is legitimate."

Rush took the paper. "He sold this for five hundred dollars?"

"Yes, sir," Gid said. "It seems he needed the money."

"Lost it in a poker game, I suppose," Rush said shaking his head. "These fools. Many a fortune has been lost on just such a play."

"Then you think the Axis is a viable claim?" Will asked.

"Of course it is," Rush said. "The gold on Lynx Creek had to come from somewhere, and the Axis may just be its source. Of course, if you men expect to find the vein, it's going to take a lot of man hours."

"We're prepared to do that," Will said. "Do we need to do anything to register our claim?"

"Give me five minutes and five dollars, and in the eyes of the law, the Axis Mine belongs to . . . Will and Gid Crockett. Are those your legal names?"

"That would be William and Gideon," Gid said.

John Rush made some entries in a big book, then produced another deed.

"The original deed with the transfer is good, but you wanted a local deed, so here it is. Just sign here and as soon as I affix my stamp, everything is legal."

"Thank you, Mr. Rush," Will said as he and Gid signed the paperwork.

"I wish you boys good luck with the Axis."

Their next stop was the Assayer's Office. Here, they spoke with Arlen Blake.

"The last report was a thousand dollars a ton," Blake said after checking his records. "But that report was from a year ago, April. There hasn't been an assay report filed this year."

"Does that mean the mine is played out?" Gid asked.

"No, not necessarily. Based upon the last assay report, it's unlikely that the mine is no longer productive," Blake said. "It's more likely that the vein changed course and Mr. Beaumont wasn't able to reestablish it."

"That's good to know," Will said with a smile.

"Hey, Will, what do you say we take a ride out to have a look at our gold mine?" Gid asked. He chuckled. "Ha, did you ever think back when we were swinging a scythe on the farm that we would one day own a gold mine?"

"Well, let's not get ahead of ourselves. At this point we don't really know whether we own a gold mine, or a hole in the ground."

Sandos took six men with him to the place where he knew he would find Connors, Dillard, and Harper. Connors met them with an ingratiating smile.

"I was just goin' to . . ."

Whatever Connors was just going to say would never be known, because without the slightest hint of warning, Sandos shot him in the forehead.

"Hey, what the . . ." was as far as Dillard got before he too, was killed.

"No, don't shoot, don't shoot!" Harper said raising his hands.

"What are we goin' to do about him?" Snow asked.

"Chapman, you and Muley take him back and put him in jail. We need to throw the people a bone, and he's going to be our bone," Sandos said, enigmatically. "Coates, you and the others stay here with me and have a look around."

Sandos and the remaining Defenders looked around for half-an-hour without finding anything, and they were growing more and more frustrated.

"What the hell did they do with the money, if they didn't hide it here?" Coates said.

"Maybe they done spent it all," Snow said.

"No, they . . . wait a minute," Sandos said. "What's that?" He pointed to some rocks that, at first glance, looked as if they had always been there, but a little closer examination showed that the rocks had extended the slide by about four feet. "Start moving some of those rocks out of the way," he ordered.

After a few minutes of moving the rocks, Coates called out. "I see somethin'."

Reaching down into the cavity formed after moving the rocks, Coates pulled out a canvas bag. The words WESTERN BANK AND TRUST were written on the side of the pouch.

"Give it here," Sandos ordered, holding out his hand.

Coates handed it over to him and Sandos opened it. He looked inside, then glanced up at the others with a large smile. "It looks like the money's here, or at least most of it is."

Back in Prescott, Sheriff Bower was grilling Nate Harper. "Where's the money you men took from the stagecoach?"

"I don't know," Harper said.

"The other two men are dead," Bower said. "So, you're not protecting them. Now, where's the money?"

"Abe hid it somewhere, only he didn't tell me or Pogue where it was that he done it."

"That doesn't make any sense, Harper, think about it," Sheriff Bower said. "What good would it do to rob a coach, 'n then have Connors hide it away from you two?"

"Abe said he wanted to wait 'till it blowed over a little afore it is that we started on a' spendin' it."

"You didn't just hold up the stagecoach, you murdered some folks, 'n murder don't never blow over," Sheriff Bower informed his prisoner.

Sandos came into the jailhouse then. "Has he told you anything about the money they stole?"

Bower shook his head. "He said that Abe Connors hid it somewhere, 'n didn't tell the other two where he hid it."

"That doesn't seem to make much sense to me, but if he did hide it, he sure picked a good spot. We searched for it and came up empty."

"Maybe when he realizes he's going to get his neck stretched, he'll remember," Bower suggested.

Before Will and Gid left town, they went by the City Feed Yard where they picked up their horses and Jack, the burro that came with the mine.

"You might want to take some grain along with you," Clem Whitehair said. "Not much grazin' land where you're goin'. And besides, why have a pack animal if you don't use 'im?"

"All right, load up a couple hundred pounds of oats," Gid said.

"Do you plan to take in any grub for yourselves?" Whitehair asked.

"I suppose so."

"Then two hundred pounds is too much weight. If you want the little fellow to stay healthy, go light on him going up in the mountains."

"Then make it a hundred pounds," Gid said.

"Not enough."

"Look mister, what are you trying to do?"

"I think I know," Will said. "Do you have another burro that you would sell us?"

Whitehair nodded his head. "I could let him go just real cheap."

"No thanks," Will said. "One Jack is enough. Besides, if we need more grain, that's a reason to come into town more often."

Gid laughed. "What my brother is saying is that the Crockett brothers will be needing more grain themselves."

"I can tell you about that, too. If you ain't never tasted any bock beer, it'll be in season here in a week or so. Them Germans at Raible Brewery brew the best in the Territory."

"We'll keep that in mind," Will said.

When they were out of hearing of Whitehair, Gid turned to Will.

"What in the hell is he talking about? Bock beer?"

"You remember—back in St. Louis, they used to brew a strong ale that they called Doppelbock. Since he said it's almost in season, I suspect he's talking about Maibock. That's a little lighter version," Will said, "but whatever, we'll check out the Raible Brewery when we get back into Prescott."

They stopped at Bashford & Company for their own supplies, picking up enough food to last what they expected to be a week.

"You boys headed up to the Axis?" the clerk asked.

"We are, but how did you know that?" Gid asked.

"Saw you're leadin' Kurt Beaumont's burro. Ever'body knows ever'thing that goes on in this place. Hear he lost his claim in a poker game."

"That's not exactly true. We bought his claim fair and square," Will said.

"Of course you did," the clerk said with a broad smile. "That's what they all say." He picked up a brown bag and began sacking horehound candy. "Kurt never forgot some candy. Woman will be expecting it if she sees Jack."

"Woman? What are you talking about?" Gid asked.

Now the clerk roared back in a loud guffaw. "Old Kurt didn't tell you about Woman? Then you can just be surprised."

The Axis gold mine was located on a slope of the north flank of the Bradshaw Mountains, which was approximately six miles east of Prescott. Will and Gid crossed Lynx Creek, then headed up the gulch. On the way they encountered several of the placer miners, who had makeshift operations in place. To a man, they recognized Jack, and each one called out asking about Kurt Beaumont.

"Seems like a friendly enough place," Gid said when they had passed the last encampment.

"It could be a lot different," Will said. "We all know about cutthroat claim jumpers."

"I suppose it helps that Beaumont hasn't been gone that long," Gid said. "I wonder what his cabin will look like."

Will chuckled. "Don't get your hopes up. Do you remember what he said? 'It's not really a cabin, but it's where I been livin'.' In my mind, that tells me it's not going to be much better than the shebangs we've been passing on the creek."

At that moment, Gid stopped and pointed toward a flat area where some of the Ponderosa pines had been cleared out and an oval shaped hut was located.

"Do you think that's our 'cabin'?"

"We won't know until we check to see if there are a couple of cans of peaches inside," Will said as he dismounted and led his horse up to the shelter.

Gid followed, leading his horse and the burro. "I guess it's better than sleeping under the stars," he said.

The door to the shelter was a hanging piece of deerskin, and once inside it was dark except for a smoke hole in the center of the structure. They saw the iron oven that Kurt had mentioned sitting in the center of the space. As their eyes adjusted to the darkness, they made out a makeshift shelf where there were a few provisions, including the two cans of peaches and a tin of coffee.

"This must be the place," Will said as he picked up the can of peaches. "Who gets the bed?" He indicated a mound of pine straw off to the side.

"That should be me," Gid said, "since I'm the biggest."

They found another hide door leading out the back. When they stepped through it, they saw a crudely made corral. Further up the mountain, they saw what they took to be the opening of the mine. It was boarded over with a "keep out" sign prominently displayed along with the initials, K B.

"This must be the place," Will said as he pulled the boards down. "You know, Little Brother, I think we may have just thrown away five hundred dollars."

"It wouldn't be the first time we've been taken. And besides, our cabin is worth at least that much."

Both men laughed as they stepped into the opening of the mine. Finding a miner's lamp and some lucifers in an attached skin bag, they soon had a light to allow them to move further inside the mine.

"This passageway only goes back about fifty feet," Gid said as he moved along cautiously.

"With only one man working it, that's quite a bit. And according to the assayer, it's already produced some gold."

"Yeah," Gid said. "But didn't Beaumont say he's had this claim since the early seventies?"

"Maybe he was digging someplace else. He must have had some reason to start a drift here, and with both of us working, I think we can get it productive again."

At the end of the drift, they saw evidence of Beaumont's last efforts, rubble on the floor and concave diggings on the back wall.

"What do you say we dig around a bit?" Will suggested.

"All right by me," Gid replied.

They found pickaxes, shovels, and a wheelbarrow just as Beaumont had said, so returning to the mineshaft, they attacked the back wall. They worked for about an hour, and pushed it back at least a foot farther, but their efforts did nothing but add more dirt and rocks to the ground.

They stopped with the pickaxe and started shoveling the ground rubble into the wheelbarrow. After they had cleared away the rubble, they returned to the cabin.

"You tend to the horses and I'll look around and see if I can find a spring head somewhere close," Will said. "If we have to haul water up from the creek, we may be giving up our fortune before we even get started."

"All right," Gid said as he disappeared into the shelter.

Will had only moved a few feet when he heard Gid yell.

Hurrying to the front of the cabin, he found Gid with the two horses.

"What's wrong?"

"Jack's gone—that's what's wrong!"

"Damn! We should have taken care of the animals before we explored the mine, but he can't have gone far," Will said. "It looks like his tracks are leading down this pathway."

They followed the tracks for about a half mile where there was a thicker stand of trees. They found the burro tied to a stake in front of a smaller version of their own dwelling.

"What's this?" Gid asked.

"I don't know, but Jack can't tie himself up," Will said

as he approached the animal.

When he got close, the burro let out a loud bray and a woman of indeterminate age, wearing a deerskin dress came hurrying out of the structure. She was carrying a club and she headed toward Will.

"Hold on there, lady," Gid said as he moved toward her.

Instantly, she turned her club toward Gid and began swinging wildly at him.

Will held up his hand. "Woman. Are you Woman?" He said it as calmly as he could.

The woman turned toward him and lowered her club. She nodded her head.

"Mr. Beaumont told us about you. He sold the Axis to my brother and me."

She got a puzzled expression on her face, but she didn't say anything.

"Jack belongs to us now." Will moved toward the donkey.

Immediately the club came up again.

He continued to move toward the animal. He opened one pack and withdrew the sack or horehound candy.

"For you," he said.

She took the bag and when she looked inside, she smiled and threw her club back toward the hut.

"It's a good thing we brought that candy," Gid said. He moved to untie the burro.

She immediately grabbed the rein and shook her head no.

"All right," Gid said, you can keep Jack here, but we need the grain and the grub."

With the packs off the burro, Will opened one again and handed her some dried fruit. "Do you know where we can find water?" He made a motion like he was drinking.

She pointed to a spot behind her hut where a wooden box had been constructed. Inside was a little pool, where good clean water bubbled. Will bent over and cupping his hands, drank the cool water.

"Do we share?" he asked, and she nodded yes.

"Then we will see you again soon. Come on, Gid, let's leave Woman alone for awhile."

The Crocketts grabbed the packs and waving goodbye headed down the path to their cabin.

"You would have thought Beaumont might have told us about his neighbor, don't you think?" Gid asked.

"If you remember, he did tell us about her. He said he had a neighbor who was old and crotchety sometimes. He just didn't tell us she was an Indian woman who apparently doesn't say a word."

"Who likes horehound candy," Gid added.

When they got back to the hut, they put the horses in the corral and put out some grain. Finding a couple of buckets, Will went back to get some water, while Gid put their few items of food on the shelf with the peaches. He also gathered some pine straw to make another bed, and bringing in the saddles and horse blankets, he made credible beds for both of them.

"I'm so tired," Gid said when Will returned. "I'm thinking jerky and coffee will be enough food for tonight."

"And peaches," Will added. "I do believe this is a first—my little brother not hungry."

Gid smiled. "It'll have to do."

After the jerky and peaches, the two men sat on the ground outside the hut, leaning back against the wall.

"Have we bitten off more than we can chew, here?" Gid asked as he threw a stone off into the distance.

"I don't know, Gid. This seemed like a pretty good idea at the time, but right now I hurt like the dickens, and it can only get worse."

***

Although Nate Harper wasn't being tried for accosting Addie Reed and her father, both Biff and Addie testified against him, the prosecuting attorney saying that would help establish the kind of person Harper was.

"Your Honor, there are no witnesses for the defense,"

Albert Blocker, the court appointed lawyer for the defense said.

"Mr. Harper, you have the right to take the stand to testify on your own behalf," Judge Briggs said. "If you are willing to tell the court where you hid the money, it might mitigate the circumstances for you."

"There ain't no need in me a' doin' that," Harper said. "I don't know where no money was hid, 'n you're goin' to hang me anyway, so let's just quit all this palaverin' around 'n get the job done."

"Very well. Jury, you may retire to consider the verdict."

When the jury reached the jury room, Amos Chapman, one of the ten Prescott Defenders who made up the jury, was selected as jury foreman.

"Let's get this over with," Chapman said. "There ain't nobody here, hell, there ain't even nobody in the courtroom but what don't know Harper's guilty."

"I'm not so sure about that," Matt Culver said. Culver was one of the two non-Prescott Defenders that made up the jury.

"How the hell can you say that, Culver?"

"There were no witnesses against him," Culver said.

"Biff Reed and his daughter both testified against him," Chapman said.

"Yes, but that testimony had nothing to do with the

robbery, or with the murder. What I mean is, there wasn't anybody who could actually put Harper at the scene of the crime."

"Yeah? Well, he knows where the money is, that should count for something," Chapman said.

"He said he didn't know where the money is," Culver insisted.

"Matt, but consider this," Dale Pollard said. Pollard was a teamster with the Prescott Freight Haulers. "He told Sheriff Bower that the reason he didn't know where they put the money, was because Abe Connor hid it. Now how would he know Connor hid it, if he hadn't been part of the robbery?"

"Yeah," Culver said. "Yeah, I guess you're right."

"All right, let's vote on it," Chapman said.

The vote was twelve guilty.

Chapman informed the bailiff, and the court was called back into session, the twelve men returning to the jury box.

"Gentleman of the jury," Judge Briggs said. "Have you selected a jury foreman?"

"Yeah, that would be me, uh, Your Honor. Amos Chapman."

"Please stand when you address the court," Briggs ordered.

Chapman stood.

"Has the jury reached a verdict?"

"Yeah, we have."

Briggs winced at the lack of decorum exhibited by Chapman, but he made no comment.

"How find you?"

"Hell, we find the son of a bitch guilty . . . uh, Your Honor."

There was a scattering of laughter in the gallery, and Briggs brought his hammer down, sharply.

"So say you one, so say you all?" Briggs asked.

No one challenged the verdict.

"Will the defendant and council approach the bench?" Briggs asked.

Harper and his lawyer approached the bench.

"Nate Harper, you have been tried by a jury of your peers, and you have been found guilty of the crime of robbery, and murder in the first degree. Have you any comment to make?"

"No."

"Very well, this court directs that a gallows be built, and that your sentence, which is death by hanging, be carried out at the sheriff's convenience not to exceed one week from today. Court is adjourned."

The trial for Nate Harper had taken less than two hours.

Within a week, Will and Gid had gone ten feet farther into the side of the mountain, but turned up no sign of color.

"I don't know, Will, I think we bought a pig in a poke," Gid said as he leaned on his pick and wiped the sweat from his face.

"I'm not ready to give up just yet," Will said.

"I'm not ready to give up either, I was just saying."

"What do you say we go back into town and have a beer?" Will asked.

Gid chuckled. "People are right, you *are* the smart one."

When they returned to Prescott, they were surprised to see a considerable gathering of the town citizens in the street. It didn't take much investigation to determine what was happening. A gallows had been erected right in front of the jail house on Gurley Street, and a sign was nailed to one of the upright beams.

ON THESE GALLOWS WILL BE HUNG THE
STAGECOACH ROBBER AND MURDERER
NATE HARPER BROUGHT TO JUSTICE BY THE
PRESCOTT DEFENDERS.

Will and Gid saw the door to the jail open, and Sheriff Bower came out, followed by a prisoner who was wearing brown pants and a white shirt. The prisoner was clean-shaven with hair the color of sun-ripened wheat. He was being brought out between two men, each one wearing the uniform of the Prescott Defenders. There was one Defender on each side, holding the prisoner's arms, and leading him toward the gallows.

"Will that's . . ." Gid started to say, but Will finished the sentence for him.

"One of the men who attacked Biff and Addie Reed."

"So, he was a stagecoach robber and a murderer too."

The expression on Harper's face, and the look in his eyes, was more of detachment than fear. It was as if he had already surrendered his life, and nothing remained but the physical, soulless body.

The four men were followed by another member of the Prescott Defenders, his uniform considerably more elaborate than that of the two men who were escorting Harper.

The somber party mounted the steps where the hangman and a priest were already waiting. When Harper was put into position, the priest stepped up to him. Harper seemed oblivious of the priest and of the hangman, as he stared straight ahead with flat, unblinking eyes.

The priest spoke so quietly that not even those nearest the gallows could hear him, then he made the sign of the cross and stepped back.

The sheriff stepped to the front of the gallows platform. Holding a piece of paper in his hand, he began to read loudly enough so that all could hear.

"In a trial conducted one week ago before a jury of his peers, Nate Harper was found guilty for robbing the Wickenburg Stagecoach, and murdering Clem Patterson the driver, and passengers Emma Joyce, and her six-year-old daughter, Christina. We are assembled here today, to carry out the court order of the execution signed by Judge Andrew Briggs.

"And now Colonel Jubal Sandos has a few words to say."

The sheriff stepped to one side, and the man in the elaborate uniform moved forward.

"Ladies and gentlemen of Prescott, you are about to see a murderer and a stagecoach robber be hanged by the neck until dead. After Nate Harper and two others, Abe Connors and Pogue Dillard, carried out the foul deed, I mobilized the Prescott Defenders and we pursued, caught, and engaged in battle with the three men. Abe Connors and Pogue Dillard were killed in that engagement, and Nate Harper was captured and brought here for trial."

"Let this be an example, and let the word go forth that if any crime is committed anywhere in Yavapai County, the Prescott Defenders will hunt you down, and we will bring the perpetrator to justice."

Sandos stepped aside, and now the prisoner and the hangman occupied center stage. The hangman offered

Harper a mask, but he refused. The hangman then walked over to the lever and looked at Sheriff Bower.

The sheriff nodded, the hangman pulled the lever, the trap door opened and Harper fell through. The gallows platform was high enough that Harper's body could be seen as it hung beneath the floor. He jerked, and pulled his legs up then pushed them down a few times, as if by that action he could relieve the pressure on his neck. The convulsions continued for almost a full minute as the crowd gasped, and a few called out prayers.

Then the convulsions stopped, and the body hung still, making a slow, quarter turn to the right.

That evening Sandos and Addie had dinner together at The Gem. During the meal other customers kept coming over to the table to congratulate Sandos and the Prescott Defenders on bringing the murderers and stagecoach robbers to justice.

"Thank you, we were only doing our duty," Sandos insisted. "Addie, you helped bring about justice too, you know. I've no doubt that it was you and your father's testimony that Harper was one of the men who accosted you was what helped find Harper guilty."

"If I had to do it again, I'm not sure I would testify."

"Why would you say that?"

"Papa and I were the only two who testified against

him, and our testimony had nothing to do with the robbery or the murders."

"Yes, but in my mind, his sin of attacking you is as great as his sin of murdering the stagecoach driver and the two passengers."

"Oh, no, I can't see a comparison between them being killed and me being made to feel uncomfortable," Addie insisted.

"But, my dear, don't you realize that if the Crocketts hadn't come along when they did, you and your father could well have been killed?"

"Oh, that's true, isn't it? That makes me even more thankful that they came along when they did."

"Yes, and though it pains me to admit it, violent men that they are, even I am glad they arrived in time to help you."

"Jubal, why do you insist that the Crocketts are violent?"

"I told you about their attack on my men who were but doing their duty. But if you want to know more, just ask Ben Weaver. He has archived issues of the *Prescott Advocate* that have stories about their exploits, and they name some of the men the Crocketts have killed."

"But, they seemed so nice."

Jubal laughed. "You'd hardly expect them to advertise that they're killers, would you?"

"No, I guess not."

Chapter Eight

Over the next few days, Will and Gid found out what they could about the Prescott Defenders, and especially about their leader, "Colonel" Jubal Sandos. They learned that, at one time Sandos had actually been a colonel, but he was cashiered from the army for dereliction of duty, and mistreatment of the soldiers under him.

"They collect taxes from every business in town," the bartender at The Beatrice told them. "In addition, we have to charge everyone in town five cents on the dollar for every purchase they make, so that means they are taxing the citizens as well."

"And the city fathers haven't given them a charter to do that?" Will asked.

"No," Ki said.

"Then that's a form of extortion."

"You could say that," Ki said, "but the plain truth is that

the Defenders have at least fifteen members and there's no way Sheriff Bower and his deputy can challenge them."

"What about Governor Fremont? Can't he do something about it?"

Ki shook his head. "There's no territorial police force, and besides . . . I hesitate to say this, but Governor Fremont is more interested in Washington than he is in Arizona."

"Then we'll go see what the army can do," Will said.

Will and Gid rode the short distance to Fort Whipple which was located on the banks of Granite Creek. They presented themselves at the gate where they were escorted to the Post Headquarters. They were met by Sergeant Major Hamilton Philpot. The sergeant major was a big man, as large as Gid. He was clean-shaven and completely bald, and because of his size, his head looked like a cannon ball perched upon shoulders.

The cannon ball spoke.

"You boys come to join up with the army, did you?"

"No, Sergeant Major, we came to speak with the commanding officer of the post," Will said.

"What do you want to talk to him about?"

"I'm afraid that is privileged information."

"You don't tell me what it's about, you don't see the general. My job is to filter out people who might turn out to be a pain in the ass."

"We have a letter from Governor Fremont, asking General Myers to meet with us."

"Let me see the letter," Philpot said.

Will showed the sergeant major the letter Fremont had given him, and after he read it, he handed it back. "Wait here," he said, his words little more than a snort.

General Myers was leaning back in his chair, with his feet on his desk when Will and Gid were shown to his office. He was smoking a cigar, but he removed it to speak.

"What does the governor want?" Myers asked.

"We have a problem in Prescott, that's more than the sheriff can handle," Will said.

"Listen, I know my men can raise a ruckus, but when you get men and alcohol together, things happen," the general said.

"I suppose that is true, General, but that is not the problem," Will said.

"Then why have you come to me?"

Will explained how the Prescott Defenders had taken over the town and were charging illegal taxes.

"But aren't they serving a purpose? Didn't they recently bring in the man who held up the stagecoach, murdering the driver and two passengers?"

"Yes, they did."

"It would seem to me that such a thing would be welcome," General Myers said.

"Some say it's too big a price to pay," Will said.

"General, we need the army to come help the town deal with the Prescott Defenders," Gid said. "Like my brother told you, they're taking over the town, and they have everyone too scared to stand up to them."

Myers reached over to his ashtray to tap off the ash. "Sorry boys, but I can't help you."

"What do you mean you can't help?" Will asked, barely keeping his anger in check.

"Posse Comitatus."

"Posse what?"

General Myers pulled out a book from his desk, then began to read. "From and after the passage of this act, it shall not be lawful to employ any part of the Army of the United States, as a posse comitatus, or otherwise, for the purpose of executing the laws, except in such cases and under such circumstances as such employment of said force may be expressly authorized by the Constitution, or by act of Congress, and no money appropriated by this act shall be used to pay any of the expenses incurred in the employment of any troops in violation of this section and any person willfully violating the provisions of this section shall be deemed guilty of a misdemeanor and on conviction thereof shall be punished by fine not exceeding ten thousand dollars or imprisonment not exceeding two years or by both such fine and imprisonment."

After reading the passage, he lay the book down. "So, as you can see, my hands are tied. There's nothing I can do to help, so the governor is going to have to deal with it, himself."

"Thank you for taking the time to meet with us," Will said. "Let's go, Gid."

"It's the judge," Sheriff Bower said when Will and Gid told him of their failure to get any support from the army.

"The judge?"

"Yeah, Judge Andrew Briggs, the worst judge in the Territory," Bower said. "He appointed Sandos as chief law enforcer, and then Sandos put together that bunch of hoodlums as deputies of the court. That means there's nothing I can do about the Defenders, even if I had the money or manpower to go after them. So, with the army's hands tied, and with the court telling me what I can do, the Prescott Defenders can't be touched."

"Yeah, so it would seem," Will said. He sighed. "Come on, Gid, this isn't our fight so let's head on out to the mine."

"Humph," Gid said. "You mean the mine that hasn't produced anything."

"We haven't given it much of a chance," Will said. "Are you ready to give up so soon?"

"California is looking better every day."

Addie stood in front of the rather small, white building crammed in between the Raible Brewery and the bank building. A large window in front of the building had painted in blue letters, outlined with gold, the words PRESCOTT ADVOCATE.

Jubal had told her that if she wanted more information about Will and Gid Crockett, she should search through old newspapers. She stood outside for a moment, steeling herself before going in. Did she actually want to find out anything negative about the Crocketts? After all, one of the men who had intercepted her father and her had been convicted of murder, so she was even more convinced that Will and Gid had saved their lives.

Taking a deep breath, she pushed the door open and stepped inside, where she was assailed by the smell of printers' ink. A rather short man, with a pleasant, though bespectacled face, came to meet her.

"Ah, Miss Reed, are you bringing new copy for your advertisement?" Ben Weaver, the editor and publisher, asked.

"Oh, no, Papa is well pleased with the results we're getting from the ad," Addie said. "But I wanted to ask you something else."

"Sure, go ahead, I'll answer if I can."

"I suppose you have met Will and Gid Crockett?"

"Of course," Ben said. "I hope they hit pay dirt out

at the Axis. Heaven knows Kurt Beaumont did his best out there, and the whole county was rooting for him. A right good fellow."

"Back to the Crocketts," Addie said. "What I want to know is, who are they, exactly? Jub . . . that is, Colonel Sandos said that you might know a little of their past."

Weaver smiled. "Well, they seem like upstanding young men, but some of their previous escapades have been picked up by the AP, and since I belong to the Associated Press, I have the option of printing the article if I want to. I admit I've printed a few. Made good copy and that sells papers."

"What do you mean by exploits?"

"That's just my word for what they do," Weaver said. "It seems like some folks consider them real heroes if somebody needs a defending angel. Sort of like what they did for you and your pa. As the AP likes to point out, the Crocketts have dealt with many an outlaw."

"By dealt with, do you mean killed?"

Weaver raised his eyebrows as he walked over to a shoulder high cabinet and, pulling open one of the drawers, he began sorting through the flat-lying newspapers until he found what he was looking for.

"Here's an article that's not too old," Weaver said, handing the newspaper to Addie. "You can read it yourself and decide what you think."

GUNFIGHT HURLS THREE MEN TO ETERNITY

Deputy Harley Peters Killed, His Widow Mourns

Gerald Tombs and Clyde Critchlow Also Slain

World is Better Off For Their Demise

Saturday night, at a time lacking fifteen minutes of eleven o'clock, the streets of Reveille became a battlefield when four desperate men threw themselves at each other in mortal struggle. When at last the smoke had cleared, only one, Will Crockett, remained alive. By his courage, and the accuracy of his shooting, the murder of Deputy Harley Peters was avenged, and two of the most pernicious desperadoes ever to walk the streets of Reveille were dispatched to their Maker, whose mercy they can only hope for, as no one who remains on this mortal coil would deign to lift a prayer on their behalf.

Addie handed the newspaper back to Weaver.

"Then Jubal was right. They are violent men."

"I suppose you could say that, Miss Reed, but from what I've read, when they've killed, it has only been in the fulfillment of justice."

"They are violent men," Addie said as she turned to leave the newspaper office.

As she returned to the apothecary, she thought about the article she had just read. What sort of man would stand up to three others in a gunfight? The article said that Will Crockett was a virtuous man for having done so, but still only a man of violence could do such a thing.

What if violence had been required to rescue her and her father?

She was troubled, because she didn't know exactly how she felt about that. She let her hand cover her pocket where she carried the very derringer given to her by the Crocketts. Would she consider herself violent if she ever had to use it? Perhaps she should return it. What if this very gun had been used to kill someone? She shuddered as she opened the door to the drugstore and went inside.

Within another week the brothers had extended the drift ten feet deeper into the side of the mountain, but still had nothing to show for their effort.

"Tell me, Will, do you think this is worth it, or are we wasting our time?" Gid asked as he was sitting on a bolder eating beans from a can.

"Getting tired of the work are you?"

"No. Well, yeah if it's going to be totally non-productive. I mean we've taken out quite a chunk of this hill, and we have nothing to show for it but dirt, rock, and blistered hands."

"What if we go into town for a couple of beers and a good supper . . ."

"At The Gem and then spend the night at Reed's--get a haircut, a hot bath and a real bed to sleep in," Gid injected.

"That's kind of what I was thinking."

Gid smiled. "Sounds good to me."

The first place they went after going into town, was The Beatrice, where they were greeted warmly by the bartender.

"So, are you two boys here with your pockets full of gold?" Ki teased as he drew a mug of beer for each of them.

"Our pockets are full, all right," Gid said. "Full of dirt and rocks."

"Well, keep at it. Arlen Blake believes the mine will pay out," Ki said.

"That's easy for an assayer to say," Gid said. "He's not the one with blisters on his hand as big as quarters."

"We're in no hurry to quit," Will said. He glanced toward Housewright who was playing the piano. "What's Nigel playing now? That's a pretty tune."

"It's a *Piano Concerto* by Mozart."

"How do you know all these pieces?" Gid asked.

Ki shrugged his shoulders. "He's played the same things so often that I just recognize them."

"You have a fascinating job, Ki. You're entertained by beautiful music as you work, and in Penny and Elaina you have pretty girls to look at. Besides you get to meet and talk with interesting people all day."

"I do enjoy the music and I do appreciate having Penny and Elaina around. But as far as meeting and talking to interesting people, some of them I would just as soon not meet. For example," he added nodding toward the front door. Four men wearing the uniforms of Prescott Defenders came in.

"Hello, Jonas, what will it be?" Ki asked.

"We'll have our free drink," Jonas replied. "But first, we have a little business to conduct with these two."

Neither Will nor Gid showed any reaction to Jonas' comment.

"Don't you want to know what that business is?" Jonas asked.

"Not particularly," Will replied.

"Well, I'll tell you what it is. We're here to collect a gold tax."

"A gold tax? What the hell is a gold tax?" Gid asked.

"It's a tax on people who own gold mines," Jonas explained. "And since you two now own the Axis mine, you have a tax to pay."

"We haven't found any gold yet."

"It doesn't matter whether you've found gold or not. You still have to pay the tax."

"And just how much tax would that be?" Will asked.

"Forty dollars. That's twenty dollars apiece."

"We aren't going to pay it."

"Forty dollars too much for you, is it?" Jonas asked.

"No, you don't understand. We wouldn't pay it, if it was only five dollars."

"Oh, I think you'll pay it all right," Jonas said.

Jonas and one of the other Prescott Defenders drew their pistols and pointed them at Will and Gid.

"What do you expect to do with those guns?" Will asked the question as calmly as if he were inquiring about the time.

"We plan to kill you, if you don't pay your taxes," Jonas said.

"Wouldn't that be counterproductive?"

"Wouldn't that be what?" Jonas replied, confused by the word.

"Counterproductive," Will said. "It means that if you kill us, you absolutely won't get your tax money."

"Are you going to pay your taxes?"

"No."

"We can't let you get away with that," Jonas said. "If you don't pay your taxes, then other people will say they don't have to pay either. I'm afraid we're going to have to kill you."

"Or I'll kill you," Will said.

"What the hell are you talking about?" Jonas asked. "Are you blind, man? Me 'n Vestal already has our guns out, and we're a' pointin' 'em at you. All we have to do to kill you, is pull the trigger."

"And you're still hell bent on killing us?"

"If you don't pay your taxes, we have to. I told you, if we let you get away with it, ever' body else'll stop payin' their taxes too. So, this is your last warning. Pay us the forty dollars or die."

"No."

Jonas shook his head. "You asked for it, mister. Kill 'em, Vestal," Jonas ordered. "Kill 'em both."

Jonas started to pull back the hammer on his pistol, but before he could do so, Will drew and fired twice. Both Jonas and Vestal went down. The other two started for their guns but Gid beat them to the draw, and they went down as well.

The sudden shooting interrupted the piano music and halted all conversation. For a long moment there was a stunned silence in the room as gun smoke drifted over the four bodies lying on the floor.

"Did you see that?" someone asked, interrupting the silence. "Jonas 'n Vestal both already had their guns in their hands 'n was fixin' to shoot when that one drawed 'n killt both of 'em."

"Yeah, 'n the big un got the other two," another said.

"I ain't never seen nothin' like it," a third offered.

"Are they dead?" Ki asked, as he looked at the bodies

lying on the floor just in front of the bar.

"Yes, they're dead," Will said. "We didn't have time not to kill them."

Now a very spirited conversation began as everyone in the saloon wanted to share their point of view on what happened.

Will picked up his beer. "You'd better drink up, Little Brother. I expect the sheriff will be here soon."

The brothers were only half-way through their beer when Sheriff Bower came into the saloon.

"I heard shooting," he said, then he stopped in mid-sentence and looked down at the four bodies lying on the floor. "Oh, oh, what happened here?"

Everyone in the saloon started talking at once, yelling out what they had seen, along with their own interpretations of the event.

"Hold it, hold it!" Sheriff Bower called out, holding up his hands to silence the shouting. He looked over at Ki Hastings.

"Ki, I take it you saw what happened, here?"

"Yes, I saw it."

"All right, tell me about it."

Ki told of the four men coming into the saloon and accosting Will and Gid, demanding forty dollars from them.

"And when Will and Gid said they wouldn't pay,

Jonas 'n Vestal there tried to shoot them," Ki said. "And get this, Sheriff, Will's gun was in his holster, but he drew and killed them before they could even pull the hammer back."

"What about these two?" Bower asked pointing to the remaining two men who, like Jonas and Vestal lay crumpled on the floor.

"They started to draw," Ki said.

"And you shot all four of them?" Sheriff Bower asked Will.

"No, sir," Gid said. "I shot those two."

"He was provoked too, Sheriff," Ki said. "Those two men started their draw first. It's just that Gid was faster."

"There won't be any charges filed against these two fine men, will there, Sheriff?" Nigel Housewright asked.

"I don't intend to file any charges," Bower said. "But I don't know how Sandos is going to take this."

"There are four of his evil brigands lying dead on the floor, and you say you don't know how Sandos is going to take it?" Nigel Housewright asked. "I don't think there is any doubt as to how he will react. Do you, really?"

At that very moment, the subject of their speculation came rushing into the room.

"What happened here?" Sandos demanded.

"It's rather obvious isn't it?" Ki replied. "The four sons of bitches that you see lying on the floor are dead."

"Who did this?" Sandos asked looking around.

"That would be me. Well, and my brother," Will said.

"You are under arrest, for murder," Sandos said. "Both of you."

"Sandos, you have no authority to make arrests," Sheriff Bower said.

"Of course, I do," Sandos said. "I've been given arrest authority by Judge Briggs. How do you suppose I was able to arrest Nate Harper?"

"It was my impression that Judge Briggs gave you limited authority for posse use only," Bower said.

Sandos smiled smugly. "Well, Sheriff, what do you think the Prescott Defenders are, if not a posse? And if you think that commission is invalid, it will be easy for me to get another one. I ask only that you keep them here, until I see Judge Briggs."

"I tell you what, Sheriff. Gid and I are going to have supper at the coffee shop in the Reed Hotel. If you need us, you'll find us there."

Once Sandos stormed out of the saloon, the saloon patrons who had been following the heated exchange without comment started a dozen brisk conversations.

"Who does that son of a bitch think he is, trying to arrest those men? It was self-defense, everyone in here saw it."

"It don't matter none whether it was self-defense or not,"

someone said. "Ole Sandos has Briggs in his hip-pocket for some reason, though I sure don't know why."

"Sheriff, we're going to our supper now," Will said.

"All right," Bower answered, giving his assent, even though it had been a declaration and not a question.

"Too bad Sandos wasn't with them when they came in," Gid said as the two of them boarded their horses at the livery. "Because I have a feeling that son of a bitch is going to be trouble."

"Well, if he is, we'll deal with it as it happens," Will replied.

Chapter Nine

When Sandos went into the apothecary, Addie was busy with a customer. She saw him and smiled as if asking him to wait for moment, and he nodded.

"You should take this nostrum just before you go to bed tonight, and then again right after you get up in the morning," she told the customer.

"Thank you, Addie," the customer replied. "Sometimes I think you give me better advice than I get from Dr. McCandless."

"That's kind of you to say, but you should follow what Dr. McCandless has to say before you listen to me."

Addie waited until her customer had left before she came over to greet Sandos.

"Jubal," she said with broad smile. "This is a pleasant surprise, but wait, you aren't coming to tell me you can't come to dinner tonight, are you? I'd be so disappointed."

"Apparently, you haven't heard," Sandos said.

"Heard? Heard what?" Her smile was replaced with a look of concern.

"If you still question whether or not your heroes are violent men, they committed murder this afternoon."

Addie gasped, and put her hand to her mouth. "You're not talking about Will and Gid are you? What happened?"

"I think you know that somehow by hook or by crook, the Crocketts say they own the Axis mine. Lord knows how that happened—nobody's seen or heard from Kurt Beaumont since he left here," Jubal said, "but according to John Rush, he says their paperwork is all in order. That being the case, the Crocketts owe the tax Judge Briggs has attached to all mine owners. But those two refused to pay their tax, and when my men approached them with a legitimate tax assessment, the Crocketts killed all four of them."

The expression on Sandos' face was one of great sorrow.

"Four men, four good and decent men, men who have dedicated themselves to the service of our community, murdered for forty dollars."

"Oh, Jubal, I'm so sorry," Addie said, putting her hand on Sandos' shoulder.

"And I'm sorry this is what it took for you to learn the truth about these two. I tried to tell you they were violent men and now you can see for yourself how you were duped by them."

"Yes, I . . . I'm afraid you were right."

* * *

When Will and Gid stepped into the coffee shop at the Reed Hotel a few minutes later, they saw Governor Fremont sitting alone at a table near the back of the room. Fremont signaled for them to come join him.

"Thank you for joining me," Governor Fremont said indicating that they should sit down. "Ben Weaver has shared some articles chronicling some of your past exploits, and I must say, I'm most impressed. You two have earned quite a reputation as paladins of the oppressed."

"I'm afraid that our reputation is bigger than our accomplishments," Gid said.

"And yet, such a reputation could not be gained, without an underlying of truth," Fremont insisted.

Shortly after they sat down, but before their orders were taken, they were joined by Nigel Housewright.

"Governor, have these fine gentlemen told you of their adventurous visit to The Beatrice?" Housewright asked.

"I don't believe we have discussed any recent adventure. What happened?"

"Four members of the Prescott Defenders accosted

them with deadly intent, but so quickly were Will and Gid able to employ their pistols and energize the balls that struck with deadly effect, that there are now four fewer members of that accursed organization who will be able to visit their evil machinations upon the oppressed citizenry of our fair community."

Governor Fremont looked at Housewright with a bemused expression on his face. "Nigel, I have no idea what you just said."

"He said we killed four of the Prescott Defenders," Gid said.

"Oh, dear," Fremont said.

"It was in self-defense, Governor, as will be attested to by everyone who was in the pub at the time," Housewright added.

Addie came into the coffee shop then, and seeing Will and Gid, walked back to the table.

"Is it true?" she asked, in a pained voice.

"What?" Will replied.

"Did you just kill four men?"

"I assure you, Miss Reed. The employment of their firearms was necessitated by self-defense. They had no choice but to engage their attackers, or die," Nigel said.

"But you did just kill four men," Addie said.

"Yes." Will offered no further explanation, and Addie, with a sense of chagrin on her face turned, and walked away.

"I wonder why she seems so upset by this?" Nigel asked. "I clearly explained that it was in self-defense."

"She's Sandos' woman," Gid replied, as if that could explain Addie's reaction.

At that moment Sheriff Bower, Jubal Sandos, and three of the Prescott Defenders came into the coffee shop and walked up to the table where the four men were sitting.

"I have a warrant, issued by Judge Briggs, for the arrest of Will and Gid Crockett," Sandos announced. "I am hereby placing you two men under arrest. Sheriff, take them to jail."

"There's no need for that," Fremont said.

"Governor, didn't you hear me? I have a warrant from Judge Briggs."

"You can arrest them, but there will be no need to put them in jail. I'm granting a limited commutation so that they may remain free under their own recognizance until such time as a trial is held," Fremont said.

"Very well," Sandos said, barely able to restrain his anger. "The trial is tomorrow."

"What's going to happen to them?" Addie asked.

"I imagine, and I certainly hope, that they pay for their crime of murder with their lives," Sandos said. "They will be tried tomorrow morning, and I've no doubt that Judge Briggs will sentence them to hang."

"Oh, but they were so . . ." Addie paused in mid-sentence.

"They were so what, my dear?"

"Nice," Addie said. "They were so nice to papa and me."

"I'm afraid they were merely playing upon your innocence. I have no doubt it was their intention to collect upon that service at some later date. And didn't you tell me that your father gave them free rooms at the hotel?"

"Yes, he did."

"See, even that was a form of extortion. They are no good, Addie; they have a long and storied history of violence. I wouldn't be surprised if they didn't come into possession of Beaumont's mine by means of some violent action."

"I suppose you're right—they did kill four of your men."

Sandos shook his head. "No, they didn't kill them, they murdered them."

"Oh, Papa, is it true what Jubal says?" Addie asked her father that night.

"There seems to be two very different stories," Biff Reed said. "The story being told by all those who actually witnessed the event say that Will and Gid reacted in self-defense."

"Jubal said his men were killed for no other reason

than asking for the mine tax to be paid. Just think. Four men dead because of forty dollars."

"There aren't any witnesses who say that," Biff replied.

"And why are there no witnesses?"

Biff paused for a moment before he replied. "Because they are dead."

"Killed by the Crocketts."

"Apparently so."

"We were fooled by them, Papa. They made fools of us."

"But they also more than likely saved our lives."

"Oh, I don't know what to think. On the one hand, Jubal tells me that the Crocketts are murderers. On the other hand, our contact with them has been positive."

"Sweetheart, have you stopped to think that Jubal may have his own reasons for turning the public against Will and Gid?"

"What do you mean?"

"Well, let's face it. Right now, Jubal Sandos has this town under his thumb. I think he sees Will and Gid as an impediment to his control."

"But, Papa, I just can't believe that Jubal would lie to me. I'm sure he cares for me as much as I care for him."

Four of the Prescott Defenders were sitting around a table in the Bit Saloon. They had been drinking pretty hard and were talking about the four of their number who had been killed.

"Jonas Cokeberry was as good with a gun as anyone I ever know'd," Amos Chapman said. "There ain't no way in hell that he already had his gun drawed 'n 'a pointin' at Crockett, 'n Crockett was still able to kill 'im. No sir, they're all lyin'. Like as not Crockett just drawed his gun 'n kilt Jonas without givin' him no warnin' a' tall."

"Folks is all sayin' that Jonas was holdin' the gun in his hand, though," one of the others said.

"Yeah, well they're all a' lyin', 'n there ain't no doubt in my mind but that them two sons of bitches is goin' to be found guilty 'n hung."

"Can't be soon enough."

Chapter Ten

Talk of the trial was on every tongue in every saloon up and down Whiskey Row. Albert Blocker and Sebastian Phelps had been summoned to meet with Judge Briggs in his office.

"One of you is going to act as prosecutor, and the other will be the defense counsel," Judge Briggs said.

"I want to prosecute," Blocker said. "There's no way I want to go against Sandos."

"Very well, as you were counsel for defense the last time, you'll prosecute this case."

"That leaves me to oppose Sandos," Phelps said.

"I don't expect it'll be much of a case," Briggs said. "I don't think you'll have to worry about Mr. Sandos. If you can get them to plead guilty, it will save us all a lot of trouble."

"Will you spare them, if I can do that?"

"If you get a guilty plea, I'll sentence them to life in prison rather than the gallows," Briggs said.

"All right, I'm pretty sure I can get them to plead guilty," Phelps said.

Voir Dire was mechanical, and no potential juror was eliminated.

Will and Gid had no input into the selection of their attorney, though they were able to discuss their case with him for a few minutes before the trial began.

Phelps pushed his glasses up his blade of a nose and looked at Will and Gid.

"I think you two should plead guilty, and throw yourselves at the mercy of the court," Phelps said. "I believe I could talk the judge into giving you a life sentence, rather than sending you to the gallows."

"We're not going to plead guilty," Will said.

"Why not? You did kill them. Everyone in the saloon saw you kill them."

"They also saw that it was self-defense."

"I'm afraid that's going to be a very difficult case to make."

"Nevertheless it's true, and we will not plead guilty."

Phelps let out an audible sigh, and shook his head, slowly. "Very well, we shall enter a plea of not-guilty. After all, it is your necks that will be stretched."

"Your confidence is most reassuring," Will said sarcastically.

* * *

The courtroom was packed for the trial, to the point that the walls were lined by those who were unable to find a seat. The courtroom buzzed with conversation.

"Jim Ed seen the whole thing, 'n he said it beat 'nything he ever seen."

"Turner said it was self-defense."

"That don't matter none. Not with this judge," another said.

The bailiff stepped out from a back room and addressed the court. "All rise for His Honor Judge Andrew Briggs."

Everyone in the court stood as Judge Briggs entered. He was wearing a robe that didn't obscure his protruding stomach. Flipping his robe back out of the way, he sat down.

"Courtroom may be seated."

Will, Gid, and Sebastian Phelps took their seat with the rest of the court room.

"Bailiff, for what reason are we gathered?"

"Your Honor, there comes now before this court William and Gideon Crockett to be tried for the crime of murder," the bailiff replied.

"Are the accused represented by council?"

Phelps stood. "Your Honor, Sebastian Phelps for the defense."

"And who is present for the prosecution?"

Blocker stood. "Albert Blocker for the prosecution, Your Honor."

To most of the people in the gallery, this was a charade. These two lawyers were always the ones chosen to argue in the Briggs court. Any one of the dozen other lawyers in town, preferred to argue before Judge Hargraves.

"Mr. Phelps, how do your clients plead?"

"They plead not guilty, Your Honor."

"Not guilty?" Briggs replied, the expression in his voice denoting his surprise by the plea.

"Not guilty," Phelps repeated, as he lowered his head, not wanting to look at the judge.

"Bailiff, you may summon the jury."

As the jury entered the court room a moment later, Will and Gid noticed that seven of them were wearing the uniform of the Prescott Defenders.

"Hey," Will said, "can't you get those Prescott Defender people off the jury?"

"I'm afraid not. The jury pool isn't that big," Phelps said.

"Well, we don't want those people," Will said.

"Your only other option is to reject a trial by jury and have the judge decide."

"All right, let's do it that way," Will said.

Phelps stood. "Your Honor, may I address the court?"

"You may."

"Your Honor, my clients object to the makeup of the jury."

"You were present for *voir dire*, counselor," Judge Briggs responded.

"Yes, Your Honor, but as they are being charged with the murder of members of the Prescott Defenders, they are concerned about having jurymen who are, themselves members of that organization."

"Do they understand that if they decline trial by jury, this will be a bench trial?" Briggs asked.

"Yes, Your Honor, they have been so informed."

Phelps looked at Will and Gid, both of whom nodded that they wished to decline the jury.

"Your Honor, my clients choose a bench trial."

"The prosecutor has the right to deny or accept that request," Judge Briggs said. "How say you, Mr. Blocker?"

Blocker nodded.

"You two men understand, don't you, that if I hear the case without jury, my decision as to your guilt or innocence is binding?"

Both Will and Gid answered in the affirmative.

"Very well. Jurors you are dismissed."

"Damn, I wanted to find that son of a bitch guilty," one of the Prescott Defender jurors said as they got up to leave.

The other Defenders laughed.

"Mr. Blocker, your opening statement," Judge Briggs said.

"Your Honor, the defendants, William and Gideon Crockett have openly confessed that they killed the four victims, Jonas Cokeberry, Roy Vestal, Chris Doolin, and Clyde Parker, fine upstanding young men, all."

"The question that we must determine is whether or not those killings were justified. I will establish through logic and lucidity of argument that the killings were in fact, acts of murder."

"Mr. Phelps?"

"Your Honor, the defendants claim that the killings were in self-defense, and we will have witnesses who will attest to that."

"Mr. Prosecutor, you may make your case," Briggs said. "Call your witnesses."

"Your Honor, as all of our witnesses are dead, slaughtered by Will and Gid Crockett, we will have no one to testify for the prosecution. However, we will cross examine witnesses for the defense."

"Very well, Mr. Phelps, you may call your witnesses."

Phelps, called his first witness, a percentage girl who gave her name as Penny Admore.

Penny testified that Jonas Cokeberry and Roy Vestal had their guns drawn and that Cokeberry had told Vestal to "kill him," but Will drew his gun and fired before either Cokeberry or Vestal could pull the trigger. She also noted that Chris Doolin and Clyde Parker attempted to draw their guns, but that Gid had outdrawn them.

Blocker rose to challenge Penny's testimony.

"If Cokeberry and Vestal were going to shoot Crockett, and they already had their guns out and pointing toward him, there is no way he could have drawn and killed them before they could pull the trigger."

"But that is what happened," Penny insisted. "I saw it with my own eyes."

"May I inquire as to how you make your living?" Blocker asked.

Penny looked at the judge.

"Answer the question."

"I, uh, work at The Beatrice."

"The Beatrice is a saloon, is it not?"

"Yes, sir."

"What do you do at The Beatrice?"

"It's difficult to describe."

"The truth is, isn't it, that you entertain the customers, the male customers, by forcing them to buy drinks for you, in order for them to be able to visit with you?"

"I don't force them to buy drinks."

"But buying drinks for you is what they do, isn't it?"

"Yes, sir," Penny replied.

"Tell me how, if you are drinking whiskey all day, you aren't too drunk to know what's going on."

"We don't actually drink whiskey."

"Oh? What do you drink all day?"

"We drink tea."

"You drink tea, and yet you lead the customers to believe you are drinking whiskey? Whiskey is more expensive than tea, yet your customers pay the full whiskey price for your drinks. Is that not true?"

"Yes, sir," Penny said quietly.

"I didn't hear you girl. Speak loudly enough for all to hear."

"Yes, sir," Penny said much louder.

"Then tell me this, if you lie to the men who are buying these drinks, telling them tea is whiskey, how can we expect to believe you are telling the truth now?"

"Phelps, aren't you going to object? What's important is what the young lady saw, not how she earns her living," Will said.

"Objection, Your Honor," Phelps called, reluctantly. "The young lady's occupation is not germane."

"Your Honor, bar girls and prostitutes have such

low standing among the good people of the population, that very little credibility can be given their testimony," Blocker said in response to the objection. "In this case, this woman is making the claim that Cokeberry and Vestal already had their guns drawn, and yet one of the Crocketts was able to draw against them and kill these good men. Now, tell me, does that make any sense at all?"

"Objection overruled," Briggs said.

"I can only tell you what I saw," Penny said. "Mr. Cokeberry and Mr. Vestal already had their guns drawn, when Will Crockett drew his gun. And Mr. Doolin and Mr. Parker were going for their guns, when Gid Crockett drew his first."

"I have no further questions of this . . ." Blocker paused for a long moment before he spoke the last word in a contemptuous tone of voice, "*witness.*"

"Witness is excused," Briggs said.

Phelps called four more witnesses, all of whom testified that Cokeberry and Vestal had their pistols in their hand, and Cokeberry had declared his intention to kill Will, for his refusal to pay the forty dollars that had been assessed as tax. Doolin and Parker had attempted to draw their guns when Gid drew his gun and shot them. After the last witness testified, Phelps made his closing argument.

"Your Honor, as the witnesses have testified, the shootings were an act of self-defense. I rest my case."

Blocker stood to make his own closing argument, and as there was no jury, he, as had Phelps, spoke from behind the prosecutor's table.

"Your Honor, what have the witnesses testified? Without exception, every witness has said that Will Crockett killed two of our citizens and his brother killed two more. These four men were good men who had dedicated their lives to providing security for our fair city, and now, to the sorrow of their friends and families, they lie dead. We are not here to argue about the details of the shooting—we are here for one purpose, and one purpose only. We are here to decide who killed these men, and neither Will nor Gid Crockett has denied that between the two of them, they did indeed, kill Jonas Cokeberry, Roy Vestal, Chris Doolin, and Clyde Parker. I ask that you find them guilty of murder in the first degree, and that you assess the maximum punishment allowed by law, which is death by hanging."

Blocker sat down and Judge Briggs stroked his chin for a moment as he stared at Will and Gid.

"I am ready to make my decision. I ask that the defendants stand," Judge Briggs said.

Will, Gid, and their attorney stood to await the Judge's finding.

"Mr. Phelps, as Mr. Blocker stated, four men are dead, and Will and Gid Crockett have confessed to killing them.

"Therefore, I have no recourse but to find both defendants guilty of murder in the first degree."

"What?" someone shouted from the gallery. His shocked outcall was seconded by at least a dozen others. Several of the spectators started talking at once, expressing their disagreement with the finding.

With repeated banging of his gavel, Judge Briggs restored order in his court. Then, when all was quiet, he pronounced his sentence.

"William Crockett and Gideon Crockett, your case having been heard, and adjudication, by your own request, made by me, I now find for guilty. This court sentences both William Crockett and Gideon Crockett to death."

Again, there were shouts of disagreement from the gallery, and again Judge Briggs gaveled them quiet.

"As the gallows erected for the execution of Nate Harper still stands, I order that it be employed as the means to carry out my sentence, which is death by hanging no later than ten o'clock tomorrow morning.

"Colonel Sandos, take as many men as you need to escort the prisoners to jail, where they will remain until the sentence is carried out."

Judge Briggs brought the hammer down hard. "This court is adjourned."

Chapter Eleven

Jubal Sandos, with a smile that could better be described as a smirk, approached Will and Gid with four of his men. With hands behind their backs, they were cuffed and two Defenders escorted each brother to jail. Will had the muzzle of a pistol pressed up against the side of his head, as did Gid.

"If you try and run, I'm going to blow your brains out," one of the men said to Will. "But I hope you don't, because I want to watch you bastards hang."

When they got to the jail, Will and Gid were both put in the same cell.

"Now you boys have a nice night, you hear?" Sandos said, laughing out loud as he and the other four left the cell area.

Sheriff Bower came back to the cell and stood there for a moment, looking through the bars. He shook his head. "I want you boys to know that I don't approve of any of this." Without waiting for a response, he turned and walked away leaving the jail completely.

Will sat down on one of the beds. "Well, Little Brother, we seem to have gotten ourselves into quite a fix this time."

"I'm not worried," Gid replied.

"Did you not listen to the judge? They plan to hang us tomorrow, and you're not worried."

"Nope. You're my big brother and you'll figure out some way to get us out of this."

"I appreciate your confidence," Will said as he ran his fingers through his hair.

The two brothers were quiet for a few minutes, then Gid spoke. "I should have gone back. I should have at least written to her. Then, when I found her, I let her go. She would have still married me . . . but we had both moved on by then. I should have married her."

Will knew that Gid was talking about Katie Ann McMurtry, the girl who had lived on the farm adjacent to the Crockett farm. Will and Gid had grown up with Katie and her brother, Tyrone.

The last time they had seen Katie, she was calling herself Cat Clay, and she had been forced into prostitution. The last time they had seen Ty, he was a sheriff. Now Katie and Ty were both dead.

"Gid, we can't look back on things as we wish it had been. We can only look back on things as they are."

"Yeah," Gid said. And in that one word was contrition, sorrow, and regret. He cast his memory back to another place and another time.

The Crockett Farm, Southwest Missouri, 1860:

Gid and Katie McMurtry were sitting on the bank of Wahite Creek, the stream of water that separated the Crockett farm from the McMurtry farm. Katie was a beautiful young girl of sixteen, Gid was also sixteen.

"Mama was only sixteen when she married Daddy," Katie said.

"Sixteen might be old enough for a girl to get married, but it's not old enough for a boy to be married," Gid replied. "I'll have to make a living for us, and who knows how fast we would have a baby?"

"I'd say within nine months," Katie said with a seductive smile.

"See, there you go. If I can't support a wife when I'm sixteen, how would you expect me to support you and a baby? And I want to do it on my own. I don't want either my pa or yours to have to support us."

"Don't you want to marry me?" Katie asked.

"You know I do, but when we're both old enough."

"Papa says there might be a war coming."

"And if it does, I'll more 'n likely go away to be in it. That's all the more reason we need to wait."

"Gid, you won't go off somewhere 'n find some other woman to marry, will you?"

"No, I promise you, that won't happen," Gid said. "I might not be old enough to get married right now, but I'm old enough to know that I don't want any other woman but you."

"Do you love me?"

"You know I love you."

Katie smiled at him. "Then give me a kiss."

"It's raining," Will said, and with his words Gid left Katie McMurtry on the creek bank that formed the border between the Crockett and McMurtry farm. He realized, almost with a start, that he was sitting in a jail cell, under the sentence of death.

"Yeah, it is," Gid said. "Normally I like to hear rain and know that I'm inside, and not outside in it. But tonight, I would gladly trade being outside in the rain."

"I can see that."

Across town, Addie was sitting in the hotel apartment that she and her father occupied, looking through the window at the rain.

"Papa, how could we have so misjudged the Crocketts?"

"Are you that sure we have misjudged them?"

"Well, yes, aren't you? I mean they have just been proven to be murderers."

"No, darlin', they were *adjudged* to be murderers, and there is a difference between judgment and proof. Every eyewitness supported the account given by Will and Gid as to what and how it happened."

"But Jubal is so certain they are guilty. And don't forget, he warned me about them before any of this happened."

"Jubal Sandos has a reason for wanting the Crocketts to be guilty. He sees them as a threat."

"A threat? How could they be a threat to him?"

"Addie, think about it. We may have a mayor and a sheriff, but Jubal Sandos controls this town as surely as any king may control his kingdom. He collects taxes, and it's a rather generous amount too. I know he gets a hundred dollars a month from me, and I'm told he gets ten dollars a week from each of the saloons in town. That's four hundred dollars a week, plus what he gets from all the other businesses in town. I wouldn't be surprised if he doesn't take in at least twenty-five hundred to three thousand dollars per month and that doesn't include the gold tax."

"But Papa, think of all the good he does for the town. And it isn't as if he is keeping all the money for himself. It must be quite expensive to pay the salaries of all those men who work for him."

"Oh, I'm sure he pays himself quite generously."

"You have never liked Jubal, have you?"

"No, I haven't."

"What if he were to become your son-in-law?"

"Is that likely to happen?" Biff asked. "Has he asked you to marry him?"

"Not yet, but I think he will."

"You're a grown woman, Addie, and I can't lead your life for you. But if you were to marry him, it would be the worst day of my life, and in my opinion, the biggest mistake you will have ever made."

"Well, he hasn't asked me yet, so this discussion is a bit premature."

"I pray that it's a discussion we never have to have."

When Addie went to bed that night, she lay in the darkness, listening to the rain. Why did her father dislike Jubal so? Jubal had never given her any reason to doubt him. He was good to her, and he was always the perfect gentleman when she was with him. She was sure that he loved her, even if he had not yet said so. And she was equally sure he was going to propose to her. She didn't want to have to choose between Jubal and her father, but it was beginning to look as if she would have to do so.

She prayed only that, when the time would come, she would know what decision to make.

A flash of lightning followed her silent prayer, as if it were an answer from God. But what was His answer? Was He giving His approval, or was the thunderclap a harsh warning against her marrying Jubal?

Sometime during the night, the rain stopped and at dawn the next morning the sun streamed in through the small window of the jail cell.

"Will, Gid, are you boys awake?" Sheriff Bower called through the bars.

"We're awake, Ed."

"I've got bacon, eggs, biscuits, gravy, and coffee if you're up to eating breakfast."

"Sounds good, thanks," Will said.

A few minutes later Ed Bower passed the plates through to Will and Gid, then he sat just outside the cell with his own plate. "I'll take breakfast with you, if you've no objection."

"Your company is always welcome," Will said.

"I hope you don't mind, but when the time comes, I'll not be going out there with you. I don't mind tellin' you that I don't think there's anything about this verdict that's right, 'n I don't want anything to do with it."

"Don't worry, Ed, there's no need for you to be there.

And we appreciate your sentiments."

After the three finished their breakfast, Ed gathered the empty plates. "I'll be in my office, if you need me just give me a shout. By the way, you might be interested in this morning's paper. I'll bring it to you, if you'd like."

"Yeah, thanks," Will said.

"Why in the world would you want to read the paper this morning, of all mornings?" Gid asked.

Will chuckled. "What else do I have to do?"

The sheriff brought the paper back to their cell.

EXTRA EXTRA EXTRA

Miscarriage of Justice

Although the trial of William and Gideon Crockett was held in a courtroom, and adjudicated by a sitting judge, it could be described as a kangaroo court in every meaning of the term. The two defendants rejected a trial by jury, and who could blame them?

They were being tried for the killing of four members of the Prescott Defenders, and yet a significant number of the jurors belonged to that contemptible organization.

Judge Andrew Briggs, (please note that I omitted the term of esteem "His Honor" by intent) heard the trial, but none of the facts. He gave no weight to the testimony of the eyewitnesses who said that the shooting was in self-defense.

Judge Briggs handed down the sentence of execution by hanging. This unjust killing, and it is both unjust, and a killing, will take place at ten o'clock on this very morning. It will be one of the low points in the history of our fair community.

While Will and Gid were reading the paper, Ed excused himself, left the jail, then walked down to the territorial capital building.

"Another somber day, it looks like," Governor Fremont said.

"Did you read the paper this morning, Governor?" Bower asked.

"No, I haven't gotten around to it."

"I brought a copy. Read Ben's story." Sheriff Bower handed the paper to the governor.

A short while after Bower left the office, Jubal Sandos, and four of his men arrived. They saw Deputy Jimmie Burns sitting at his desk.

"Where's the sheriff?" Sandos asked.

"Gone," Burns answered.

"Gone where?"

"He didn't say."

"It doesn't make any difference. We're here to take the prisoners out to be hanged. You can escort us just as well as the sheriff."

"I ain't escortin' you," Burns said.

"What do you mean, you aren't escorting us?"

"I don't like anything about this, so I ain't goin' along with it. Besides, you claim you're all deputies, why do you need me?"

"You are quite correct, Burns. We don't need you. All we need from you is the key to the cell."

"Get it yourself," Burns said. "It's hanging there, on the wall."

"Get the key, Chapman," Sandos ordered.

After Chapman got the key, Sandos and the others went back to the cell occupied by Will and Gid.

"Good morning," Sandos said with a bright smile on his face. "It looks like a beautiful day, but it could rain again this afternoon. Oh, but I don't suppose that would make any difference to you two, because after justice is done this morning, you won't be here to see if it rains or not, will you? Turn around and put your hands behind your backs."

Will and Gid turned around and put their hands behind them to be handcuffed.

"All right, time to go," Sandos said, his voice still full of cheer. "There's already a crowd outside. It's like they're here to see a show, but I don't know what that would be. Oh, wait, now that I think about it, you two would be the show, wouldn't you?" Sandos laughed out loud.

As Will and Gid were taken from the jail to the gallows,

the town plaza, as Sandos had said, was filled with citizens of the town. But, unlike the celebrating crowd that had watched Nate Harper hang, there was a melancholy about the people who had gathered today. The accounts of the eyewitnesses had spread all over town, and even those who hadn't heard directly from the witnesses, had read the morning *Prescott Advocate.* It was obvious that those who were gathered this morning, believed that an injustice was being done.

"Bless you boys," an old woman in the crowd said.

"God be with you," another called out to them.

There were several more blessings called out until they reached the gallows.

They climbed the steps that led up to the platform, then stood to one side as they waited to be moved onto the trapdoor, which was big enough to accommodate both of them at the same time.

Gid chuckled. "I wonder if they'll hang us with a new rope."

"What?"

"Don't you remember? You used to tell me I would bitch if I would be hanged by a new rope. I wonder if this is a new rope."

Will laughed too. "I guess we'll just have to find out."

"And if it is a new rope, I'll bitch, just for you."

"I appreciate that, Little Brother. I really do.

Hey, Gid, do you remember when ma caught you 'n me riding on those two old sows, Flossie and Florette? Whooee was she mad or what?"

Gid laughed out loud. "Do you also remember that you talked me into it, and because you were my big brother, I went along? Damn, Big Brother, here we are about to get our necks stretched, and you remember that?"

"Yeah, well, it just popped in my mind for some reason," Will said, laughing as well.

"Look at the two of 'em," someone in the crowd said. "They're laughin' at death. I ain't never before seen nothin' like this."

"They've got to be the two bravest men I've ever seen," another added.

Sandos stepped to the front of the gallows platform and began to read the order of execution.

"We are assembled here today, to carry out the court order of the execution of William and Gideon Crockett, for the murders of Jonas Cokeberry, Roy Vestal, Chris Doolin, and Clyde Parker, four good men and community servants. This order was signed by Judge Andrew Briggs, after William and Gideon Crockett were both found guilty of those crimes in trial, which by their own request, was adjudicated before Judge Briggs."

"Let us through, let us through," someone began calling out, doing so with a sense of urgency and authority.

"It's the sheriff," someone said.

"And the governor," another added.

"Let us through," Sheriff Bower said again then, reaching the bottom of the steps, he and Governor Fremont climbed up to the gallows platform.

"Here, what is this?" Sandos asked, obviously irritated by the interruption.

"Hold up this execution, Sandos, the governor has something to say."

"By all means, go right ahead," Sandos said sarcastically, making a sweep of his hand.

Fremont walked to the front of the platform, then began to read from a sheet of paper he held in his hand.

"Convinced of the injustice of the verdict and sentence rendered in court yesterday by Judge Andrew Briggs, and certain as to the innocence of William and Gideon Crockett, I, John C. Fremont, Governor of the Territory of Arizona, do order that the sentence be set aside. I hereby grant a full pardon, providing the freedom of, and restoring all rights of citizenship to William Crockett and to Gideon Crockett."

Governor Fremont looked over at Sheriff Bower. "Set these men free."

"Yes, sir!" Bower said happily.

The gathered crowd cheered as the handcuffs were removed and the two men left the gallows.

Shy's Apothecary, as were most of the other businesses in town, was closed for the hanging. Despite the fact that the store was closed, Addie had come to work anyway, and she was standing in the back of the store.

She was supposedly taking inventory, but the reason she was standing in the back was because she didn't want to see Will and Gid hanged. She knew that Jubal was convinced that they should hang, and she felt a degree of guilt for not agreeing with him. After all, she had known Jubal a lot longer than she had known the Crocketts.

And she believed herself to be in love with Jubal Sandos.

On the other hand, the editor of the newspaper was convinced that Will and Gid were innocent. And she couldn't forget that they had saved both her and her father from either death or at least depredation. That being the case, she couldn't just cavalierly stand by and watch the two brothers hang.

"Addie! Addie!" her father shouted rushing into the store.

"Is it over?" Addie asked in a tight, pained voice.

Addie was surprised to see a broad smile on her father's face. "Yes, daughter, it's over. And Will and Gid have been set free."

"What?"

"They are free! Governor Fremont pardoned them at the last second. And I mean the very last second. They were both standing on the gallows with their hands cuffed behind them, and the execution order had already been read when the sheriff and the governor came rushing in to save them."

"Oh, Papa!" With a smile that matched her father's, Addie hurried to him, embracing him happily.

"You know your friend is going to be very upset by this."

"I don't care if he is. We don't have to agree on everything."

"That's true, sweetheart, you don't have to agree on everything, and I hope you remember that."

"In celebration of an injustice being righted, drinks are on the house," Housewright said.

With a hurrah, the customers rushed to the bar,

"Your Excellency," Housewright said, addressing the governor, "you, Sheriff Bower, and Will and Gid are our guests of honor, so sit at this table. Penny, Elaina—bring out our best bottle to celebrate."

"Why, thank you, Mr. Housewright, that is most generous of you," Fremont said.

"Gentlemen, once your glasses are charged, hold them aloft for the toast I intend to propose," Housewright called out.

Once everyone had their glasses filled, they turned toward the table and held them up as Housewright gave the toast.

"Ladies," Housewright said with a nod of his head toward Penny and Elaina, "and gentlemen, let us lift our glasses to Will and Gid Crockett, staunch gentlemen of courage who were prepared to face death, unjust though the sentence was, with admirable stoicism, to Sheriff Bower who solicited intervention from the governor, and to Governor John C. Fremont, who by executive action, righted a terrible wrong that was about to be committed."

"Hear, hear!" someone shouted, and everyone drank.

Chapter Twelve

After the celebration in The Beatrice, Governor Fremont asked Will and Gid if they would mind coming to his office. He said he had a favor he wanted to ask of them.

"Governor, after what you just did for us, whatever the favor is, the answer is yes," Will said.

"Is two o'clock this afternoon convenient?"

"We'll see you at two o'clock in the morning if that's what you want," Gid said.

Fremont laughed. "Well, please don't come waking me up at two o'clock in the morning. I'm afraid my Jessie wouldn't take that too kindly."

After the governor left, Penny came over to the table still occupied by Will and Gid. "I was so scared," Penny said. "I just knew they were going to hang you."

"Would you have missed me?" Gid teased.

"I would have cried all day," Penny replied with a smile.

"Just one day?"

"Well, I do have to make a living." Her smile broadened when she realized Gid was teasing. "I saw you two laughing while you were standing up there. Weren't you afraid?"

"Well, I admit I was afraid but I was more concerned if they were going to hang us with a new rope."

"What?"

"That was my little brother's idea of a joke," Will said.

"I'll tell you who's scared now," one of the nearby customers said. "Sandos and all those bastards who belong to the Prescott Defenders. They've been ridin' roughshod over this whole town, but when they tried it with these two boys, they killt all four of 'em."

"I'd like to buy these boys a drink," one of the others said.

"That won't be necessary," Nigel Housewright said. "For the rest of the day their drinks will be on the house." Housewright smiled. "As a matter of fact, everyone here can have yet another drink on the house."

"You're going to go broke if you keep providing free drinks for everyone," Will said.

"I could think of no more worthy reason to go broke, than in the celebration of an injustice being righted," Housewright said. "But thanks to a Sovereign Allowance, the chances of me going broke are rather miniscule."

"Sovereign Allowance?"

"It is a story of indiscretion, intrigue, and bribery, best not discussed," Housewright said.

"The Governor wants to see us at two this afternoon," Gid said. "Do you think he's going to ban us from Prescott, or worse, ban us from the whole territory? We haven't turned up any color in our mine yet, but I'm not quite ready to give up on the Axis."

"Oh, I'm quite sure that is not his intention," Housewright said.

As the conversation continued, two members of the Prescott Defenders came into the saloon.

"Excuse me for a moment," Housewright said, and getting up he walked up to the bar to address the two uniformed men.

"You gentlemen are welcome in my establishment," Housewright said, "but from this point forward, there will be no more free drinks."

"What are you talkin' about?" one of the men asked. "It's the rule that the first drink is free."

"No, that is Jubal Sandos' rule—it isn't mine. You are welcome to stay, but there will be no free drinks."

"Yeah? Well, we're just the people who can enforce Sandos' rule," the same man said.

"Pete, look over there," the other one said, pointing

toward Will and Gid.

"What?"

"Them's the two that kilt Jonas 'n the others."

"Yeah, that is them, ain't it," Pete said. He called over toward Will and Gid. "I want you two bastards to know that Jonas 'n them other boys was all friends of our'n."

"It's too bad they were so . . . careless," Will said, setting the word careless apart.

"Yeah, well they . . ."

"Come on, Pete," the other man said, interrupting Pete in mid-sentence. "There are plenty of saloons on Whiskey Row. We can get as many free drinks as we want."

"Don't hurry back!" one of the saloon patrons called as the two men left the saloon. The other patrons cheered.

"None of them ever pay for a drink," Housewright said. "This ridiculous policy of first drink free, means they can go from saloon to saloon, staying only for the first free drink." He smiled. "Of course, there is an advantage to that. It means that none of them will stay in the same saloon very long. And now that I've said I would no longer be providing drinks for any of the Prescott Defenders, it may have the advantage of keeping any of them from coming in here."

"How is it that the town caved in to them?" Will asked.

"There are too many of them," Housewright said. "The sheriff has only one deputy, so he can't control them, and they have Judge Briggs on their side. I've no way of knowing for sure, but I would be willing to make a rather significant wager that the judge gets a portion of the tax they collect."

"What about the people of the town?" Gid asked. "What do they think of the Prescott Defenders?"

"There, I believe the opinion is mixed," Housewright said. "Some actually believe that the Prescott Defenders are a legitimate law enforcing agency and are worth the tax that they charge. But most believe that the taxes are oppressive and that the Prescott Defenders are arrogant and heavy-handed in the way they deal with people."

At two o'clock that afternoon Will and Gid, as requested, went to the governor's office in the territorial legislative building which was located on Plaza Square.

When they stepped into the building, they encountered a man sitting behind the desk. He was thin, bald, and wearing wire-rim glasses. He looked up as they came in.

"Ah, the Crocketts," he said as he rose and offered his hand. "Jerome McCoy."

"Mr. McCoy," Will said, shaking his hand. "My brother and I are here at the governor's request."

"Yes, sir, I'll tell the governor you're here."

"What do you think the governor wants with us?" Gid asked after McCoy had left.

"No doubt he wants to tell us to stay out of trouble," Will replied with a chuckle.

"The governor will see you now," McCoy said when he returned.

"Governor," Will said, as he and Gid shook hands with Fremont.

"I know you men are wondering why I asked you to come see me, and I didn't want to leave you just hanging, so we'll get right to it."

"Just hanging," Will said with a laugh.

Fremont joined him in laughing. "I'm glad you acknowledged my choice of words."

"Forgive me for not laughing at your joke," Gid said as he rubbed his neck.

"I suppose it was a bit unthinking of me," the governor said. "My reason for asking you to meet with me concerns the Prescott Defenders."

"Sheriff Bower has told us the Defenders are not connected to his office in any way. He says they are definitely not his deputies," Will said.

"That's right, they are deputies of the court, appointed by *Judge* Briggs." Fremont twisted the word 'judge' as an indication of his contempt for the man and his title.

"Do you have the authority to revoke the deputy appointments the Prescott Defenders hold?" Will asked.

Fremont smiled. "I'm not sure that I do, but who's

going to tell me that I can't. Therefore, I will inform Briggs that I'm revoking the authority of the Prescott Defenders. That also means that I am rescinding the repressive tax that Briggs has imposed on the citizens."

"Everyone is going to be glad to hear that," Will said.

"Yes, well, they'll have to actually know about it to be glad. So, as I told you yesterday, I'm going to ask you men to do me a favor, if you would."

Gid chuckled. "Governor, after what you did for us, I can't think of anything you could ask that we wouldn't do."

"I was hoping you would say that," Fremont said. "I would like to appoint the two of you as special territorial deputies. This would give you authority over every other law enforcement officer in the territory, except for that authority held by United States Marshals."

"Is there such a thing as territorial deputies?" Will asked.

Fremont chuckled. "There is now."

After Will and Gid left the governor's office, they went to the *Prescott Advocate.* As soon as they stepped through the door, they were met by Ben Weaver, the editor of the newspaper.

"Can I help you gentle . . ." Weaver stopped in mid-sentence. "Will . . . Gid . . . how happy I am to have you stop by the *Advocate.* Even though I don't know you that well, the whole town knows who you are. The two men who cheated the hangman."

"You can't exactly say we cheated. The governor gave us a full pardon." Gid said.

"And I and every decent citizen in the county can only say bully for him."

Will nodded his head. "My brother and I would like to thank you for your editorial expressing that sentiment."

"What I said was the truth," Weaver said. "Now, what can I do for you gentlemen?"

"Actually, it's what you can do for Prescott," Will said. "The governor has issued an executive order relieving all citizens from any form of oppression, passing itself off as law enforcement."

Weaver smiled. "Would you be talking about a group like the Prescott Defenders?"

"We aren't talking about a group *like* the Prescott Defenders—we are specifically talking about *the* Prescott Defenders. They are no longer valid deputies, and because of that, they will no longer be able to collect taxes."

"That is great news," Weaver said with a welcoming smile. "Now, you just tell me how I can help, and I'll do whatever you ask."

"We'd like for you to print up a poster to be displayed in every public place there is. It will say that the Prescott Defenders no longer have the right to collect taxes," Will said. "I'm not sure how many posters that would be."

"There are forty saloons, fifteen businesses, two churches, the courthouse, the territorial capitol building, the post office, the city hall, and the jail. That would be sixty-one."

"Better make it a hundred," Will said. "It can't hurt to have a few extra."

"Not only will I print them for you, I'll do it for free. Do you think the governor would mind if I write an article about this? I think it would be welcome news," Weaver said.

"I'm sure he wouldn't mind, and Mr. Weaver, after the favorable article you wrote about us this morning, I would be in support of any article you would write."

Weaver smiled. "Of course, the first amendment gives me the right to write anything I wish, but in this case, I do appreciate your support."

Ben Weaver printed the posters first, then hired two young boys to deliver them to every business in town.

TAX REPEALED

By order of

Governor John C. Fremont

All taxes here before assessed by the organization known

as

Prescott Defenders

are henceforth revoked.

The very next morning news of the change in status of the Prescott Defenders was made known as soon as the *Prescott Advocate* appeared on the streets of Prescott.

Chapter Thirteen

EXTRA EXTRA EXTRA

PRESCOTT DEFENDERS AUTHORITY REVOKED

HARSH TAXES ANNULLED

For some time now the businesses and citizens of this city have suffered from the effects of an unfair tax levied upon us to support a tyrannical "peace keeping" force calling themselves the Prescott Defenders. While it is true that the Prescott Defenders have, from time to time, acted as an arm of the law, the truth is, any good they may have done has been offset by the oppressive nature of their organization.

Territorial Governor John C. Fremont has revoked the deputyship of the Prescott Defenders, and appointed William and Gideon Crockett as special territorial marshals. In addition, he has declared an end to the tyrannical taxation assessed by them. Posters have been printed and distributed so that every business and citizen of Prescott will be apprised of this welcome change.

This newspaper now believes that with this yoke of oppressive tax removed from our necks, the continued success of area mining, the growth of the cattle industry, and the prospective arrival of the railroad, Yavapai county in general, and Prescott in particular, can only but increase in wealth and industry.

"So, the governor has made you two territorial marshals, has he?" Sheriff Bower asked.

"Yes," Will said.

"What exactly does that mean?"

"I think he just wants to have someone available to help you, if you ever need it," Will said.

"We're not taking your place, Ed," Gid added.

"We do have a claim to work and the governor has freed us to go to the Axis," Will said. "But, if you need us, come get us. After all, we owe you and Governor Fremont our lives."

"Part of me wishes I could just step back and let you two handle everything. But it's good to know that I'll have some backup if I need it," Sheriff Bower said.

From the sheriff's office, Will and Gid went to The Beatrice where they were greeted, joyfully, not only by

Housewright, but by Ki, Penny and Elaina. In addition to those greetings, the saloon patrons, many of whom were businessmen, added their own happy comments.

"I tell you what, gettin' out from under these taxes, is like getting free of leg irons," Bill Gillespie, the owner of the leather-goods store, said.

"That will, no doubt be the end of the Prescott Defenders," Ki said.

"I hope so," Nigel said. "Unfortunately, history has shown that evil, though sometimes abated, is rarely subdued."

Throughout the afternoon as more and more people learned that the Prescott Defenders had lost their authority, and that the taxes had been lifted, they began to celebrate their freedom. Many of the celebrators came to The Beatrice to celebrate, and the crowded room reflected the cheer in laughter, drinking, and vocal exclamations of joy.

During the festivity Will happened to glance over at a table where Nigel was sitting alone. He stepped up to the bar.

"Ki, what does Nigel prefer to drink?"

"That would be Glenlivet Scotch."

"Give me a beer, and a glass of Glenlivet."

Will walked over to Nigel. "May I join you?"

"Yes, please do."

Will handed Nigel the glass of Scotch. "Ki said you like Glenlivet."

"It's the preferred drink of the Royal family," Nigel said.

"Ah, I see. So, you want to drink what the Royals drink."

"And why shouldn't I?" Nigel replied. "I am of the Royals."

"What?"

"You might say I am the king."

Will laughed, then he saw the expression on Nigel's face. "Wait a minute, you aren't kidding, are you?"

"King George had seven sons. Queen Victoria's father, Edward was fourth in line of succession, but he was the oldest to have a legitimate issue, which was Victoria. Notice that I said, legitimate issue."

"William the Fourth, Duke of Clarence, had three legitimate children, Charlotte, who was born and died on the same day, Elizabeth, who lived but a year, and twin boys, unnamed, who were born and died on the same day."

"But, as it turns out, the Duke of Clarence was actually, quite virile, and he produced ten illegitimate children, six boys and four girls. Had they been legitimate, the oldest boy would have been king."

"As it turns out, the oldest boy of those ten, Percival Housewright, was my father. He would have been king, and now that he has died, I would be."

"What are you doing in America?"

"I didn't learn of all this, until after my father died. Sir Charles Grey, secretary to the sovereign, asked me to come see him. I thought it was to be given another award for my music, but I was mistaken."

Buckingham Palace, October 5th, 1867:

"Her Majesty, Queen Victoria, wishes to extend her condolences to you, upon the death of your father."

"The Queen?" Nigel replied, surprised by the announcement. "I'm honored, and I know that my father would have been. My mother too, if she were still alive."

"You have no issue?" Grey asked.

"No, I'm childless. I'm not married, actually."

"As it turns out, marriage isn't necessary in order to have children."

Nigel laughed, politely.

"As your grandfather would know."

"I beg your pardon?" Nigel replied, somewhat piqued by the comment. "Why would you say such a thing?"

"What do you know, of your grandfather?"

"I know very little of him. I never met him."

"Your father was the illegitimate son of William the Fourth, Duke of Clarence. By bloodline you would now be the king. That can never be of course, but just to preclude any future unpleasantness, it is your duty to leave the country. We are prepared to provide you with a Sovereign Allowance of one hundred pounds per month."

"No, I can't do that. I have no intention of giving up my music career."

"I'm afraid you don't understand, Mr. Housewright. You no longer have a music career."

"I have three concerts scheduled and . . ."

Lord Grey held up his hand.

"Your concerts have all been cancelled, and there will be no new ones. As I said, you have no music career."

"Where would I go?"

"We will give you enough money to relocate and allow you to get established in a new country. In addition, of course, there will be a lifetime allowance of one hundred pounds per month. Might I suggest America? One hundred pounds is five hundred American dollars, and I'm told that one can live quite well in America on five hundred dollars per month."

"Tell the Queen I have no intention of trying to establish legitimacy for the crown."

"It would be better if you leave."

"There was a young woman, Beatrice Sutherland, with whom I was very much in love. When the Secretary to the Sovereign ordered me out of the country, I asked Beatrice to marry me. She agreed, until she learned that I would be coming to America."

"Beatrice couldn't understand why I would give up a successful concert tour and, by agreement with the Queen, I couldn't tell anyone. I asked her to trust me, and come with me, but she couldn't find it in herself to do so. Thus here I am, in the American West, playing my music in a pub that is named for her," Nigel said, concluding his story. He smiled. "Of course, it helps, that I own the pub."

"It must be very difficult for you to know that, by rights, you should be the King of England," Will said.

"It isn't difficult at all. A sovereign does not own himself, or in the case of the Queen, herself. What I regret, is losing my music career."

"What were you and Nigel talking about?" Gid asked, when the two of them left the saloon.

"You mean, what were the King of England and I talking about?"

"What? What do you mean, King of England?"

Will told Gid the story Nigel had told him.

"Do you believe him?" Gid asked.

"You know, if almost anyone else had told me such a preposterous story, I would just laugh at him. But for some reason, don't ask me why, yes, I believe Nigel."

Chapter Fourteen

The next morning dawned relatively cool in Prescott, though the cloudless sky gave warning of the heat that would develop later in the day. Morning smells pervaded Montezuma Street, the smell of liquor from Whiskey Row, the aromas of coffee and bacon from breakfasts being cooked, as well as the underlying, but not overpowering stench of horse apples on the street.

Ike Snow and Dan Coates, members of the Prescott Defenders, were laughing over some shared joke as they stepped into Goldwater's Department Store.

"Can I help you gentlemen?" Morris Goldwater asked.

"Yeah, you can help us," Snow said. "We're here to collect the tax."

"And what tax would that be?"

"What do you mean, what tax would that be? The ten dollar a week tax you owe for keeping your store open. That's what tax."

"Oh, but haven't you heard?"

"Haven't we heard what?" Coates asked.

Goldwater showed the two men the poster that was attached to the wall behind them.

"Read it," he said.

"They can't neither one of us read," Coates said. "What does it say?"

"Gentlemen, it says that I owe you no taxes, because that tax has been repealed," Goldwater said.

"Repealed? What does that mean? I've never heard the word," Snow said.

"It means I don't have to pay the tax anymore."

"What the hell is this?" Jubal Sandos bellowed when Snow and Coates brought him a copy of the poster.

"Repealed means there ain't no more taxes," Snow said.

"I know what repealed means, you dumb son of a bitch!" Sandos said, angrily. He grabbed the poster, wadded it up, and threw it in the trash can.

"That won't do no good, Colonel, hell these things is all over the place," Coates said. "They say it's even in the newspaper."

"Give me that paper," Sandos said snatching it away from Coates.

Sandos read the article, growing angrier with every

sentence. Then, folding the paper over, he left the building used by the Prescott Defenders and hurried across town to the town plaza. A large, two-story, pink brick building, surmounted by a cupola, stood right in the center of the plaza, which was surrounded by a white picket fence.

When Sandos reached the courthouse, he went right by the court clerk's desk and into Judge Briggs' office.

"What the hell is this all about?" Sandos demanded, showing Judge Briggs the article.

"Apparently the excise tax has been removed by gubernatorial decree," Briggs replied.

"Hell, can't you do anything about it? May I remind you that you have been getting twenty percent of the money? What do you think we are paying you for, if not to take care of issues like this? Put the tax back on."

"A governor's act supersedes anything I can do."

"Yeah, well, find something to do about it," Sandos demanded, then, without waiting for a response from the judge, Sandos left the office.

***

It was less than an hour's ride from Prescott to the Axis mine. When they arrived, they unloaded the few supplies they had brought with them and put the horses in the pen behind the hut.

"This is no place for a fine horse like Prince," Gid said as removed the saddle. "It's no place for a fine man like Gid, either.

"I heard that," Will said. "I think you're the one who said he wasn't ready to give up on this venture."

"That was when I thought we were going to be put in prison or worse than that, hanged," Gid said.

"Don't you think it's better to work on our own rock pile, than work on one in a prison?" Will asked. "If you're up to it, let's set a powder charge this afternoon and see if we can find anything that looks promising."

"Will, tell me something—do you know enough about gold mining that you'd actually recognize pay dirt if you found it?"

"Are you calling me a tenderfoot?"

Both men started laughing. "What else would you call us? Back in Missouri, we'd be called rubes, especially by our own pa," Gid said.

"Maybe we should look around and see if we can find a buyer for this hole in the ground."

"Not yet. You said we should set a charge this afternoon. What if after we did that, we found gold nuggets as big as hen eggs that just fell into our hands?"

"I don't think that's how it works, Little Brother, but I'm willing to give it another try. Grab your pickax, and let's go hit a bonanza."

Back in Prescott, Jubal Sandos was holding a meeting of the Prescott Defenders in the headquarters building. At one time part of the space had been a tobacco store, and a slight aroma of tobacco remained.

"Gentlemen, I'm sure you've heard by now, that we won't be collecting taxes anymore," Sandos said.

"Yeah, we heard," Amos Chapman said. "Does this mean the end of the Defenders? If we don't bring in no money . . ."

Sandos held up his hand. "Just because we can't tax the businesses, doesn't mean we can't collect money from them." He smiled. "In fact, I have an idea that might work out even better."

"All right, we'll listen," Ike Snow said.

"We're going to sell them insurance."

"Insurance? You mean like if one of their buildings burn down, we have to pay them for it?"

"Not exactly," Sandos said with a sly, smile.

Earlier in the day, Addie had agreed to have supper with Jubal and now she was sitting in the coffee shop where they were to meet. She felt bad about being so curt with the men who had saved her life, but those same brothers had killed four of Jubal's friends and escaped hanging only because of the governor's pardon. And because of her relationship with Jubal, she felt that she couldn't be friendly with Will and Gid.

Sandos stepped into the hotel coffee shop, and seeing Addie headed toward the table where she was sitting. He had a big smile on his face, and when he reached her, he bent down and kissed her cheek before he sat down.

Addie's face colored because she wasn't used to such a public display of affection from Jubal.

"My, my, you seem chipper today," she said as she touched her cheek. To cover her embarrassment, she continued. "It seems strange to see you without your uniform."

Sandos chuckled. "Do you mean you were attracted to me only because of my uniform?"

"Who said I was attracted to you?" Addie teased.

"Well, I hope you are, because I have big plans."

"Jubal, speaking of plans, what are your plans? I mean, now that the Prescott Defenders are no longer official."

"I'm turning the Defenders into a private detective agency."

"A detective agency?"

"Yes, like the Pinkertons."

"Oh, dear, does that mean you will be leaving Prescott? Will you work for the railroads?"

"No, nothing like that, but I'm happy to see you would be upset if I were to leave."

"I don't want you to go anywhere," Addie said as she

put her hand over Jubal's. "But what I know about the work of the Pinkertons is that it is dangerous. Remember when they were trying to get Jesse James and his gang and some detectives were killed?"

Sandos became quite serious. "Need I remind you that four of the Defenders were murdered by the Crocketts. There is a lot of danger in this world, and right here in Prescott, I might add. That's why I intend to provide a service that protects people."

"Protect? What does that mean?"

"You'll see," Sandos said without elaboration.

Addie raised her eyebrows. "Can you make a living that way? Without collecting taxes."

"We'll be paid for our protection services," Sandos said. "The way I have it figured, we'll make more money doing this than we did when we were collecting taxes."

Addie shook her head. "If you say so, but I don't see how that can be possible."

When Jubal Sandos went into the apothecary, he was in uniform, and he was greeted by Gerald Shy.

"Hello, Mr. Sandos, what brings you by?" he asked.

"He came to visit me," Addie said as she moved toward Jubal, a smile on her face. She slid her finger along the front of his uniform tunic.

"I did indeed," Sandos replied.

"I thought you weren't going to be wearing a uniform any longer," Gerald Shy said. "It was my understanding that the governor put the Prescott Defenders out of business."

"Yes, he did remove us from duty—I might add quite unceremoniously—in spite of all the good we did for this town. At the time, I felt there was no need, nor even justification, for wearing the uniform. But now, under our reorganized arrangement, though my men will no longer be wearing a uniform I, as their leader, believe that I have not only the right, but the obligation to wear the uniform. My uniform will instill discipline, loyalty, and even a sense of pride among my followers."

"You have reorganized? In what way?" Shy asked.

"Oh, in a way that I think you and the other merchants will appreciate, and you will be more than willing to continue to pay us."

"Pay you? Pay you what? I thought the tax had been suspended."

"That is true, but what you are being asked to pay now, isn't a tax," Sandos explained. "It's a private enrollment fee. For your business, it will be ten dollars a week."

"But that's as much as you were charging when you were collecting the tax," Shy said.

"I'm not charging you anything," Sandos said. "When we were charging a tax, we were officers of the court, and the tax was mandatory. But we are no longer officers of the court, so no tax. And, if you choose not to enroll in our program, there's no way of forcing you. Your participation will be strictly voluntary."

"And what program would that be?" Shy asked.

"It's an insurance program."

"Insurance? You mean like fire insurance?"

"No. Rather than being an insurance that pays you if something happens, we are an insurance that will make sure nothing does happen."

"I don't understand."

"It's simple, really. By subscribing to this insurance, we will see to it that your business is never vandalized, nor robbed. And if anyone does rob your store, we will hunt them down, bring them to justice, and if possible, recover what they might have stolen."

"I think it would be a good idea, Mr. Shy," Addie said. "It won't cost any more than you've been paying, and I'd feel a lot safer."

"All right," Shy said. "You're right, it won't cost me any more than I've been paying. And if you can keep something like that from happening, it'll be worth it."

Sandos offered his hand. "You've made a good decision, Mr. Shy. You won't be sorry."

Three days later, the Cook and Bell Jewelers was broken into in the middle of the night. The back door was pried open and four hundred dollars worth of jewelry was taken.

Sandos visited the Bashford and Burmister grocery store that same day.

"We talked with Cook and Bell and tried to get them to subscribe to our services. But they didn't do it and look what happened to them. Yes, they saved the ten dollars a week, but it wound up costing four hundred dollars in lost merchandize, plus the cost of having to replace the door. All the smarter businessmen are subscribing to our service."

"I thought we didn't have to pay you taxes anymore," Bashford said.

"As I have explained to all the others, this is not a tax. This is just a charge for a service the Prescott Defenders plan to continue doing in order to serve the community, but since we can't assess a tax, then we are forced to sell our services."

"Is it legal for you to do that?" Bashford asked. "I mean sell you services as the law, when you don't have any authority,"

"Are you familiar with the Pinkertons?"

"Of course. They're the railroad investigators, aren't they?"

"Indeed they are, but they do a lot more than that," Sandos said. "A lot of times, they do the same thing that sheriffs and marshals do, only they do it more efficiently because they aren't tied to one location. But since they aren't a part of the government, they charge for their services. And those who hire them are more than willing to pay for their services."

"All right," Bashford said shaking his head. "I'll give it a try. If you can keep what happened to the jewelry store from happening to us, then it's worth the money."

Chapter Fifteen

Penny and Nigel were having a cup of coffee together in the morning quiet of The Beatrice.

"Thank you," Penny said.

"For hiring you?"

"That too, but also for the music you play."

"You mean you like it, even though it isn't the cowboy ditties played in so many of the saloons?"

Penny smiled. "Especially because it isn't that kind of music. I saw Gustave Satter when he stopped in Memphis on his concert tour of the country."

Nigel nodded. "I've heard him play. He is very good."

"Yes, he is, but Nigel, you're even better."

Nigel put his hand across the table to lay it on Penny's hand. "I thank you, my dear. Your appreciation of my music means a great deal to me." He smiled. "Especially as I realize that most of the time I'm playing for my own enjoyment. I'm well aware that most of our customers merely tolerate the music I play."

"When you performed in England, and in other countries in Europe, did your audience just 'tolerate' your playing?"

"Actually, if you will forgive me for a bit of braggadocio, my audiences seemed to appreciate it. I did play before packed auditoriums."

"I know what," Penny said with an enthusiastic smile. "Let's do a concert here. I know that I'm not the only one in town who appreciates classical music."

"I'd love to play a concert, but where in Prescott, would I find a venue for such a thing?"

"I'll speak to Mr. Howey about getting the opera house. He is a regular customer, and I know he enjoys your music," Penny said.

"I appreciate this, Penny, but don't be disappointed if you can't get this arranged. Not everyone in town accepts a foreigner who plays classical music in a saloon."

"Just leave it to me. If I can't get the opera house, I'll find someplace else."

Penny went to every conceivable venue in town, trying to find a place for the concert. The temperance agitator, Francis Murphy, was speaking at the Grand Opera House, the Knights of Pythias had a piano that was so out of tune, she knew it wouldn't work, and as Nigel had predicted, the churches didn't want to open their sanctuaries to a saloon piano player.

As she was walking back to The Beatrice, she had an idea.

"Let's have the concert right here in The Beatrice."

"My dear, I play here every day."

"No, you don't understand. You play every day for miners and cowboys who are here to drink. Let's turn The Beatrice into a concert hall for one night and play for people who would genuinely appreciate it. Move the tables out of here, line the chairs up as they would be in a theater, and invite the whole town, to include ladies and children, and people who have never been here before."

"And what should we charge for this musical extravaganza?" Nigel asked.

"Nothing. Anyone who wishes can attend for free," Penny said. "They'll see what The Beatrice has to offer every day."

Nigel was quiet for a moment, then he reached both hands across the table to take her hand in his.

"Penny, thank you, my dear," he said, with great emotion. He stood up. "I need to get my music together."

Penny remained at the table after Nigel left. Elaina

came over to stand beside her.

"Does he know yet?" she asked.

"Does he know what?"

"That you are in love with him?"

"No, of course not. How could that ever be? He is a grand gentleman, and I am a . . . you know what I am."

"Indeed I do, honey. Indeed I do."

"On the other hand, had circumstances not brought me here to this place and time, I would never have met Nigel."

For a moment, Penny replayed in her mind, the circumstance she had spoken of to Elaina.

Memphis, Tennessee, two years earlier:

Penny stepped out of the hired hack in front of the Filbert Mississippi Riverboat Company. Damon Filbert, owner of the riverboat company, was not only the wealthiest man in Memphis, he was one of the wealthiest men in the tri-state area of Tennessee, Arkansas, and Mississippi. He was also the father of Julius Filbert, one of Penny Admore's fifth grade students.

Julius, aware of his father's wealth and position, bullied the rest of the children in the classroom, and he treated Penny more like his servant than his teacher. It was for that reason that Penny had come to this office building on the river, to speak with Julius' father.

When she stepped into the office, she saw a man

sitting behind a desk. He was, she thought, a very handsome man, and she stared at him for a moment until he looked up.

"Something I can do for you, Miss?"

"I came to speak with Mr. Filbert."

"I'm Damon Filbert."

"You? I'm sorry, I thought there would be more people here."

"One of our boats, the *Delta Mist*, is preparing to depart, and the others are down at the docks. Why do you want to speak with me?"

"Mr. Filbert, I'm a school teacher and your son, Julius, is one of my students. I'm here to talk to you about him."

"What about him?"

"Julius has been, well, the nicest way to put it is, a distraction."

"As I'm sure you know, he is very intelligent, and intelligent young men can be a bit high-spirited at times."

"Yes, sir, but it's more than being high-spirited. He bullies the other students, he is disrespectful of me, and he is disobedient."

"Why don't you come into my private office, and we can discuss this more," he paused before he spoke the last word, "intimately."

There was something about the look in Filbert's eyes that made her uncomfortable. But she went into his private office because Julius was a problem, and she hoped he could help her.

Once inside the office, Filbert closed the door behind them.

"How much?" he asked.

"Mr. Filbert, I have no intention of selling a passing grade for your son."

Filbert smiled, but there was no humor in his smile. "I'm not talking about a passing grade for Julius. You can fail him as far as I'm concerned. I mean, how much do you charge for sex?"

"Mr. Filbert, what are you talking about? How dare you make such an insinuation?"

"You want me, Miss Admore, I saw the way you looked at me when you came into the office. How much? Three dollars? Five? Ten? I've never paid any whore ten dollars before—you should be flattered I'd be willing to pay you that much."

Filbert reached down to grab a handful of Penny's skirt. Penny put both hands on his shoulders, then pushed him away from her, and because he was off-balance, he fell to the floor. Running to the door, she opened it, then slammed it behind her as she fled the office.

"You'll be sorry you ran out on me, you bitch!" Filbert shouted.

The next day, Penny was summoned to the office of Mr. Twitty, the school superintendent.

"Miss Admore, I want you to return to your classroom and remove all your personal items, then depart the school grounds, never to return. Your services have been terminated."

"What? But Mr. Twitty, why?" Penny asked in a high, shocked voice.

"It has come to our attention that you approached the father of one of your students, who also happens to be one of the most important men in our city and offered to sell him sexual favors."

"But I did no such thing, he . . ."

"There will be no further discussion of this matter," the superintendent said. "You are dismissed."

Now, as Penny was standing in front of Elaina, those awful memories brought tears to her eyes.

Elaina handed Penny her handkerchief. "You are thinking of that Filbert bastard?"

Penny nodded as she used Elaina's handkerchief to dab at her eyes.

"Honey, he's not worth one tear," Elaina said, putting her hand on her friend's shoulder.

Will and Gid had spent the entire week working in the

mine going through the rubble that had been dislodged by the blasts they had set off, then loading the rock and dirt into the wheelbarrow so they could haul it out.

"We're going to see some color this time, I just know it," Gid said as he tipped up the wheelbarrow and made a close examination of its contents. Will joined him in the perusal.

After a few minutes of close study, Will sighed, and looked over at Gid. "You swore you were going to see some color this time. Have you?"

"Yeah, I have," Gid replied. "I mean, brown is a color, isn't it?"

Will chuckled. "I'm glad to see you haven't lost your sense of humor. That way you can keep your spirits up."

"You know what would really keep my spirits up?" Gid asked.

"What?"

"A beer. Maybe even two or three of them. What do you say we ride into town tonight and visit with a few friends?"

"Now see there, Gid, you actually can come up with a good idea from time to time," Will said.

"We can't go into town like this, though," Gid replied. "If I'm goin' to be around the ladies, I don't intend to smell like a pig lot. I'm goin' to boil some water and take a bath."

"Two good ideas in a row," Will teased. "Who would have thought it?"

Addie was in the hotel lobby when Will and Gid came in to get a couple of rooms for the night.

"Why hello, Addie," Will said with a welcoming smile

"Hello," Addie replied in a flat, dismissive tone.

"How are you doing this fine evening?" Will asked.

"Fine," she replied in the same, flat tone. "I have to go."

"Hmm, she didn't seem all that happy to see us, did she?" Gid commented as Addie left. "Do you think she wanted to see us hang?"

"No, I think she'd just as soon have us go away," Will said. "Let's get our rooms, have some real food, then go have a couple of beers."

"I'm for that," Gid replied enthusiastically.

Chapter Sixteen

When Will and Gid stepped into The Beatrice after supper, they were met by Penny and Elaina.

"Oh, good you are back in town," Penny said. "I hope you can stay for the concert."

"Concert?" Will asked. "You mean Nigel playing the piano? Doesn't he do that every day?"

"No, not like that. I mean a real concert," Penny said.

"It's going to be wonderful," Elaina said as she gave Gid a hug.

"What concert are you talking about?"

"It was my idea," Penny said proudly. "Nigel didn't want to do it at first, but I talked him into it."

"And when is this concert going to happen?" Gid asked.

"Friday night," Penny said. "We're goin' to put an ad in the paper before then. Ki said he's sure Governor Fremont will come, and also Major Willis and all the other officers and wives from Fort Whipple."

"Do stay for it," Elaina said. "I think it would mean a lot to Mr. Housewright if you were here."

"What do you say, Gid?"

"Hmm, let me think about it. Would I rather dig dirt and haul rocks, or look at pretty girls and hear pretty music? That's really a hard decision to make." Gid said, putting his finger on his jaw.

The two girls laughed.

"Only thing is, you won't be able to buy anything to drink while you're listening to the concert, because the bar will be closed until the concert is over," Elaina said.

"There's nothing that says we can't buy drinks now, is there?" Gid asked. "I mean I do see other folks in here drinking."

Penny laughed. "This is a saloon, or a pub as Nigel calls it. And drinking is what people do in a saloon."

"I thought you said we couldn't drink."

"That's during the concert, silly. You can drink now."

"Well, good. Get us a couple of beers, something for yourselves, and join us," Gid said. "I want to think about something besides dirt and rocks for a while."

Penny and Elaina retrieved the drinks, then joined Will and Gid at the table.

"Are any of Sandos' goons still coming around?" Will asked.

"From time to time," Penny said.

Elaina laughed. "But they aren't getting free drinks anymore."

"Nor taxes," Gid added.

"Well, that's not quite true," Penny said.

"What do you mean? I thought the taxes had been rescinded," Will said.

"The taxes have, but the protection hasn't."

"Protection?"

"Sandos is charging people to protect them. Of course, people don't have to pay for the protection, but what happened with the jewelry store scared some people," Penny said. "So, several businesses signed up for their insurance."

"What happened to the jewelry store?"

Penny explained that the jewelry store had not bought protection and was robbed and vandalized.

"Doesn't that seem a little too convenient?" Gid asked.

"Nigel made that same observation," Penny replied.

The next morning Will and Gid called on the governor.

"It's good to see you boys," Fremont said. "How goes the mining?"

"Tiring and non-productive," Gid said.

"Don't give up on it. There's color all around that slope, and I can't believe the vein played a cruel trick on the Axis," Fremont said. "You've got to be patient, and I'm speaking from experience. At one time, there was a five-mile quartz vein on my Mariposa ranch." He stopped talking, a faraway look in his eyes. "Oh, what could have been . . ."

"What happened?" Gid asked.

"Greed—that's what happened. I wasn't satisfied with what I had, so I speculated in railroads that went broke, then when the panic hit in '73, I lost even more money." He shook his head. "It's hard to believe, you are looking at a man who twice ran for President and now I'm the appointed governor of the Territory of Arizona drawing a pittance. Poor Jessie. Why she puts up with me, I'll never know."

"Sir, this nation owes you a debt of gratitude. We all know what you did to map this country," Will said.

"Ah, yes, the Great Pathfinder," Fremont said.

"Well, how are things going here in Prescott?" Gid asked as he felt a little uncomfortable discussing the governor's past. "Have Sandos or the Prescott Defenders caused any trouble?"

"I'm not exactly sure whether we're having problems with them or not," Fremont said.

"We've heard about the protection racket they're running," Gid said.

"A racket, yes, that's what I call it, but there's no law

against selling protection services per se' unless they're actually the ones who vandalized the jewelry store."

"To switch to a happier note, have you heard about the concert Nigel Housewright is giving?" Will asked.

"Oh, yes, and Jessie and I intend to be there. We already have our seats reserved. What about you two?"

"We plan to be there," Will said.

The next morning, an article about the concert appeared in the *Prescott Advocate.*

GALA CONCERT

Were we to gather in the finest theaters and concert halls of London, Paris, Vienna, or New York, we would not be able to enjoy more beautiful music, or a more accomplished pianist than is in store for us.

On Friday evening next, The Beatrice, heretofore known as a purveyor of the finest liquors and a warm atmosphere conducive for the exchange of convivial conversation, will undergo a transformation. No longer will men gather there merely to drink and exchange tall tales, for on that night The Beatrice Pub will become The Beatrice Theater, welcoming ladies, and even children, as its four walls will be graced by music as beautiful as anything found in the finest theaters of the world.

The artist will be Sir Nigel Housewright, knighted by Her Majesty, Queen Victoria, and presented with The Most

Excellent Order of the British Empire for his contribution of talent and culture to the arts.

The concert will begin at eight p.m.

"During a what? During a concert?"

"Yes, that's a perfect time. Half the town will be at the concert, the rest will either be home, or in one of the other saloons."

"How much money will be there, do you reckon?"

"There'll be enough for us both to be happy with an equal share."

"All right, we'll do it."

The Beatrice closed at noon on the day of the concert, so the pub could be turned into a concert theater. Will and Gid showed up to help Ki, Penny, and Elaina make the conversion. Nigel offered to help as well, but Penny insisted that he study his music and select the pieces he would be playing.

"The first thing we need to do is get rid of all the tables," Penny said.

"What will we do with them?" Elaina asked.

"If we stack them all up, we can get them in the liquor storeroom," Ki suggested.

"What about the chairs? I'm worried that we won't have enough," Penny said.

Ki smiled. "Don't worry, they'll be here within half an hour."

"Be here from where?"

"I'm getting them from the Plaza Bit, the Sazerac, and the Sample Room."

"Other saloons are offering to help?" Gid asked.

"Yeah." Ki chuckled. "They said if people are sitting here listening to Nigel's music, they won't be drinking his whiskey."

Under Penny's direction, the tables were all removed, to be replaced with chairs lined up as in a theater. Although most saloon piano players played on an upright, Nigel performed on a Steinway baby grand piano. Because of that, the piano was already present, and needed only to be moved into a more centralized location.

The shelves of liquor behind the bar were draped with cloth, and pots of ferns were placed on the bar, which added even more to the transition of saloon into theater. When all the work was done, Will, Gid, Penny, Elaina, and Ki sat in the front row to take a short rest.

Nigel came down the stairs from his living quarters, then looked at what had been done.

"Oh, my," he said, softly. He stood perfectly still for a long moment. "Oh my, this is absolutely unbelievable. You have actually transformed a pub, into a theater. I will have more pride in playing here tonight, than in any theater where I have performed."

"You can thank Penny," Elaina said. She took in the room with a broad wave of her arm. "This was all her idea, and she directed every move."

"I . . . I must go back to my room for a moment or two," Nigel said. He turned quickly, but not before the others could see that his eyes had filled with tears.

That evening, wheeled conveyances deposited their passengers at the corner of Gurley and Montezuma Streets. Among the first to arrive in a liveried carriage, were Governor and Mrs. Fremont. This was the first time either Will or Gid had seen Jessie Fremont.

When the arrivals stepped into The Beatrice, they saw that it had undergone a complete change. Men, women, and children made up the audience, and there was a quiet buzz of conversation as everyone stared at the empty piano.

Will and Gid were in the back row sitting with Penny and Elaina.

"I'm happy that we were able to do this," Ki said. "Mr. Housewright is such an accomplished piano player that everyone in town should be able to hear him, not just those of us who hear him all the time."

"Tonight, he isn't a piano player," Penny said.

"What do you mean he isn't a piano player?"

"Tonight, this is a theater, and the piano is a grand piano, and that means that Nigel is a pianist."

"What's the difference between a piano player and a pianist?"

"Someone who plays piano in a saloon is a piano player. Someone who plays the piano in a theater is a pianist," Penny said.

"Penny, how did someone who knows all the stuff you know, ever wind up doing the kind of work you do?" Gid asked.

"We all have histories we'd rather keep to ourselves," Penny replied enigmatically, sharing a glance with Elaina.

All the lanterns were turned low, and a spot-light found the piano as anticipation grew within the audience. A moment later, Nigel appeared wearing a tuxedo and tails. A blue sash angled across the front of his ruffled white shirt, The Most Excellent Order of the British Empire hung from a red ribbon around his neck, and other medals were just above his left pocket.

"Oh, my, look at him," Elaina said, quietly. "I have never seen Sir Nigel Housewright look so handsome."

Penny reached over and squeezed Elaina's hand.

"Yes," she said, "doesn't he?"

The audience consisted of officers and their wives from Fort Whipple, businessmen, women, and children, miners and clerks, cowboys and wagon drivers, housewives, laundresses, and ladies of the evening. As the audience applauded his entrance Nigel bowed, then moved to the piano and sweeping the tails back from his tuxedo, sat down and began to play the dulcet strains of Bach's *Prelude in C Major.*

Bach was followed with pieces by Grieg, Chopin, and Liszt, and all sat spellbound as the beautiful music caressed their souls.

The concert lasted for an hour and a half, then after finishing the last piece, *Bach's French Suite Number 2 in C Minor,* Nigel stood and acknowledged the applause of the crowed with a deep bow.

Suddenly the applause was interrupted by the ear-shattering sound of a nearby explosion.

The applause stopped and several in the audience called out in surprise.

"What was that?" someone shouted.

"Will, the last time I heard anything like that, we were being bombarded with cannon," Gid said.

"It truly does sound like that, but I'm pretty sure that's not cannon fire."

At that moment, Jubal Sandos stepped into The Beatrice. "The bank has been robbed!" he shouted at the top of his voice. "Prescott Defenders with me! We're going after them!"

Half a dozen men who had been at the concert, stood

up and hurried toward the door to join Sandos.

The six men who responded were not wearing the uniform of the Prescott Defenders, and they were joined by several others from the audience, men women and children, drawn by the excitement.

"What do you think, Will, should we go after the bank robbers?" Gid asked.

"Not yet," Will said. "I want to see what Sandos and his bunch do about this."

When Will and Gid went out front, they stood back with those who had poured out of The Beatrice. By now Sandos and the others were mounted and at a call from Sandos, they started out at a gallop, nine strong. Because the saddled horses were those of the Prescott Defenders, they were the only ones who made up the posse. The rest of the men of the audience stood out front and watched them ride away.

"Go get 'em!" someone shouted.

"Bring 'em back so we can hang 'em," another added, his shout as loud as the first.

"I'll tell you this, whoever it was that blew up that safe in the bank don't have a chance of getting away now that Sandos and the Prescott Defenders are after them," someone else said.

"There warn't none of 'em wearin' uniforms. Did you notice that?"

"Well, that's because they were here listening to the concert."

"No, that ain't it. There ain't none of 'em been wearin' a uniform ever since they couldn't collect tax no more."

"I reckon it's a good thing that the concert's over now," someone said.

"Well, hell yeah, there isn't anybody who would want to listen to music when the bank is being robbed right under our very eyes."

"How about several different ones of us get out of here and go find us a drink?" someone suggested.

"How 'bout we go down there 'n get a lot of drinks?" another said, and many laughed.

"Mama, is the concert really over?" a young girl asked.

"I'm afraid it is, darlin'."

"That music was pretty, wasn't it?"

"Yes, dear, it was very pretty."

"Do we have to go home now?"

"Yes, it's time to go home now."

Will and Gid watched the others drift away, then they went back inside. There, they saw Governor and Mrs. Fremont, Nigel, Penny, Elaina and Ki, sitting together in what had been the front row of the audience area. Will and Gid walked over to join them, pulling a couple of chairs out so they could face the others.

"So much for trying to bring culture to Prescott,"

Nigel said. "The robbers knew there would be a lot of people here tonight."

"Don't sell yourself short, Nigel," Penny said. "I was watching the audience and they were enchanted by the music."

"That's very sweet of you to say, my dear," Nigel replied. "Once in London I had a concert interrupted because a string broke on the violin that was accompanying me." He paused for a moment, then inexplicably, he laughed. "I wonder if anyone else has ever had their concert interrupted by an explosion."

"You were finished though, weren't you?" Will asked.

"Technically I was finished, yes. But I was prepared to play an encore, Beethoven's *Fur Elise*."

"Will you play it for us now, please?" Elaina asked.

"Yes, do play it for us," Jessie Fremont added.

Nigel returned to the piano, took his seat, paused for a moment, then began to play. He played as if the audience had not left, caressing every note. When the song was finished, he stood, turned, and bowed as if he was before the Queen of England.

Penny, unable to restrain herself, got up from her chair and hurried up to Nigel where she gave him a warm embrace.

"I am so proud of you, Nigel," she said.

"This is because of you, Penny," Nigel said. "Everything, from the idea, to the getting the theater set up. At the conclusion of my encore, I was going to make a public declaration, that I was dedicating the concert to you. But alas, the audience is gone."

"No they aren't," Elaina said. "The audience that matters is still here."

Nigel chuckled. "I suppose you are right at that." Nigel reached out to take Penny's hands in his, and he stared into her eyes.

"Penny, my dear, with all my heart and soul, I dedicate tonight's concert to you."

"Hear, hear," Governor Fremont called as he began clapping, as the others joined him in his applause.

Chapter Seventeen

"The outlaws who robbed the bank only got eight hundred and nine dollars," Sol Lewis said, as he made the bank report on their loss. Lewis was president of the Bank of Arizona. "They blew the daily working safe, instead of the accounts safe. If they had blown that one, they would have gotten close to twenty-five thousand dollars."

Sheriff Bower was at the bank to hear the report, as were Will, Gid, and Governor Fremont.

"Sandos and his men are after them," Sheriff Bower said.

"Do you really have any hope that they'll find them?" Will asked.

"I don't know," Bower said.

"They may be successful," Fremont said. "After all, they need something to prove their relevance."

"All their horses were already saddled," Will said.

"What?" Bower asked.

"It was barely two minutes between the sound of the explosion, and the time Sandos came in to call out the Defenders. And yet when they got outside, all their horses were standing there, already saddled. Seems to me like that was awfully quick."

"Yes, come to think of it, it was," Governor Fremont agreed.

"Are you suggesting something, Will?" Sheriff Bower asked.

"Only that as fast as they got the horses saddled, and gathered in front of The Beatrice, it was almost like they were expecting something to happen."

"We can't prove that, though," Bower said.

"No," Governor Fremont said, "but we can certainly speculate."

When Oscar Pugh and Clovis Meachum reached the slope of Mingus Mountain they stopped.

"How much did we get?" Meachum asked.

"I ain't had time to count it yet, but it don't seem like very much," Pugh said. "It sure ain't as much as we was told it would be."

"Yeah, and we only get to keep half of it," Meachum said. "Sandos is goin' to take half the money back, so it'll look like they done somethin', even if we get away."

"Have you give any thought to just runnin' off 'n keepin' all of it?" Pugh asked.

"No, we don't want to do that. This way, we get away clean, with half the money, 'n nobody comin' after us," Meachum said.

"I guess you're right. Here comes Sandos and the others."

"Damn, they's a lot of 'em," Meachum said. "Ain't you glad this ain't for real?"

"Howdy!" Pugh said, stepping out and raising his hand in greeting. "We don't think we got all that much but climb down 'n we'll split it with you."

"No need for that," Sandos said, drawing his gun and pointing it at the two men.

"What? Look here, what are you a doin'? I told you we'd split just like you said."

Sandos pulled the trigger as did at least half a dozen other Prescott Defenders. Both Meachum and Pugh went down with multiple bullet wounds. They were dead by the time they hit the ground.

"All right boys, drape them over their horses. They've just helped us put the Prescott Defenders back in business."

"What about the money they took? Seein' as they're dead, we'll be gettin' all of it now, won't we?" Coates asked.

"Yes, we'll be getting all of it, and we'll be giving it back to the bank."

"What? What are we going to do that for?" Ike Snow asked.

Sandos looked into the sack containing the money. "It's only a little over eight hundred dollars or so. It'll be worth more to us if we give it back to the bank, than it will if we keep it."

"I sure don't understand that," Snow said.

"No need for you to try and understand it," Sandos said. "I'll do the thinking for all of us."

When the posse rode back into town the next morning their return caught everyone's attention, not only because that many horses made quite a parade, but also because there were two additional horses with them. And each of those two extra horses had a body draped over the saddle.

The little parade came to a halt in front of the bank, and by now a dozen or more people had gathered.

Lewis came out of the bank to see what the commotion was out front.

"Here you go, Mr. Lewis," Sandos said, tossing a bag toward him. "This is the money that was stolen from your bank, and we're about to take the two hombres who did it down to the morgue."

"Who are they?" Sheriff Bower asked as he stepped up.

"I've never seen either one of them before," Sandos said.

"Hey, I know them two," one of those who had gathered around the front of the bank said. "That's Oscar Pugh and Clovis Meachum. They ride for the Circle K ranch."

"You mean they did ride for the Circle K," Dan Coates said with a little chuckle. "They don't ride for 'em no more. They don't ride for nobody, 'lessen they're belly down over a saddle the way we brung 'em in this morning."

After the show in front of the bank, Sandos' men spread out among all the saloons along Whiskey Row. Only The Beatrice was spared a visit from any of the Defenders. Although the requirement that saloons give them their first drink free had been removed, in most cases the saloons gave them a free first drink anyway.

"You boys recovered the money and brought in the sons of bitches who robbed the bank, so your money is not good here, at least not today," Fred Williams, owner of the Sazerac Saloon, said.

Coates and Kramer lifted their drinks in toast.

"To the Prescott Defenders," Coates called out loudly.

To the Prescott Defenders," a few others said.

In saloons all along Montezuma Street, the recovery of the bank's money and the Prescott Defenders, were the subjects of discussion, and debate, some of it heated.

"There ain't no more Prescott Defenders. I mean, not for real, seein' as they don't wear them uniforms no more," someone in the Plaza Bit Saloon said.

"You're right, there ain't no more Prescott Defenders 'n as far as I'm concerned, good riddance," another replied.

"Why would you say that? Hell, the bank was robbed yesterday 'n they done found the ones that done it, 'n they brung the money back," still another said, adding to the debate.

Over in The Beatrice, Ki observed that none of the members of the Prescott Defenders had made a visit.

"I'm not sure why we have been spared a visit from an arse-orifice like Sandos or any of his despicable minions, but I'm thankful for it," Housewright said.

"But they did kill the two men who robbed the bank, and recover the money that was stolen," one of the customers said.

"If I was Lewis, I'd count every dollar to make sure the bank got it all back," Ki said.

"Every penny," Sol Lewis told Sheriff Bower. Will and Gid were there as well.

"I'm surprised the sons of bitches brought the money back," Sheriff Bower said, "especially since they're no longer being paid. And there was no reward for Pugh and Meachum either, so why do you suppose they did it?"

"It's probably worth more to them bringing it back than it would have been if they had kept it," Will said.

"Why do you say that?" Bower asked.

"They're trying to sell their protection service to people, and after bringing in the bank robbers and the money, the whole town is going to be treating them as heroes."

"You've got that right," Bower said. "And I see what you mean about it helpin' 'em sell their protection."

"Well, whatever they are, and for whatever reason, I'm happy to say that we got every dollar back. And that's good not only for the bank, but for our depositors," Lewis said.

"I need to get back to the office," Bower said. "Mr. Lewis, if you need me for anything, just send word."

"I will, and thanks, Sheriff."

Will and Gid went back with Bower.

"Ah, good, Jimmie, you made coffee," Bower said when they stepped into the sheriff's office.

The deputy began pouring coffee for the three men.

"You know, there's something very strange about all this," Will said as he wrapped his hands around the coffee cup.

"You mean other than the fact that Sandos and the Defenders went after them?"

"Well, that's strange enough, but I'm talking about

how quickly they had the horses saddled and ready to go. I ran outside as soon as I heard the explosion and Sandos and the others were there with their horses already saddled."

"Yeah, you mentioned that, but basically they're a bunch of lazy bastards," Bower said. "I wouldn't be surprised if they hadn't just left their horses saddled that night."

"No, they knew the bank was going to be robbed," Will said.

"How could they know that unless they . . ." Sheriff Bower paused in mid-sentence. "I'll be damn. You're thinking they planned it themselves, aren't you?"

"Could be."

"But I don't understand. If they did plan the robbery, why did they bring the money back? Every penny of it, according to Lewis."

"I don't think they had any intention of ever keeping the money," Will said. "I think this was all planned to buy back some of the credibility they lost when the governor took away their appointments as deputies of the court."

"So, they can sell themselves as protectors," Bower said.

"Exactly."

"Well, they're passing themselves off as private detectives, and I don't see that as being much different from the Pinkertons," Bower said.

"The Pinkertons have a reputation for honesty," Will said. "I'm not willing to say that the Prescott Defenders have earned that yet."

Apparently, Will's skepticism as to the Prescott Defenders' motivation in returning the money wasn't shared by Ben Weaver, as he stated in the next issue of the *Prescott Advocate.*

Prescott Defenders Recover Stolen Bank Money

Nobody has been harder on the Prescott Defenders than this newspaper. We criticized them for the onerous tax with which they were burdening our businesses, and the arrogance they exhibited as they paraded about on our streets and sidewalks.

But perhaps we have been too quick to judge. On the 7th, Instant, two men, Oscar Pugh and Clovis Meachum, formerly riders for the Circle K, grew tired of honest labor, and put into motion a plan to enrich themselves by robbing the Bank of Arizona. That their plan was ill-conceived is best demonstrated by the fact that they were hunted down and killed. According to Sol Lewis, president of the bank, every cent of the stolen money was recovered. And all that came about due to the quick action of Jubal Sandos and the Prescott Defenders.

It may well be that what has been perceived as arrogance, is in reality, self-confidence. When one puts one's self in harm's way, as do the members of the Prescott Defenders in bringing to justice those who would do us harm, self-confidence is a necessary trait. Kudos to the Prescott Defenders for recovering the money stolen from our bank.

"That's what we are now. We are a private detective agency and we're charging for our services. But, of course, you will only pay us, if you sign up for our protection. I would remind you though, of what we did for the Bank of Arizona. We chased down the robbers, and when they turned their guns on us and refused to surrender, we were forced to bring them to a summary justice. And let me remind you, we returned every penny that was taken from the bank," Sandos said as he made his pitch to Murray Bashford.

"Yeah, folks have been talking about that ever since," Bashford said. "That was a good thing you did. But what does this insurance you're selling have to do with that?"

"Maybe if I explain it this way, you'll understand. If you've noticed, none of the businesses that have subscribed to our protective services have been hurt. So far, the only business in town that has encountered any problems is the Cook and Bell Jewelry Store, and I'm convinced that if they had signed up with us, nothing would have happened to them. The criminal element is well aware of what we did to Pugh and Meachum, and they'd rather not encounter the men of the Prescott Defenders. We will defend any of our clients."

"All right, you've convinced me," Bashford said. "We'll enroll in your program."

Chapter Eighteen

Over the next two weeks there were nearly as many businesses subscribing to the Prescott Defenders Protective Insurance, as there had been those paying the tax. The fee for the insurance exactly equaled what the businesses had been paying when taxes were being levied against them, except for now, Judge Briggs did not get a share of the money.

In addition to the jewelry store, there were two more businesses, Dunnigan's Grocery Store and Chip's Shoe Alley, that were refusing to pay the insurance fee.

Dunnigan's had been broken into in the middle of the night and more than half of their groceries had been destroyed. Cans were opened and sacks were sliced so that sugar, flour, and coffee covered the floor.

Chip's Shoe Alley had also been broken into, and finished shoes and boots were destroyed, while rolls of unused leather and all the tools had been stolen.

During that same two weeks out at the Axis, Will and Gid had made some improvements on the little hut Beaumont had built. As a result, the place was considerably more habitable than it had been when they first arrived.

"This is the end of our bacon," Gid said. "And Woman hasn't been around to supply us with any game she's snared."

"And we're running low on flour and coffee too," Will added. "I think it's about time we went back into town."

"And maybe drop into The Beatrice for a visit," Gid said.

"Just a visit? You mean no beer?" Will teased.

Gid smiled. "Well, using a pickax all day long, day in and day out, can give a man a powerful thirst."

"So then, you're all right with us getting a beer."

"Or maybe two," Gid added.

The two brothers were quiet for a few minutes as they were eating their lunch. Then Gid broke the silence.

"Are we wasting our time here, Will?"

"I don't know the answer to that question. My mind tells me that almost two months of work, without the slightest bit of color might be telling us something."

"Huh, uh," Gid said with a shake of his head. "It's been more than that. Don't forget the years Beaumont put in here without finding much of anything."

"We know he took out more than a thousand dollars year before last, so there must still be something here. We just don't know where it is," Will said. "And as I look at it, if we're frugal, we have enough money to stake us for quite some time. In a way, doing this is better than being shot at, don't you think?"

"What we need is more dynamite," Gid suggested.

"I suppose you're right, but if we do that, we're going to have to get some timber to shore up the drift," Will said. "I'd hate to blast open an area, only to cause the rest of the mine to collapse. That would be a disaster."

"Yeah, especially if we were in the mine when it collapsed," Gid said.

Will chuckled. "No, Little Brother, in that case it would be a total disaster."

"How are we going to get the lumber out here?"

"We'll have to buy a wagon while we're in town. We're probably going to wind up having to get one anyway, especially when we start hauling all our gold out," he added with a teasing laugh.

"Jack can't pull a wagon," Gid said. "Should we buy a mule?"

"No, our horses can pull the wagon. They won't like it, but they'll do it."

When they arrived in town, the first place they went was to the freight company where they managed to buy an old wagon. As Will had suggested, they used their riding horses to pull the wagon. And as he had said, the horses didn't like it. They weren't used to being used in such a way, and they felt restricted when they were in a harness and attached to a wagon. They were a little restless, and that had made it difficult to hitch them up, but eventually they calmed down and gave Will and Gid no trouble when they left the yard.

Their next stop was Guthrie's Hardware store.

"Well now, it's good to see you boys again," Sam Guthrie said. He chuckled. "You're lookin' a lot more chipper than you were the last time I saw you. You was standin' on the gallows, as I recall."

"Yeah, well the only reason we were standing there was because we thought we could get a lot better view of the town that way," Will replied.

Guthrie got a surprised look on his face which he held for a moment, then he laughed out loud. "A better view of the town," he said. "You two are a couple of jokers. Now, what can I do for you?"

"We've come to get some supplies," Will said. "Hey, wait a minute. What's that?"

Will pointed to a silver-plated pistol that was being displayed in a glass case.

"Ain't that a beauty, though? That's a Colt Model 1861 pistol that was once owned by Custer his ownself."

"How did you get it?"

"Fred Benteen got it. He's my cousin, and he sold it to me."

"Frederic Benteen? Yes, he was there when it happened, wasn't he?"

"Yeah, fortunately though, Custer had broke off from my cousin's unit, so he wasn't directly with him during the actual battle."

"I'm surprised the Indians left something like this on the battlefield."

"Oh, they didn't. Fred bought this from Custer long before the battle."

"That's quite a souvenir to have. I'm surprised your cousin was willing to give it up."

Guthrie laughed. "Fred hated Custer. He thought he was a glory-seeking son of a bitch. I don't think he minded giving it up at all."

"Well, to get back to the reason we're here, do you have any dynamite on hand?"

"I only have six sticks left," Guthrie said. "The Jersey Lily bought all the rest, and I ain't got my new order in yet, but I expect it in the next day or two if you can wait."

"If that's what you have, then we'll take all six sticks and some shoring timber," Will said.

"All right, drive your wagon around back, and we'll get you loaded up," Guthrie said. "If you need more'n I got, drive on out to the sawmill at Thumb Butte. They's a guy named Virgil Earp tryin' to get rid of his stock. Says his brother tells him the real place to be is down in Tombstone. He says they's a lot of money to be made down there, and he aims to clear out and join his brother."

"Thanks for the information," Gid said.

During the loading, the three men took up a conversation, and Sam Guthrie spoke of a new girl that had gone to work at the Palace. "She's a pretty one all right. Too bad she's what she is. She'd make a body an awful pretty wife, so one of you ought to go by and see her—that is if you'd look at anybody besides them two at The Beatrice."

Will laughed. "Thanks, Sam, but I don't think either one of us is looking for a wife right now. Just dynamite and lumber."

"Have you tried the ice cream they's a servin' at the Palace? They got it most ever' day."

"Now you're talkin'," Gid said. "I could be persuaded to go to the Palace for that."

They continued loading the wagon and when they were finished, they saw Jubal Sandos standing on the boardwalk across the street from the hardware store.

"What's happening with the Prescott Defenders now?" Will said. "Are they still selling protection?"

"Yeah, insurance, they're a' callin' it. They come aroun' tryin' to sell me their insurance, but I told 'em to go to hell. I don't plan on givin' them sons of bitches nothin'," Guthrie said. "I figure what's the sheriff for, if it ain't to look out for us?"

Shoring timber filled the wagon, and because it was too late to go back out to the mine, they parked the wagon in front of the Reed Hotel.

"Hello, boys," Biff Reed said with a welcoming smile. "I see you have a wagon out front. Do you need it to haul out all your gold?"

"I wish that was true," Gid said. "Do you have a room for us?"

"For you, we'll always have a room," Biff said, "even if we have to put you up in our quarters."

"Before you do that, you'd better make sure Addie agrees with you," Will said.

Biff had a questioning expression on his face. "Oh? Is there something I don't know about?"

"No, no," Will said, "it's just that we get the feeling—well, she's not as friendly as she once was."

"Probably something Sandos has said," Biff said shaking his head. "If you want to pull that wagon around back, you can put it in my shed."

"Thanks," Gid said, "and we'll be leaving our horses in your stable as well."

"You're paying for it so go ahead."

With the wagon parked and their horses stabled, Will and Gid walked down to the sheriff's office. Sheriff Bower and Deputy Burns were playing checkers.

"So, here are the gold miners," Bower greeted with a smile.

"No, here are the dirt diggers," Will replied.

"Well, you know what they say around here; you have to move dirt in order to find gold," Bower said. "You haven't given up, have you?"

"Not yet, but every day that time comes closer," Gid said. "We're going to do some more blasting to maybe speed up the process, that is if we don't collapse the whole mine."

"That happens," Jimmie Burns said. "Just this week we got word that a man fell forty feet down a shaft at the Black Warrior."

"That's not likely to happen to us," Will said. "We're just going straight back into the mountain."

"Maybe you should change direction," Bower said.

"Speaking of which, we were talking with Sam Guthrie, and he tells us the Prescott Defenders are still collecting money from all the businesses in town."

"You were right about them using the bank robbery to promote themselves. Now, they're callin' what they're sellin' a private detective service, and far as I can tell, it's legal for any fool who wants to pay out good money." Sheriff Bower opened his desk drawer and pulled out a poster.

"I can't see that it's any different from what Pinkerton does. Sandos puts these here posters on the front of their business, 'n tells them this will put the word out that anyone that's thinkin' about breaking in think twice about it."

WARNING

This Store is Protected by

PRESCOTT DEFENDERS

Will glanced at the flyer then handed it back to the sheriff. "Guthrie said he's not buying the service."

"Not everyone has," Sheriff Bower said.

"I thought that once they lost their court deputy appointments, that they'd just go away, but I can see now that I was very naïve."

"I think we was all thinkin' that," Bower said. "Who knew that a town like Prescott could be taken over by these thugs."

"And it all started with one judge," Gid said.

"Yeah, old Judge Briggs," Burns said. "He and the governor haven't been on speaking terms since you boys cheated the devil."

"Hold it right there," Gid said, "how do you know where we were going?"

Burns laughed. "I don't know where you were going, but all I can say is you were damned close to finding out."

"Closer than we ever want to be again," Will said. "And both Gid and I can't thank you enough, Sheriff, for walking out of that jail when you did."

"Part of my job," Bower said. "Will you be in town overnight?

"Yes, we'll be at the Reed," Will replied.

"But now we're going to call on some friends at The Beatrice," Gid said.

Deputy Burns chuckled. "Would those friends be what you can find in a glass?"

"No, what are you talking about?" Gid challenged.

"I'm sorry, I was just teasing," Burns replied apologetically.

"They're in a mug," Gid said with a chuckle.

Burns' laugh was one of relief, as much as it was of humor.

Chapter Nineteen

Penny and Elaina greeted them the moment they pushed through the swinging doors of The Beatrice.

"It's so good to see you again," Elaina said. "You are our favorite customers, you know."

"Because we're so good looking?" Gid teased.

Elaina laughed. "Well, that too. But mostly it's because you were the only ones who helped us turn a saloon into a theater for the concert."

"What have folks been saying about that?" Will asked.

"Oh, everyone has been talking about how great it was," Penny said. "And why shouldn't they? Nigel is one of the best pianists in the world."

Gid chuckled.

"You doubt that?" Penny said.

"No, it isn't that," Gid said quickly. "It's just that I used to think that word meant something else."

Penny looked confused for a moment, then she too, laughed. "Oh my goodness, you were thinking it meant someone who pees a lot?"

"What can I tell you, Penny, my brother is easily confused," Will added with his own chuckle.

At that moment the subject of their conversation came over to them.

"Have you come to tell us you've hit a vein?" Nigel asked.

"I'm afraid not," Will replied.

Without having to ask for it, two mugs of beer appeared on the bar in front of Will and Gid. Will put a dime on the bar, but Nigel reached out and gave it back to Will.

"Since I no longer have to give free beer to the Prescott Defenders, I can afford to give a beer to my friends."

"I've been hearing about the Defenders charging businesses money for their protection service," Will said. "Have you fallen into that web?"

"They are now calling it a protection agency, and no, I haven't fallen into their web, if by that, you mean am I paying them anything. The way it's supposed to work is, you pay them money, and they make certain nothing happens to your business. If you don't pay them, all sorts of evil things could occur."

"Has anything happened lately?" Gid asked.

"Oh yes, a few businesses that didn't subscribe to

their service have been vandalized and robbed."

"Hmm, that's a rather convenient selling point for the insurance, isn't it?" Will asked.

"Have you read the latest edition of the *Advocate?*"

"No, we have no way of getting the paper out at the mine."

"Do you remember how supportive Ben Weaver was of them after they brought in the bank robbers?"

"Yes."

Nigel held his hand out toward Ki, who reached under the bar, then brought up a copy of the paper. "Read what he thinks about them now."

Two More Businesses Vandalized

As had been suffered by the Cook and Bell Jewelry Store earlier, two more Prescott businesses have subsequently been attacked and severely damaged by person or persons unknown. The businesses in question are Dunnigan's Grocery Store, which suffered over five hundred dollars in damage, and Chip's Shoe Alley, which sustained damages in excess of three hundred dollars. The fact that neither the Cook and Bell, nor Dunnigan's Grocery Store, nor Chip's Shoe Alley were subscribers to the Prescott Defenders Protective Insurance service can't be mere coincidence.

Jubal Sandos would have us believe that these businesses were attacked because the villains who did so, were well aware that those establishments didn't enjoy the protection of the Prescott Defenders, and therefore they could act with impunity.

But is there more to it than that? Is it impossible to think that perhaps these businesses have been struck as an inducement to others to enroll in the protective insurance program? If that is so, it would mean that the Prescott Defenders are themselves, guilty of these barbarous attacks.

In an earlier edition of this newspaper, we praised the Prescott Defenders for their quick and effective action in the recent bank robbery. As all our readers know, they chased down the perpetrators, recovered the money, and brought the bank robbers to a quick and final justice. Let us hope that these earlier accolades were not misplaced.

"It sounds to me like Mr. Weaver is suggesting the Prescott Defenders are connected with the vandalized businesses," Will said after reading the article.

"So it would appear," Housewright replied.

"Do you think . . ."

"Do I think the Prescott Defenders are the ones who attacked those stores?" Nigel finished the question for Will. "It is possible, but then it is also possible that someone decided that without the protection, the stores might be easy prey. Sandos has been quite public in letting everyone know who hasn't enrolled, and of course there are the posters. And in my book that makes him as culpable as if he and the Defenders had actually done the damage."

"We saw one of the posters," Will said. "What about The Beatrice? Anything suspicious going on?"

"I am not paying for their . . . *protection*," Nigel said.

"How long will you be staying in town?" Penny asked.

"We've got everything we need," Will said. "I expect we'll be heading out first thing in the morning."

"No, you must stay one more day," Elaina insisted. "The miners' ball is tomorrow night."

"The miners' ball?" Gid asked.

"Yes. And you are miners, so you must come to the ball," Penny added.

"Well, if digging up dirt and rock counts as mining, then I guess we qualify," Will said. "So, I reckon we'll be there, and it'll give me a reason to get a haircut."

"Good. Nigel, you'll be there, too, won't you?" she looked at him with an expression that could be easily read.

"Well now, wait a minute," Will teased. "I thought only miners could go."

"I am a miner."

"You're a miner?" Gid asked.

"My dear boy, I assure you, what do I do if I don't mine the miners' pockets?" Nigel replied with a laugh.

* * *

While the Crocketts were enjoying a beer and visiting at The Beatrice, Sam Guthrie was recording in his inventory book, the lumber and dynamite he had sold. He had already ordered more dynamite, but it should have arrived a week ago. He thought it would be wise to go out to Fort Whipple to have the telegraph operator send a message to check on the status of his order.

The freight wagons were being held up on a regular basis as they came up from Maricopa, and he thought dynamite would be a useful item to target. If it hadn't been shipped, perhaps he could ask Will and Gid to go down and meet the train and act as an escort for his shipment.

When he heard the front door open, he looked up to see Jubal Sandos coming in.

"What do you want, Sandos?" Sam asked.

"Is that any way to greet a friend?" Sandos replied. He had a fixed smile on his face, but the smile didn't reach his eyes.

"What makes you think we're friends?" Sam asked.

"Let's just let it go that we are business acquaintances. I mean, you have a very nice store here, and you provide goods and services to the whole town. Have you ever stopped to think that it's because my group has protected your store all this time?"

"Is that what you've done, Sandos? You've protected my store?"

"Yes, of course. Why did you think you were paying fifty dollars a month in tax?"

"I thought it was a nuisance fee."

"No, Mr. Guthrie, it was a fee to compensate the Prescott Defenders for providing protection for your business. I'm sorry to see that, so far, you have refused our offer to provide you with continued protection. And this for a subscription fee that won't cost you a penny more than what you were paying."

"I told your men, I ain't interested in anything you got to offer," Sam said. "I know what you're up to, Sandos, and I know you've buffaloed some of the other businesses into signing up. But as far as I'm concerned, you ain't doin' nothin' more than chargin' a tax, and I don't intend to pay it."

"I would think that you would care enough about keeping your business safe, that you wouldn't mind spending a few dollars," Sandos said. "I mean look at it like this. When you were paying the tax, your business was still profitable."

"That's true, but now it's more profitable," Guthrie said with a confident smile. "I ain't a payin' you nothin'."

"All right, Mr. Guthrie, have it your way," Sandos said. "But, if you find your store robbed, or maybe torn up in some way, I want you to remember that it was you who turned down the protection of the Prescott Defenders."

After a few beers, and a friendly card game at The Beatrice, Will and Gid had supper at The Gem, then returned to the Reed Hotel. They were met in the lobby by Addie.

"Will and Gid Crockett," she said, greeting them with a smile. "How nice to see you again. How long will you be staying with us?"

"We'd planned to start back at daybreak," Gid said, "but we've been told there's a shindig tomorrow night, so we'll stay at least one more night if you've got room for us."

"Oh good, I'm glad you'll be staying for the ball."

"Save a place for us on your dance card," Will said.

"I will. Dad's upstairs in our apartment," she said as she finished writing in the registration book. "Why don't I go get him and you two can come and have a cup of coffee with us? And I think Doris has a pie that just came out of the oven, if you're up for a piece. I'm not sure, but I think it's cherry."

"I'm always up for a piece of pie, especially cherry," Gid replied with a smile.

"Good."

"That's strange," Will said as they watched Addie hurry up the stairs.

"You mean because she's being so nice?" Gid asked.

"Yes, I wonder what brought about the change."

"I don't know, but I'd rather her be friends with us,

than have her mad at us," Will said.

"Yeah, you've got that right."

Over coffee and pie, Will and Gid answered a lot of questions about what was happening with the gold mine.

"I know there's gold out there," Will said. "The next mine over on the same slope is bringing in a lot of it."

"Yes, but the Jersey Lily has twenty people working around the clock, and we have only us," Gid said.

"Us, and dynamite," Will added.

"You're using dynamite?" Biff asked.

"Yes, we've used powder once or twice, but I think dynamite will work better," Will said, "but we only have six sticks. That's all Sam Guthrie had."

"Would you be willing to listen to a little advice from someone who has dabbled in mining?" Biff asked.

"I don't know, how successful was your dabbling?" Will replied with a smile that denoted he was teasing.

"Not as good as a lot of folks, but I did take out enough to open this hotel," Biff said.

"All right, I'd say that's good enough. Tell us what you think."

"Instead of continuing straight ahead, go back to as far as Kurt had advanced. He was successful for a while, then the vein played out. But it might be that the vein didn't actually play out, it just curved away from him.

Make your drift go at a hard right angle, first in one direction and then in the other. If the vein is there, you might come across it that way."

"You said as far as Beaumont advanced. We've gone close to seventy-five feet farther. Shouldn't we make the turn from there?"

"No, if Kurt had been working a vein, you're probably closer to it starting from where he was, than from where you are. If the vein did curve away, the deeper you go into the mine, the farther you will be from it."

"Yes!" Will said enthusiastically. "That makes sense; it's a great idea, so good that I don't know why I didn't think about it myself."

"Don't worry, Will, if it's successful, you'll try to convince me that it was your idea," Gid said. "And you'll say all these calluses on my hands were just to toughen 'em up for when we hit pay dirt."

Biff and Addie laughed.

Eventually the discussion swung to what was going on in the town, and that gave Will the opening to bring up something that was on his mind.

"I understand that Sandos is collecting a tax again."

"It isn't a tax," Addie said, quickly. "It's more like an insurance policy."

"I've heard about the *insurance policy*," Will said, emphasizing the words.

"Yes, they did charge taxes, but when our esteemed governor took that away from them, they had no recourse but to start charging a fee," Addie said. "After all, we can't expect them to do all that they do, for nothing."

"My dear, do I have to remind you that those people had these two men standing upon the gallows, staring into the abyss?" Biff asked. "And if it had not been for our governor . . ."

"Jubal and I have spoken of that. I let him know that I credit the two of you with saving our lives, and he says now that he is convinced that the shooting of his men was in self-defense. He says he regrets letting it go as far as it did, and he's glad the governor intervened."

Gid chuckled. "I have to say I agree with him on that, but it's probably the only time I'll ever agree with something Sandos says."

When Governor Fremont learned that Will and Gid were in town, he sent Jerome McCoy to invite them to come to his home the next morning for breakfast.

When they arrived, they were greeted by Jessie Fremont, a slender woman whose gray laced hair didn't detract from her attractiveness.

"Misters Will and Gid Crockett," Mrs. Fremont said. "It is wonderful to see you again, and welcome to our home."

"Thank you for the invitation, Mrs. Fremont."

"It is my pleasure," she said. "I have heard that you were instrumental in organizing Mr. Housewright's concert, and for that I am grateful. It was a most enjoyable evening."

"I'm afraid we provided little more than the muscle to move furniture around," Will said. "The concert was Penny Admore's idea."

"Admore? That name doesn't sound familiar," Mrs. Fremont said.

"Penny is one of the women who works at The Beatrice," Gid said.

"Oh my, I wouldn't think she would know about classical music, much less enjoy it."

"Ma'am, I'm sure you would have no reason to know this, but classical music is played at The Beatrice every day," Gid said.

Mrs. Fremont took a deep breath. "I'm sorry. Perhaps I misjudged Miss Admore without ever having met her."

At that moment, Governor Fremont came into the room, and put one arm around Jessie, pulling her to him.

"Jessie is my pillar of strength," Fremont said. "She's the daughter of Senator Thomas Hart Benton, who was . . ."

"A senator from Missouri, our home state," Will said.

"Indeed. But she's quite the lady in her own right. It is said that her writings about my exploits have caused more Argonauts to head west than any other publications."

"Come, John, these men didn't come here to talk about

me," Jessie said. "I'm sure Ah Chung has breakfast ready."

Over a breakfast of buckwheat cakes with blackstrap molasses, eggs, cured ham, and coffee, Will caught the governor up on their mining operations, or lack thereof.

"Have you considered selling your claim?" Fremont asked.

"That thought has occurred to us more times than you can imagine," Gid said. "We were on our way to California, you know."

A wan smile came over Mrs. Fremont's face. "California was beautiful."

"Mrs. Fremont, it's my turn to apologize," Gid said. "The Governor told us about Mariposa and I'm sorry if I brought up something unpleasant."

"My dear man, nothing about being a millionaire was unpleasant." She smiled at her husband. "John and I have had a good life, blessed with three loving children . . . and now we are here in Prescott, Arizona. What more could I ask?"

"Indeed, Mrs. Fremont," the governor said as he reached across the table to take her hand. "What more could we ask?"

Ah Chung appeared at that moment to begin clearing the table.

"Shall we go into the living room, or would you prefer to sit on the porch?" Jessie asked.

"I prefer the porch," John said. "I never get tired of smelling all the pines and looking at the mountains."

"Especially San Francisco Peak," Will said. "It's hard to believe that mountain is more than a hundred miles from here."

"Yes, Prescott has everything. It's too bad there is that element that wants to destroy it," Jessie said.

"Are you talking about the Prescott Defenders?" Gid asked.

"Of course I am," Jessie said. "I don't know why the sheriff doesn't arrest them all and stop all this extortion that's going on."

"My dear, Sheriff Bower says he has no way of proving it, but he thinks these businesses that are being damaged, are the result of Sandos."

"Humph," Jessie said. "Isn't it odd that one business after another is being vandalized, and then afterwards, a half dozen more businesses pay for his protection service? What a fraud Jubal Sandos is."

"Apparently, Ben Weaver agrees with you," Will said.

"Yes, I read his article, and appreciate his opinion," Jessie continued. "I wish more people agreed with him."

"Governor, what about the deputy commissions you gave Gid and me?" Will asked. "Do you want to activate them?"

"They are active now," the governor said, "but as to

any specific duty you might perform, I'd rather wait to see when it would be best to use you."

Will nodded his head. "We can understand that."

"Will you be attending the miners' ball tonight?" Jessie asked.

"Yes, in fact, we're staying in town an extra day, just for that purpose. Will you and the governor be there?"

"We'll be there all right," Governor Fremont said with a smile. "We've been invited, and it would behoove us to be seen among the people."

Jessie laughed. "You know what John is talking about—people say he spends too much time in Washington, but he's only trying to get more investors for Arizona."

"Would that be investors for mines?" Gid asked.

"Of course," Jessie said, "and for a railroad to connect us to either Ash Creek or Maricopa. It's ridiculous to have the capital of this territory not have rail service or even a telegraph line."

"Now, Jessie, get off your high horse," the governor said. "I guess you can tell, Mrs. Fremont is very interested in the politics of our state. She could run things a lot better than I do, if she would just takeover."

"Let's get back to the ball," Jessie said. "Can I expect to have either of you as a dance partner?"

"Yes, ma'am," Gid said. "You can count on us."

The Onie Crites band that would be providing music for the ball arrived that afternoon, after a two-day trip from Phoenix. There were six of them, filling up a special, unscheduled stagecoach that had been arranged by the Prescott Miner's Association.

Some of the youngsters had been awaiting the arrival of the band, and now they ran alongside the coach until it reached the newly built Luke's Hall, where the dance would be held. The hall had been donated to the community by one of its most recent millionaires.

When the band began rehearsing that afternoon, the same children who had run alongside the coach as it arrived, now danced and laughed to the music that could be heard out on the street.

That evening, almost everyone in town was seen heading for the dance. As Nigel would be escorting Penny to the dance, Elaina asked Will and Gid if they would escort her, and they agreed. Because there were so many more men than women in Yavapai County, their presence at the dance, as well as the girls from the other saloons, were all welcomed.

"Nigel, this music's going to be a little highfalutin for you, isn't it?" Gid teased.

"Everyone can profit by increasing their repertoire," Nigel replied.

"Does that mean you'll be playing some of these songs in The Beatrice?" Will asked.

Nigel smiled. "One never knows, now does one?"

Jubal Sandos arrived, splendidly attired in his Prescott Defenders uniform, complete with gold braid and the eagle insignia of a colonel. A smiling Addie Reed was holding his arm as they entered. Sandos wasn't the only one in uniform. Even though the Prescott Defenders had stopped wearing uniforms in general, there were several in uniform that night.

In addition, there were soldiers from Fort Whipple present for the dance, including Major Willis, the commander, and his adjutant, Captain Chambers. All those who had their wives at the fort were in attendance as well as many men who had come alone.

"Ladies and gentlemen, we welcome you to this beautiful new facility that has been donated to the community by the Honorable C. A. Luke," Governor Fremont said as he stood on a platform near the front of the hall. "Mr. Luke gives all of you reason to continue working your claims. He has proven that the Sierra Prieta still has . . . gold in them thar hills!"

There was an eruption of applause from everyone. Then the governor introduced Onie Crites.

Crites stepped to the platform. "No more talkin' folks,

form your squares and let the dancin' begin!"

The music began playing then, the strum of the guitar, the high skirling of the two fiddles, and the thumping of the base fiddle. As the caller started his calls, he danced around as if he too, were in a square. He barked out his calls in a sing-song voice.

Roll promenade a shady lady.
Gents roll back, but only one,
Promenade, you're gonna have a little fun.
It ain't no sin to swing and sway,
An' you pickle up a doodle in the middle of the day.

There were around a hundred or more miners, as well as the soldiers and town folks, so all of the women, including Penny and Elaina, were kept busy with every dance. Addie, on the other hand, danced but a few times, and only with Sandos. Once, when Will looked over toward her, she was watching the dance, swaying lightly and keeping time by tapping her toe. Sandos, who had temporarily abandoned her, appeared to be in a deep conversation with some of the other Defenders.

Will walked over to her.

"Would you like to dance? Or, do you think it would cause a problem with your beau?"

Addie smiled. "I doubt that it would cause a problem,

but I don't care if it does or not. And I'm sure, you don't care either."

"It's nice to know that we agree," Will said, returning her smile, and offering his arm.

Will danced two squares with her, then Onie Crites held up his arms. "Folks, if you don't mind, the band and I are going to take a little rest here, maybe enjoy a cup of punch. You folks could probably use a little rest as well, so visit among yourselves and we'll get started again in fifteen minutes."

When Will returned Addie to where he had picked her up earlier, Sandos was standing there with an expression of irritation on his face.

"The proper thing for you to have done, Crockett, would be to ask my permission to dance with my girl."

"Jubal, I don't need your permission to dance with whomever I please," Addie said resolutely.

"No, of course not," Sandos said quickly and apologetically. "I was just suggesting that among gentlemen, that would have been the proper thing for Mr. Crockett to do."

"You seemed to be pretty busy, going over your plans with the other Defenders."

"What do you mean going over my plans? Are you insinuating something?" Sandos asked, his irritation growing more intense.

"No, I wasn't present at your meeting," Will said, "but

it's plain to see, you've been spending more time with your men than you have with your girl."

"Will," Gid called, and looking toward him, Will saw that Gid was motioning for him to come over. He was standing in a small group of men.

"Excuse me, my brother's calling," Will said. "Addie," he said, nodding at her but ignoring Sandos.

One man, whom the others seemed to be listening to, looked to be in his late-fifties, slim, and a bit stoop-shouldered. His eyes were dark blue and deep-set. He had heavy eyebrows and a mouth framed by a full white beard, although his hair was brindled.

"Will, this is Joseph Reynolds. Do you know who he is?"

"Of course," Will said offering his hand. "The Diamond Jo Lines. Anybody who knows anything about the Mississippi River has seen your sternwheeler."

"It's a pleasure to meet you, Mr. Crockett. These gentlemen tell me that your claim separates the two of them."

"I'm Ivan LaGrange and I'm the foreman at the Jersey Lily, and this is Frank Bugbee who has just bought the Hidden Treasure claim."

"I see," Will said. "That means we're neighbors."

"We are," Bugbee said. "I'm hoping that it won't be long until the Hidden Treasure shows as much color as the Jersey Lily."

"Perhaps the vein you find might be running right through the Axis," Gid said.

For a few minutes, the conversation stopped, as the five men stood together awkwardly.

"Mr. Reynolds," Will said in an attempt to make conversation. "What brings you to Prescott? I doubt Granite Creek could even float one of your barges."

"I'm always looking for new enterprises where I can invest," Reynolds said. "I now have a railroad in Arkansas, and Mrs. Fremont has told me, you folks could use a railroad coming into Prescott."

"She's right about that," Gid said. "So are you going to do that?"

"I don't know about that. I was told Jay Gould has been visiting with your governor, so I think I'm going to consider something else," Reynolds said.

Gid looked at Will. "That's very interesting. Would you be interested in a mine above Lynx Creek?"

"I might be," Reynolds said, "but right now I've been told there's a new mining district a little south of here. I think it's called Date Creek and I intend to go look into it before I head home."

"Perhaps you could remember us and we could do some business before you leave," Will said.

"I will," Reynolds said.

When the conversation ended, Gid turned to Will.

"What was that all about? You can't believe that someone as savvy as 'Diamond Jo' Reynolds would be interested in the Axis?"

"Maybe not," Bugbee said, "but he may be interested in the Hidden Treasure, the Jersey Lily, and the Axis."

LaGrange shook his head. "Don't include the Jersey Lily in any deal. Mr. Dabney is about ready to invest in a smelter."

"Are you saying the Jersey Lily is paying out enough color that Morris Dabney is willing to spend that much money?" Frank Bugbee asked.

"I'd say," LaGrange said. "I'm about to hire fifty more men as soon as I can find them."

"Do you hear that, Gid? If these two claims are on either side of us, what would have kept just a little tiny vein from running through the Axis?"

"Fire! Fire!" Deputy Burns shouted as he ran into the community hall.

"What?" Sheriff Bower called out to him. "What are you talking about, Jimmie?"

"There's a fire, Sheriff! Guthrie's Hardware is on fire!"

Chapter Twenty

With shouts of concern and fear, everyone responded to the warning. Many of them started toward the door, but Sandos stood there with raised hands.

"Hold it, hold it!" he shouted. "Snow, Coates, get the pumper truck down there and do it fast. Muley, you and Chapman help me organize a bucket brigade to keep the pumper full of water. The rest of you, if you want to help, grab buckets so you can bring water to the pumper!"

By the time Will and Gid reached the hardware store many of the people who had not been present at the ball, were gathered there, staring in shock at the high-leaping flames.

"We were just told about this," Gid said. "How the hell did the fire get this big, so fast?"

"There's all that lumber stacked in there, 'n also there's at least a hunnert 'n fifty gallons of coal oil,"

Sheriff Bower said.

"Here comes the pumper!" someone shouted.

The wagon-mounted pumper, pulled by a team of galloping horses came speeding down Gurley Street with the two uniformed Defenders on the front seat. Coates was driving, and Snow was clanging the bell, the loud bongs echoing back from the store fronts.

"Make way, make way here!" Sandos shouted, waving people out of the way to allow the pumper wagon to approach. By now several had gathered with buckets, and Sandos organized them into three lines: one from the nearest watering trough, one from a nearby resident's windmill, and one stretching all the way to Granite Creek.

With Snow and one of the other Defenders operating the pump handles, Coates started directing a stream of water toward the burning building.

"My cash box!" Guthrie shouted. "My cash box is in there!" He started toward the flaming building.

"No!" Sandos said, grabbing him, and holding him back.

"I've got over a hundred dollars in my cash box. I can't just leave it in there," Guthrie said.

"Snow, turn the water on me," Sandos said, and Snow directed the water hose toward him, drenching him. Then, with water dripping, Sandos ran into the burning building as the crowd gasped in surprise and concern.

A moment later he came out, holding the cash box aloft. The crowd cheered and applauded.

"Boys, it's too late to save the hardware store," Sandos shouted. "Let's try to save the buildings on each side."

Within an hour the hardware store, its flames further fueled by stacks of lumber and kerosene, was totally destroyed. The two neighboring buildings, thanks to the spray of water from the pumper hose, were saved. Unlike Guthrie's Hardware, Rafferty's Grocery and McGill's Tobacco store were enrolled with the Prescott Defenders Protective Insurance policy.

The next morning Will and Gid were visiting with Sheriff Bower when Jubal Sandos and Ike Snow came into the office. Snow was carrying a spouted container and a damp rag.

"It was arson," Sandos said. "We found this kerosene can and this kerosene-soaked rag behind Sam Guthrie's place."

"I'll be damn. I wondered how that fire got started," Sheriff Bower said. "Sam swore he hadn't left a lantern burning or anything like that."

"It wouldn't have made any difference if he had or not," Sandos said. "Like I said, it was arson. So now, what are you going to do about it?"

"Well, I . . . I don't really know."

Sandos glared at Will and Gid. "Maybe you can deputize these two, *gentlemen,* to find out who did it." Sandos said sarcastically.

"You're the one selling insurance to the merchants. Aren't you supposed to take care of things like this?" Will asked.

"Unfortunately, Mr. Guthrie wasn't one of our subscribers,"

"You mean like Cook and Bell, Dunnigan's Grocery Store and Chip's Shoe Alley weren't subscribers?" Gid asked.

"What are you suggesting?" Sandos asked.

"Not a thing," Gid said, "but it seems mighty peculiar that the only business that have had any kind of problem, are those that don't subscribe to your protective service."

"What you said just proves our worth," Sandos insisted. "It stands to reason that anyone who's going to strike at a business, would choose one that isn't enjoying our protection."

"Why would someone burn the building, but not steal the money?" Will asked.

"I'm not sure what you're talking about."

"Guthrie left his cash box in the store, but whoever burned and looted it, didn't take the cash box."

"And who ran into the flames to recover that box? I do believe that was me if you recall," Sandos said.

"Yes, I do recall. That was pretty convenient for you, wasn't it?" Will asked.

"What do you mean?"

"I mean the cash box was so located that you were able to go inside, grab it, and be back outside in a manner of seconds. As if conveniently, it had been left just inside the door."

"Crockett, are you suggesting that I had something to do with where that cash box was put?"

"Well, it did make you into quite a hero, didn't it? And it should help you convince others that if they don't sign up for your services . . . why, who knows what will happen to their businesses?"

"That's ridiculous. You were there, last night. You saw how my men and I worked to save that hardware store," Sandos said.

"No. I saw how hard you worked to save the two adjacent businesses-- businesses who have signed up with you. You let Guthrie's burn to the ground."

"We'll see what the rest of the town thinks," Sandos said as he turned angrily, then left the sheriff's office.

"You have to give the son of a bitch credit," Bower said after Sandos was gone. "He and his men were right in the thick of it."

"Yeah. In the thick of it," Will said.

When Will and Gid returned to the hotel to check out, Biff and Addie were sitting in the lobby.

"Are you going back to the mountain?" Biff asked.

"Yes, thanks to your suggestion, we've got more work to do. By using dynamite to turn our drift, we may hit the vein again."

"Don't get in too big of a hurry," Biff said. "Make sure you've got your tunnel well shored up before you start blasting."

"We'll make sure we work together," Gid said.

"You could learn something from the Prescott Defenders about that," Addie said. "Did you see the way Jubal and his men worked together last night? I think maybe now the town will appreciate them a little more."

"I hate to say this, Addie, but I'm afraid you're being quite naive," Will said.

"I can't believe you said that," Addie said. "What will it take to convince you that Jubal is only doing what is best for Prescott? You were there last night. You saw how, as soon as Jimmie Burns gave the alarm, even before Jubal left the ball, he started organizing his men. The pumper, the bucket brigade, why, you could see the Defenders uniforms everywhere."

"Yes, you could see the uniforms everywhere," Will said. "Strange, don't you think, that none of them had worn uniforms for almost a month, but last night, while they were manning the pumper and organizing the bucket brigade, they were all in uniform so that they just happened to stand out?"

"I don't think that's strange at all," Addie said. "Jubal looks important in his uniform, and so do all the others. I think they wore them just for the ball."

"Perhaps, but as you said, it also made them very visible while they were at the fire. You couldn't have planned to have had that fire at a more convenient time than when they were all in uniform so they could show off for the town."

"You have him all wrong. Jubal is as fine a man as I have ever met," Addie said. "You saw how he risked his life to run into the fire to save the cash box. And don't forget, he didn't have to do that, because Sam Guthrie refused to sign up for the protection."

Will and Gid exchanged glances, then Gid spoke. "You know, Will, we need to get going."

"Yes, we do. Biff, thanks for making us feel welcome once again. Addie, it was nice to see you," Will said with a slight nod of his head.

"Ooh," Addie said, scathingly, after Will and Gid had gone. "Those two men can make me so angry."

"Addie, need I remind you that those two men saved our lives?" Biff replied.

"Yes, I know, Papa, but that doesn't give them the right to say such hateful things about Jubal. Especially in front of me."

"Darlin', they aren't being critical of you. They've never been anything but respectful of you."

"No, but they've been very critical of the man I love, and as far as I'm concerned, that's the same thing as being critical of me."

"I don't know what we can do about Addie," Will said as he and Gid started up Lynx Creek with the loaded wagon. "Nothing good can come of her relationship with that bastard Sandos, but it's not our place to say anything to her."

"Have you noticed something here?" Gid asked. "We have a habit of running into women who fall for the wrong man."

"You're thinking about Julia," Will said.

"Yes, and if it hadn't been for us, I think Jamie Kincaid would have killed her."

Will and Gid were talking about the time they had delivered several horses to Colonel John Abernathy, a wealthy man whom they had known during the Civil War. He had asked them to ride with his daughter on a trip because he feared she might be kidnapped and held for ransom. They had got her to her destination safely, but then Julia had been convinced that Kincaid loved her. She ran off with him voluntarily, only to have him bargain with her father for ransom.

"We tried to warn Julia, but she wouldn't listen to us, and now, Addie thinks that suck up Sandos is in love with her," Gid said.

"And we're not going to talk her out of it," Will said. "I just hope she's smart enough to not let him hurt her."

"Yeah," Gid agreed.

As they wound their way up Lynx Creek, the pathway got more and more narrow. When they reached the last placer, they were greeted by Hoss Martin.

"You boys been gone a bit," he said. "We was all a bettin' ya done quit on us."

"Not yet," Will called back. "This week is going to be the week we get rich."

"Ha, that's what we all think," Hoss said. "I spec you gonna be workin' quite a bit." He pointed toward the lumber in the wagon. "First off, how ya gonna get them boards up to the Axis?"

Will looked at Gid and raised his eyebrows. "We're just going to take the wagon up there."

"Uh huh," Hoss said, "and then you're gonna be walkin' cause them ridin' horses ain't gonna pull that load up that slope."

"All right," Gid said, "what's your suggestion?"

"Go get Jack. He'll get your boards up to the mine."

For the next two days, Will, Gid, and the burro made countless trips up the slope. When the last board was up the mountain, they took Jack back to Woman's wickiup.

They found her out back bending over a primitive oven made of stones that were sunk in the ground. She was adding more charcoal to the pit. Lying beside the oven were several heads of the maguey plant. Picking one head up, she began pulling an outside spine off, then putting it between her teeth, she began pulling the insides out. She handed a leaf to both Will and Gid, and they did as she had done. When they tasted the sweet substance, they saw Woman smiling at them.

"Damn, this is good!" Gid said.

Woman disappeared into her wickiup and returned with a jug and two tin cups. She poured a small amount of the clear liquid into the cups and handed one to each of them.

When Will tasted it, he thought it was not unlike the drink popular in border towns all over the Southwest.

"Is this tequila?"

"Tizwin." That was the first sound either Will or Gid had heard Woman speak.

"Well tizwin or tequila, I'll take some more," Gid

said as he held out his cup.

Woman shook her head and took the jug back inside.

"I think she's trying to tell us this is one potent drink," Will said.

"I believe it," Gid said. "Do you feel a little tipsy?"

"I'll tell you one thing," Will said as they headed back to their place. "I won't have any trouble sleeping tonight."

"So, what do you say, Will? Blast first, or shoring first?" Gid asked when they headed up to the mine opening.

"Let's shore the whole opening in," Gid suggested. "That way we won't be in any danger of it collapsing on us.

"You're probably right."

Once the two got started, they decided to continue the shoring farther back into the mine, supplementing the lumber they brought from town with sturdy pine saplings they found growing on the mountain. That took them almost a week. When they were finished, they were sitting outside their hut eating a roasted rabbit Woman had brought to them.

"I think Woman's beginning to like us," Gid said, "or maybe she just wants us to keep bringing her candy."

"If that's what it takes," Will said as he tore off a piece of the rabbit.

"I sure hope we aren't wasting our time," Gid said. "I haven't worked this hard since we were back on the farm."

"Have you ever wondered where we'd be now, if it hadn't been for the war?" Will asked.

"I know where I would be. Katie and I would be married, probably with a couple of kids, and I would be farming half-way between Pa's land and the McMurtry farm," Gid said. He laughed. "You'd probably be here, right now, doing the same thing you're doing, only without me."

"What makes you think that?" Will asked.

"Well, maybe you wouldn't be right here looking for gold, but you'd be wandering around somewhere. Will, you never were one to settle down, and you know it. Even when we were kids working on the farm, you used to say that you couldn't wait to get out of there."

"Yeah, well, Pa had me pitching hay and mucking barns. Who wants to do that forever?"

"If it would bring Ma and Pa back, I'd do it, and you would too."

Their mother and father had been killed by Kansas Jayhawkers. That was the catalyst for an odyssey that began with their time in the war and had continued long after.

Will put his hand on Gid's shoulder. "You're right about that, Little Brother. I would do it in a heartbeat."

When Jubal Sandos and half-a-dozen of his Prescott Defenders came riding into town, they looked tired from a long day's ride.

"Where have they been?" someone asked.

"Hell, haven't you heard? They've been out lookin' for the son of a bitch that burned Guthrie's store down."

"What for? He wasn't even signed up with 'em, is what I heard."

"Maybe they're better men than lots of folks have been givin' 'em credit for."

All the men who were riding with Sandos rode on down to the Plaza Bit, but Sandos stopped at The Beatrice. Stepping up to the bar, he slapped a nickel down.

"Glad to see you're paying for your drinks now," Ki said as he drew a mug of beer.

"Just give me the beer and hold the talk," Sandos said. "We've been out three days lookin' for the son of a bitch that burned Guthrie's store, and we haven't had any luck."

"How do you even know where to start looking?" Ki asked as he put the beer before Sandos.

"I have a witness who gave me some valuable information," Sandos said.

"Oh? Who?"

"Huh, uh," Sandos said. "He made me promise not to tell. I think he's afraid."

"I hope you find your man," Ki said, as he moved down the bar to tend to another customer.

Chapter Twenty - One

"There they are," Coates said, pointing to the two men who were camped on the side of Wet Beaver Creek. They had a rabbit speared on the end of a green willow branch and were holding it over a fire.

One of the two men had gray skin, heavy-lidded eyes, and a shock of lusterless brown hair that fell across his forehead. The other had a flat face and a wedge of a nose over thin lips. They smiled at Coates and Snow as the two men rode up.

"You come with the money?" the man with the heavy-lidded eyes asked. "What's took you so long?"

"What money?" Coates asked.

"What money, hell, you know what money. The money we're s'posed to be gettin' for burnin' down Guthrie's store."

"Wait a minute," Coates said. "McKinney, are you

confessin' that you 'n Wilson here burnt down Guthrie's store?"

"Yeah, I'm tellin' you we done it. Now, where at's what we got comin' to us?"

"Funny you would ask for what you got comin' to you," Coates said. Coates nodded toward Snow, and both men drew their guns.

"Wait a minute, hold on here! What are you doin'?" Wilson shouted and he and McKenney held out their hands in a vain attempt to stop them.

Coates pulled the trigger, the gun roared, and a red hole appeared in Wilson's forehead. McKenny went down with a bleeding chest wound.

"Check 'em out to see if either of 'em is still alive," Snow said. "If he is, kill 'im."

"What? Why . . .?" McKenny gasped.

There was no need for a follow up with Wilson. He was dead. Snow put two more bullets into McKenney.

"Let's throw 'em over their horses 'n get 'em back to town," Coates said.

"Get the pistol," Snow said.

"Damn, I'd like to keep that. Why do we have to give it back?"

"Because we have to," Snow replied.

After draping the two bodies over the horses, Snow and Coates started back toward town.

"Snow, you ever think what we're a doin' is for peanuts?" Coates asked.

"What do you mean?"

"Hell, we got us a damn army here, 'n we ain't doin' nothin' but scarin' all them people into signin' up for somethin' Sandos is a callin' insurance."

"What do you think we should be a doin'?"

"Hell, with as many men as we got, we could be robbin' 'bout anything-- stage coaches, banks, gold shipments, purt' nigh anything we want, then come back to town where ever' one thinks we're the law."

"I've thought about that too. But Sandos is pretty smart, hell, he's the smartest man I've ever knowed, so I reckon he purty much knows what he's a' doin'."

"Yeah, I reckon you're right," Coates agreed. "But it wouldn't hurt to say somethin' to him."

"Run!" Will shouted, as he lit the fuse then started running. Gid, who wasn't as fast as Will, had stayed close to the opening. He watched as the fuse sparked and glittered, then there was a heavy, stomach-shaking bang as the stick of dynamite exploded. The explosion was followed by a blast of hot air, dust, and small particles of residue.

The two men waited until the mine-shaft was clear enough to breathe without coughing before they went back inside. With each of them carrying a lantern, they examined the side wall, into where they had blown a two-foot-deep concave. They began loading dislodged rocks and dirt into the wheelbarrow, then took turns pushing it outside where they dumped their load into the light of day where they made a closer examination.

"See anything?" Will asked.

"I don't think so," Gid said. He reached down and picked up a few rocks. "These look different."

Will took a rock from Gid. It was a purplish rock with traces of rusty red and brassy yellow.

"I see yellow, but I don't think it's gold," Will said, "but I'm not sure we would recognize gold if we saw it."

"I have a suggestion. Why don't we take a saddlebag full of these rocks into town and have Arlen Blake take a look at them. We'll have to pay for the assay report, but then we'll know." Gid said.

"Then I say we go into town now, get a room and take a bath, then come back when we're fresh and rested. That is, unless you'd rather work a little longer."

"You didn't mention having a good meal and a couple of beers, but if that's included, then I'm on my way."

"Look over there," Gid said, pointing to one of the other tables in the Reed Hotel coffee shop. "Addie's having supper with Jubal Sandos."

"It's none of our business," Will said, dismissively.

"I know," Gid said. "It's just that it makes me sick at my stomach to see her throwing herself away like that. You know damn well he's no good for her."

"You plan on walking over there and telling her that?"

"It wouldn't do any good if I did."

"Now you're getting the picture."

Shortly after the brothers ordered, Sandos left, and Addie came over to their table.

Will and Gid both stood.

"Sit down, sit down," Addie said with a smile. "How are you doing?"

"If you mean how are we feeling, we're feeling fine. But if you're asking for a progress report on our riches, we're not doing so well."

"I'm sorry to hear that. You aren't planning on giving up right away, are you?"

"Not for a while," Will said. "We've brought some samples in to be assayed, but I don't have my hopes up."

"Oh, I forgot, since you've been gone, you haven't heard the latest news have you?"

Will shook his head. "We just got here, so no, we haven't talked to anyone yet."

Addie had a huge smile on her face. "Jubal and his men found the ones who set fire to Mr. Guthrie's store. Isn't that wonderful?"

"And how do they know they're the ones?"

"Because one man had Mr. Guthrie's pistol. You know, the one that belonged to Custer?"

"I remember seeing that pistol," Will said. "Well, I admit, that's pretty conclusive evidence. They shouldn't have a problem proving it in court."

"Oh, they won't have to prove it," Addie said.

"What do you mean? Why won't they have to prove it?"

"Because the men are dead. They put up a fight when they were caught, and both of them were killed."

"Sandos killed them, did he?"

"No, Jubal wasn't even there. It was Dan Coates and Ike Snow who found the arsonists."

"I suppose that's sort of boosted Jubal's standing in town," Will suggested.

"You would think so," Addie said as a frown crossed her face. "But that awful Ben Weaver writes terrible articles about the Prescott Defenders. I want Papa to cancel our advertising, but he won't do it."

"Thank goodness, not everyone has been taken in by Sandos and his so-called Defenders," Gid said.

Addie glared at Gid, then turned and quickly left the coffee shop.

"You could have left that last line unsaid, Little Brother."

After they were finished eating, they walked down to The Beatrice where they were greeted by Ki Hastings and Nigel Housewright.

"You just can't stay away," Ki said as he set two mugs of beer in front of Will and Gid.

"I need some conversation," Will said. "All Gid says is, 'do you think we made a mistake,' and Woman doesn't say anything. I think she's mute."

"That's not true, Big Brother," Gid said. "I heard her say tizwin as clear as day."

Ki started laughing. "That old woman didn't get you drunk did she? You know there was a time when the Indians started drinking that stuff, the soldiers knew they were heading out on the warpath."

"She only let us have one cupful and then she took her jug away," Gid said.

"Well, she was doing you a favor," Ki said. "You wouldn't be over your headache yet, if she would have let you get drunk on that stuff."

Will and Gid finished their beer, and Ki refilled their mugs. "Have you heard what the Defenders have done since you've been gone?"

"Addie told us they found the arsonists, but nobody will ever know if they really fired the hardware store . . . because they just happen to be dead," Will said.

"You sound a bit skeptical, my friend," Nigel said

joining the conversation. "Perhaps you've read Mr. Weaver's editorial?"

"No, but Addie told us it's not too complimentary to the Defenders," Gid said.

Ki smiled, and pulled a copy of the paper from under the bar. "Not complimentary," he said. "Mr. Weaver gave 'em hell."

Will read the article, chuckled, then handed it to Gid.

Questions about the Destroyed Guthrie's Hardware

When the hardware store belonging to Mr. Sam Guthrie burned two weeks ago it was a loss, not only to Mr. Guthrie, but to the entire town. Sam could have named his store the "yes, I have it store," because so well stocked was his hardware store that whether you needed something for your business or your home, the chances were very good that Sam would have it.

But Sam Guthrie's livelihood, as well as the town's convenient market, was taken away in a fire that destroyed everything. As it turned out, the fire was an act of arson. Poor Sam. He had not subscribed to the protective service offered by Jubal Sandos and the Prescott Defenders. There are many in town, this newspaper included, who believe the fire might have been set by the Prescott Defenders as an object lesson for those of us who refuse the service.

Sandos announced that, even though Sam Guthrie had not subscribed to his "protection insurance," the Prescott

Defenders would find the guilty parties and bring them to justice. Conveniently, the alleged arsonists were caught and brought back to town by a couple of the members of the Prescott Defenders.

Proof of their guilt is said to be that the Custer pistol, belonging to Mr. Guthrie, was found on the person of one called McKenny. That begs the question. Why would they take the pistol and not the money?

Was this all part of a plot to intimidate other businesses into subscribing to the protection service? We will never know, because like the bank robbers, Pugh and Meachum, the arsonists, McKenny and Wilson, were brought back dead. And dead men don't talk.

"I wonder how many more businesses Sandos has signed up since the fire," Gid said, laying the folded paper down on the bar.

"From the placards displayed in the windows, I would say there are few holdouts left," Nigel said. "When Jow Hop signed up, I'd say Sandos is close to taking over the whole town."

"That is revealing," Will said. "I would think the Chinese would take care of their own people."

"In the past, they have," Ki said, "but I suspect Jow doesn't want to risk someone stealing his fancy goods."

"You mean like teas and silk handkerchiefs," Gid

said as he mimicked drinking a cup of tea.

"Don't laugh, where do you think the women on Granite Street get their fancy clothes?" Ki asked. "They don't buy them from Goldwater's."

Chapter Twenty – Two

"What do you think this assayer's report means?" Gid asked as he and Will were riding out to the Axis.

Will laughed. "Arlen said we probably had a ledge or as he called it 'a green stone trap,' whatever that is. He said most of the color was iron pyrite, but we shouldn't give up just yet."

"A fancy name for fool's gold," Gid said as he took off his hat and wiped his brow. "I'm thinking I miss Texas. What do you say?"

"I have a better idea. Do you remember who we met at the miners' ball?"

"We met Diamond Jo Reynolds," Gid said. "Surely, you're not going to try to pawn this hole in the ground off on him?"

"Wrong man," Will said. "I think it's time to go to the other side of the mountain. You remember Ivan

LaGrange said he was going to be hiring another fifty men to work the Jersey Lily."

"Yeah, he said that, but what about it?"

"If you need that many more people, there has to be a lot of promise in the Jersey Lily. I say we go call on him."

The road to the Jersey Lily went behind the charcoal pit, and the first thing they noticed was that there was a real gravel road—not a winding pathway like the one they used to get up to the Axis. When they got to a higher elevation, the pine trees were thinning out and juniper and scrub brush was the general vegetation. There were several frame buildings and numerous tents surrounded by mounds of rocks and dirt.

"Whooee," Gid said when he saw the tailings. "That's a lot of trips with a wheelbarrow."

"I guess that's why he needs fifty more men."

As they got closer, they were met by a man holding a shotgun.

"You can stop right there," the man said as he raised the gun. "We're not hirin' anymore men, so you two can just turn around and skedaddle on down the mountain."

"We're not here looking for a job," Will said. "We'd like to see Mr. LaGrange, if he's here."

"Oh, all right. He's over by the office—that's the building off to the left."

"Thanks," Will said.

Leading their horses, Will and Gid made their way through tools and pieces of timber and the ever-present mounds of rock. When they were within earshot of the office, they heard shouting.

"Damn it, Damon, I said find the money. Dabney's on my ass and you can tell the son of a bitch I'm not firin' these men. You can't treat the help like that."

"Then get them down in that hole. Work them twelve hour shifts if that's what it takes, but Mr. Dabney says we have to show more of a profit, or they'll be no smelter."

"Fine, I'll make the penny-grubbin' bastard eat his words!"

Just then the door slammed and Ivan LaGrange came stomping out of the office to see Will and Gid standing not ten feet away.

"We're not hiring so whatever you men want, get out of my sight."

"Yes, sir, Mr. LaGrange," Gid said as they turned their horses around and started to walk away.

"Wait, do I know you two?"

"Not really. We met you at the miners' ball," Will said, "when you were talking to Diamond Jo Reynolds."

LaGrange snapped his fingers. "The Axis—the Crocketts."

"Yes, I'm Will and this is my brother, Gid."

"Well, what brings you to the Jersey Lily?" LaGrange asked, his demeanor so completely changed from what had just been in evidence.

"We have an assay report, and we're not entirely sure what it means," Gid said. "Arlen Blake tells us we may have a green stone trap."

"You don't say," LaGrange said. "Did you come to put your claim up for sale, because I'll bet I can convince Morris Dabney to consider buying you out."

"So, you're saying that the Axis does have potential?"

"Oh, yes indeed."

Will and Gid both smiled. "Well, thanks, that's what we came to find out," Will said. "But we're not ready to sell out, at least, not yet."

When Will and Gid got to their side of the mountain, they stopped to chat with several of the placer miners on Lynx Creek.

"Well if it ain't the Crocketts come back for another day or two," Hoss Martin said. "You boys know they's several of us on this here creek that ain't been to town in six months."

Both Will and Gid laughed.

"I guess we've got wandering feet," Gid said.

"Or you got some little ole girl you're sniffin' around," Lute Winfred said.

"Don't I wish," Gid said.

"You can't tell me you ain't been on Granite Street. Josie Roland runs the best house they is," Lute said. "I'd be a lot richer if I could stay away from her place when I find a nugget or two."

"Me and the boys are thinkin' about goin' together to find us a rich man so as we can put up a stamp mill right here on Lynx Creek," Hoss said. "Would you boys know anybody that fits the bill?"

"What about Mr. Dabney?" Will asked.

"You talkin' about the bastard who owns the Jersey Lily?" Lute asked.

"I guess he's out of the question then."

"Hell, yes," Hoss said. "He, or at least that asshole of a manager over there, treats his mules better'n he treats his men."

"We don't want no part of that place," one of the other men said.

"That's good to know," Will said, "but now we'd better go on up to our place. Our guard may be waiting to get paid."

"You're jokin'," Hoss said, "but nobody goes near your place without Woman comin' to pester 'em."

"Then it's worth every dried apple and piece of horehound candy we can bring her," Gid said as he patted his saddle bag.

After putting away the meager supplies they had brought from town and then calling on Woman, they headed for the entrance to the mine.

"Did you notice the change that came over LaGrange when we told him what Blake told us?"

"I noticed that, too," Will said. "Everybody's telling us to go at a right angle from where Beaumont was working, but I'm thinking we should be going down."

Gid shrugged his shoulders. "Has anybody ever told you, that you don't know a damn thing about gold mining?"

"And you know more, I suppose?"

"Sure, I say we blast a hole in the ground," Gid said, as his mouth formed a grin.

When the dynamite was in place and the fuse was lit, Will and Gid stood just outside the mine entrance waiting for the explosion. Dust, smoke, and a column of hot air rushed out of the mine.

"You know we've only got four sticks left," Gid said.

"When we run out, we'll have an excuse to go back to town and get some more," Will said. "Let Hoss make fun of us then."

"All right," Gid said, "let's get our wheelbarrow and go in to pick up all the rubble. I wonder if there's a market for rocks and clods."

"There must be. We bought 'em, didn't we?" Will asked.

"What?"

"We bought this mine. What has it produced?"

Gid laughed. "Come on, Will, that's not a bit funny."

"Then why are you laughing?"

"I don't know, it beats the hell out of me."

The two men got the wheelbarrow then pushed it down into the mine and began filling it.

When Gid rolled the wheelbarrow out, he dumped it on the growing pile of they already had taken from the mine.

"Will!" Gid called out. "Will, come quick!"

There, in what Gid had just dumped from his wheelbarrow, was a small, twisted piece of yellow metal.

"Damn, little brother, I think we've found something," Will said, excitedly.

Hurrying back into the mine, this time with pick axes rather than dynamite, they studied the hole that the last dynamite blast had exposed.

Gid held the lantern up so they could examine it more closely. They saw a narrow streak of yellow angling through the rock. Will traced his finger along the streak.

"Here," he said, "let's take out as much of this as we can."

For the rest of the day, the two brothers hacked away at the wall of the hole, not even stopping for lunch. By the end of the day, they had taken out a fairly substantial pile of rock, some with narrow, shallow veins of gold.

That night, over a tin of tomatoes and mescal cakes

from Woman, they discussed what their next move would be.

"First, I think we take a few samples into town to be assayed, then if we have what we think we have, we'll have to figure out a way to extract it," Will said.

"For that, we'll need an ore stamper," Gid suggested.

"Not necessarily. The Jersey Lily has a stamper," Will said. "I'm pretty sure we could make a deal with LaGrange to handle the ore for us. Remember, the gist of the argument coming out of that office was about money."

"Or we could go in with the placer guys and put up a stamper ourselves. I'll bet we could raise enough money to do that?"

"If we do, it sort of ties us to this place for awhile," Will said. "I recall you saying you missed Texas."

"I did, but that was before we struck it rich."

Will was quiet for a long time, and then he turned to Gid with a pensive look on his face.

"Do you want to spend the rest of your life here, working this mine?" Will asked.

Gid paused for a moment before he answered. "No," he said. "I'm afraid if I stay in one place too long, I'll grow mold."

"I think the best thing to do would be to prove it out, then sell the Axis."

"For how much?"

"Well, let's face it. Anything over five hundred dollars is a profit."

Gid grabbed his shoulder, then began moving his arm. "A profit we've had to work for."

"I'll agree with you there."

Will and Gid had come into town and as was their custom, had taken a couple of rooms in the Reed Hotel.

"Good, I'm glad you finally found something," Biff said when they showed him their samples. "And it couldn't have happened to two nicer people."

"It may not be much to crow about," Will said, "but this time it looks like the real thing."

"If it is, you'll be building a big house just off the Plaza," Biff said. "You'll be hiring a manager and everything else. You won't step foot in the Axis except when your bookkeeper tells you you're making so much money, you need to shut down a drift just to keep up."

"Can't build a house close to the Plaza," Gid said. "It would have to be up in the hills."

"And why not? You know Jessie Fremont has the whole town planting trees around the place," Biff said. "Someday the Plaza will be a beautiful park."

"Would she promise to shut down the town clock in the courthouse?" Gid asked. "That thing is loud enough from my hotel room. What would it be if I was right on top of the tower?"

Biff laughed. "You might have a point, but you'd sure keep up with all the latest pokes Ben Weaver takes at Jubal Sandos."

"Another editorial, I suppose," Will said.

"This one might be the worst one yet," Biff said as he pushed the paper over to Will. "I don't know what keeps the *Advocate* from being blown to smithereens."

"Ben does have a way of putting things," Will said as he began reading the piece aloud.

"Not since the tyranny King George visited upon the innocent citizens of Colonial America just over one hundred years ago, has there been an oppression against the people to match what the residents of Prescott are enduring today. Our despots are not the red coat soldiers of the British Army but the blue coated faux military of the Prescott Defenders.

"It was bad enough when we had to endure the draconian tax put upon us by law and enforced by the Defenders. The tax has been repealed, but the subjugation remains. A protective fee is being extorted from our businesses, and those who refuse to pay have experienced mysterious disasters. And while in many cases the alleged perpetrators have been brought to justice, the justice is always summarily applied without a word from the accused. Not since Nate Harper was sent to the gallows has anyone

lived long enough to testify.

"Though the evidence is circumstantial, the sequence of events suggests, strongly, that the businesses vandalized, looted, and in the case of Guthrie's Hardware Store, destroyed, are not by random. It is the belief of this newspaper that those incidents are intentionally applied as punishment for those who have refused to pay, and as a threat to others."

"That's telling it like it is," Gid said, "but I don't understand Weaver—sometimes he's praising Sandos and sometimes he's attacking him."

"What does Addie think about this article?" Gid asked.

"She's very upset with Ben, as you can imagine. For some reason, Addie thinks Sandos can do no wrong."

As usual, Ki, Nigel, Penny, and Elaina gave Will and Gid a warm welcome when they showed up at The Beatrice that evening.

"Well now," Ki said as he filled two mugs of beer. "Didn't we just see you three or four days ago?"

"No," Will said as he held up his hand stopping Ben from putting the beer in front of them.

"What?" Ki asked, confused by Will's rather short response.

A broad smile spread across Will's face. "Axis has shown some color. My brother and I are buying drinks for the house."

"Did you hear that fellas?" Ki called out to the other customers in the saloon. "Will and Gid Crockett are buying drinks for the house!"

Chapter Twenty – Three

"I have no intention of publishing a retraction," Ben Weaver said. "You can ask all you want—my answer will still be no."

Jubal Sandos and Amos Chapman had come into the office of the *Advocate* to complain about Weaver's most recent article.

"You don't understand, do you, Weaver?" Sandos said. "I'm not *asking* you to retract the story, I'm *demanding* that you do so."

"Demanding? Demanding, sir? I suggest you read the first amendment. And in case you can't find a copy, I will, for your edification and enlightenment quote it for you.

'Congress shall make no law respecting an establishment of religion or prohibiting the free exercise thereof; or abridging the freedom of speech, *or of the press;* or the right of the people peaceably to assemble, and to petition the Government for a redress of grievances.'

And in case you don't understand, sir, *that is the law of the land*." Weaver practically shouted the last seven words.

"We aren't discussing something that was written a hundred years ago," Sandos said. "We're discussing something that was written less than a week ago, specifically, your slanderous article about the Prescott Defenders. Now I'm telling you one more time—print a retraction."

"I'm glad you're only telling me one more time," Weaver said, "because I have no intention of complying with your demand, so we can end this conversation right now. And so, gentlemen, and believe me, I am using that in its most generic and non-specific way, I'm going to ask you to leave. I have a paper to get out."

"You will rue this day, Weaver," Sandos said, resolutely.

"Gentlemen," Arlen Blake said when Will and Gid stepped into the assayer's office. "The breakdown of the samples you brought in show iron, sulfur, and antimony."

Will looked at Gid and raised his eyebrows. "I guess that's the end of our fortune hunting, and now I'm ready to walk away."

"Me, too," Gid said. "Thank you, Mr. Blake."

"Don't you want to hear the rest of my report?"

"What else is there?" Will asked.

Blake picked up a couple of the samples they had brought in. "These could bring as much as eighty dollars to the ton if there is a significant vein, and this one—well it is very rich. I would say this could be as much as one thousand dollars per ton."

Both Will and Gid's mouths dropped open simultaneously.

"You mean we really have discovered gold?" Will asked.

"If these samples came from the Axis mine, I would say that, yes, gentlemen, you have discovered gold."

Gid slapped Will on the back and then began to dance a jig, but then he was embarrassed and immediately stopped.

"I suppose that wasn't very mature of me," Gid said.

Blake was smiling. "At least you didn't start screaming, or worse yet, fire off your guns." He pointed to a hole in the ceiling. "That was a result of one exuberant miner."

"Well, it is exciting," Will said, "but what do we do now?"

"To start with, if you have more ore like this, you can bring it in to me. I can melt small quantities into bars and have them stamped. Then I can give sight checks or telegraph transfers for gold at par. These checks will be drawn on the Nevada Bank in San Francisco," Blake said. "Would you like to do that?"

"Yes, sir," Gid said.

"Depending upon how large your find is, the next step is to get equipment in to sink a shaft or excavate into drifts. There are several outfits, like the Peck Mining Company, for example, that would do that for you, but it will take quite a bit of capital to get started."

Will took a deep breath. "I see. I think my brother and I have a lot to think about."

"Yes, my lad, I would say that is true."

Will and Gid went into The Beatrice. Gid was waving the assay report a big smile on his face.

"Is it true?" Ki asked. "Did you really strike gold?"

Will nodded his head. "And now we'd like to take all our friends out for dinner."

"Sorry," Ki said. "Some of us have to work."

"I don't think you have to work if The Beatrice is closed," Nigel said as he stopped playing the piano and came off the stage. "This is cause for a celebration!"

"Indeed it is," Will said. "The ladies at The Gem will lay a fine table tonight."

When they stepped into the restaurant, they saw Ben Weaver sitting alone, at one of the smaller tables.

"Mr. Weaver," Will said, "my brother and I are buying supper for these fine folks. Why don't you join us?"

Weaver smiled. "Well, I can't turn down an invitation

like that, now, can I?"

"It's more than just an invitation," Penny said. "It's a true celebration. The Crocketts have struck gold."

"Then I'm very happy to join you," Weaver said.

They went to the biggest table in the restaurant, a round table that could seat all of them. It took a while for the ladies to get out their food, because everyone ordered pan broiled steaks and cheese potatoes. The conversation was very jovial as everyone congratulated Will and Gid on their discovery.

Sol Lewis, the president of the Bank of Arizona, along with his wife, was at another table. When they finished their meal, they stepped by the boisterous table.

"We couldn't help but overhear your conversation," Sol said. "You know the bank buys bullion—with promptitude and fidelity."

"Said like a true banker," Ben Weaver said.

"Of course," Sol said. "The Bank of Arizona is the strongest bank in the Territory, and we'd love to have your business."

"We'll keep that in mind," Will said.

They continued making small talk until Mrs. Lewis addressed Ben Weaver directly.

"That was a very good article you wrote about the Prescott Defenders. And truthful."

"Aren't you afraid?" Penny asked.

"Afraid of what?" Weaver asked.

"Jubal Sandos. You've written some very critical articles about him, accusing him of being responsible for damaging those businesses that haven't signed up for his services."

"I don't consider them accusations, Miss Admore. I consider them statements of fact," Weaver said.

"That's all the more reason why I think you should be afraid. I mean, if they really are doing all that you say," Nigel said, "and I believe they are, aren't you just opening yourself up for such an attack?"

Weaver smiled. "Ah, but that's where I have them, you see. If my office is attacked now, after my accusations, it would be proof positive that I've been telling the truth all along. They can't attack me, without giving away their own guilt."

"One thousand dollars?" Nate Crowley said.

"Only if you kill both of them."

"So, that's five hundred dollars apiece."

"No. There is no apiece. You get nothing unless you kill both of them."

"When do you want it done?" Crowley asked.

"As soon as possible. That is, as soon as you can after they leave town. They've leased a pair of mules and a wagon from the livery, so I expect they'll be going back out to the mine, tomorrow. It shouldn't be that difficult to set up an ambush somewhere on the road."

"Can I ask you something?"

"You can ask. I may not answer."

"How come you don't kill 'em yourself?"

"Because that's what I'm paying you to do."

****

After Will, Gid, and the others returned to The Beatrice, Will and Gid decided they'd have another drink before going back to the hotel for the night. Nigel excused himself and went to the piano to begin playing, and Penny said she had to go to her room for a few minutes.

Elaina sighed. "I just can't understand those two," she said. "Why won't they talk to each other?"

"What do you mean?" Gid asked. "They were talking to each other over supper."

Elaina chuckled. "No, they weren't. Not really."

"Little Brother, I think she means something more than just talk," Will said.

"Exactly," Elaina said. "Penny loves Nigel and Nigel loves Penny, but they're both too afraid to say it to each other."

"How do you know?" Gid asked.

"In Penny's case, she's told me as much" Elaina said.

"And all you have to do is see the way Nigel looks at her to know that he's in love with her, too. But they're afraid to say anything."

"Why don't you tell them?" Will asked.

"It's really not my place," Elaina said. "If this is going to work out between them, they have to do it themselves."

"I suppose you're right," Will said.

Will and Gid finished their beers, then set the empty mugs on the bar. "Ki, Elaina, we'll see you next time we come into town," Will said. "Tell Penny and Nigel we said goodnight."

"We'll be glad to," Ki said. "I hope you boys find a lot more gold."

"From your lips to God's ears, as our sainted mother used to say," Will replied.

After the two brothers left, Elaina sighed. "Those two are going to make a couple of lucky women, good husbands."

"Not necessarily," Ki replied.

"What do you mean, not necessarily?" Elaina said, surprised by Ki's response. "Do you know something about them that I don't know?"

"Apparently so," Ki replied. "They are very good men, both of 'em, as fine as anyone who's ever come through that door. But I can't see either one of 'em ever settling down, at least for a long, long time. They'll be chasing the sun for the next twenty years."

Elaina nodded. "Even if they're rich?"

Ki nodded his head. "Yes, even if they're rich. I have a feeling a lot of money doesn't mean the same thing to them as it would to you and me."

Chapter Twenty - Four

Will and Gid had breakfast in the hotel dining room the next morning. "Do you think we'll find the vein?" Gid asked.

"If we haven't found it already, I'd say we're close," Will said.

"Well, we've got a case of dynamite, two pick axes, muscles, and. . ." Gid started, but he paused in mid-sentence, then smiled. "That is, I have muscles. I don't know what you have."

Will smiled as well. "Feet fast enough to get me away from a burning fuse."

"Oh, yeah, well, if you want to put it that way."

"But I know this. We're not going to find any gold in the bottom of our coffee cups," Will said. "I think it's time we get back to work."

When Will and Gid started back to the Axis Mine

they had, in addition to the case of dynamite, twenty feet of primer cord, more shoring lumber, another shovel and wheelbarrow, a side of bacon, a keg of butter, several cans of beans and tomatoes, bags of flour and sugar, a tin of coffee, dried apples and of course, the horehound candy for Woman.

It was the apples that fueled the discussion.

"What makes you think you can make a pie?" Will asked.

"Well, it won't be as good as something Sara Sue and Millie Jean would make, but if I make a crust from the flour and butter, and stew the apples in sugar, you know it's going to be better than what we have now," Gid replied.

"Better than what we have now? You don't set your target very high, do you, Little Brother, because we don't have anything now," Will replied with a chuckle.

Gid joined his brother in laughter. "Then you agree, whatever I make will be better than what we've got."

The laughter was interrupted by the buzz of a close-passing bullet, followed by the sound of a rifle shot.

"Gunshot!" Gid shouted, his announcement totally unnecessary.

The two brothers bailed out of the wagon, then dashed to the side of the road, opposite from where the shot had come. There was a ditch alongside the road. It was shallow, but deep enough to give them some cover, though not enough to feel comfortable in their position.

"I guess I got your attention, didn't I?" the shooter called out to them. "And now you boys ain't got nowhere to go. That little ole ditch you're in ain't doin' that much for you."

The shooter fired again, and the bullet clipped the top of the ditch, kicking up dirt and sand.

"Damn, that'n was close, warn't it?" the shooter said. "This'll be over for you right soon."

"The shots are coming from those rocks," Will said pointing toward an outcropping. "Fire a couple of shots up there so he'll keep his head down long enough for me to get into position."

"Position to do what?" Gid asked.

Will smiled and held up a stick of dynamite. "Change the position of your gun when you're shooting, so he'll think both of us are still here."

Gid nodded, then fired his first shot as Will started wriggling down the ditch staying low.

Gid fired a second shot, this time repositioning his pistol.

The rifle shooter fired again, and again the bullet clipped the edge of the ditch.

"Damn, them bullets is comin' so close to you boys that if either one of you sneeze, you'll more 'n likely get your brains blowed out."

Will managed to crawl about ten yards away from Gid, then as the shooter fired again, Will raised up high enough to see the smoke from the last report.

"This here ain't nothin' personal boys," the shooter called out. "It's all business, but I bet you think you're worth more'n a thousand dollars to kill both of you."

He took another shot, this time the bullet coming so close to Gid his impulse caused him to fall back.

Seeing Gid fully exposed, Will lit the fuse to the stick of dynamite and held it for a couple of seconds, then running across the road, he tossed it so that the dynamite landed behind the rocks, just where he had seen the last puff of smoke.

"Son of a bitch!" the shooter shouted in panic, the explosion coming immediately thereafter.

Will pulled his pistol, then dashed toward the rocks. If the dynamite hadn't killed the shooter, Will was taking the chance that the shooter would be too disoriented to engage him.

When Will leaped over the rocks, no further action was necessary. What was left of the man who attacked them was beyond identification.

"What are we going to do with him?" Gid asked.

"We can't take him in to the sheriff, not looking like this," Will said. "We picked up a new shovel while we were town. We'll bury him, then go tell Bower."

When Will and Gid returned to town, they went first to the sheriff's office where they saw Bower sitting at his desk, playing a game of solitaire. He looked up in surprise when he saw them come in.

"I thought I saw you boys pullin' out this mornin'," Bower said. "What happened?"

"We ran into a little trouble along the way." Will went on to tell the sheriff about being ambushed on the road by a lone shooter. He also told the sheriff that he had killed and buried the shooter.

"I'll be happy to show you where he's buried," he concluded.

"Who was it?" Bower asked.

"I don't know."

"Why didn't you bring the body in?"

"There really wasn't enough of the body to identify," Will said. He told Bower how he had eliminated the threat by using a stick of dynamite.

"Damn," Bower said. He chuckled. "I guess it's not funny blowing somebody up like that, but damn." He chuckled again. "That's funny."

"He told us he was getting paid a thousand dollars to kill us," Gid said.

"Someone was paying him a thousand dollars to kill you, you say? Do you know anybody that hates you enough to spend that kind of money to kill you?"

"Quite a few, actually," Will said.

"I reckon with the lives you boys have lived, that could be true," Sheriff Bower suggested.

"But there's only one man in this town," Gid added.

When Will and Gid left the sheriff's office, they headed to the headquarters building of the Prescott Defenders. When they went inside Jubal Sandos looked up. When he saw them, he got an expression of shock on his face.

"What . . . what are you doing here?" he asked.

"I can see why you're asking that question. You never expected to see us again, did you?" Will said.

"No. I mean, yes, of course, why wouldn't I expect to see you again?"

"Why indeed? Perhaps it's because you paid someone a thousand dollars to kill us."

"Who told you that? Whoever it was, he was lying, and I'll tell him that right to his face."

"You can't do that," Will said.

"And just why do you think I can't do that?"

"Because the man you paid to kill us has no face. Apparently, he got too close to a stick of dynamite."

"Did you see Sandos' face when we told him the man who attacked us was getting paid a thousand dollars to kill us?" Will asked.

"Yeah, I saw it," Gid replied. "There's no doubt Sandos is the one who paid the guy, but how do we prove it?"

The visit of Will and Gid Crockett left Sandos unnerved. How could they possibly have known that he had agreed to pay Nate Crowley a thousand dollars? Crowley must have told them, but why would he do such a thing?

Sandos was glad the son of a bitch was killed. Anyone dumb enough to tell his targets that he was being paid to kill them, deserved to be killed. Sandos thought about it for second and smiled. Since Crowley was dead, the Crocketts had no way to prove their claim no matter what they thought.

"As long as we're back in town, what do you say we just wait until tomorrow to go out to the mine?" Will suggested.

"You know what I'm gonna say," Gid said enthusiastically.

Will chuckled. "You're so easy. It's a damn good thing you aren't a woman, you never would be able to say no."

Not wanting to leave the remaining sticks of dynamite in the open wagon, they put the wooden crate in a sack to carry with them.

"What are we going to do with this dynamite?" Will

asked. "I can't see us carrying it around with us all day."

"Why don't we ask Nigel to keep it for us?" Gid suggested.

"That's a great idea," Will said.

"You mean you're surprised I can have a good idea every now and then?"

"Somewhat," Will replied with a chuckle.

When they pushed through the swinging doors of The Beatrice, Nigel was playing some piece of classical music that neither Will nor Gid could name, though both could appreciate.

"It's you, what happened this time?" Ki asked as he drew beers for both of them.

"Yes," Elaina added. "We didn't expect to see you again for at least two more weeks."

"Well now, let's see," Will said. "Spending two weeks looking at this big lug," he pointed to Gid, "or coming back to town to look at you. That's not a hard choice to make."

Penny came up to visit with them for a few minutes, as did Ben Weaver.

"Here you are again," the newspaper editor said. "I don't know if it's the convivial ambience of The Beatrice, or our company that you like."

"Ben, you seem to be here a lot, too," Will said. "Could we ask the same thing about you?"

"Young man, they like to say there are forty saloons

on Whiskey Row," Ben Weaver replied. "But they're wrong. There are thirty-nine saloons and one pub."

Will chuckled. "Indeed, The Beatrice is a pub."

After a grand crescendo, Nigel finished the song he was playing, then stepped down from the piano and started toward the bar.

"And speaking of pubs, here is just the man we came to see," Will said.

"I thought you two would be picking through the detritus of your efforts now, looking for more gold. I am pleasantly surprised to see you here," Nigel said, "but I'm sure there is a reason more compelling than good company that brings you back."

"Good company would be reason enough, but you're right, there is a good reason for us being here. Nigel, I wonder if Gid and I could meet with you somewhere in private."

"Of course. Come to my office."

With Weaver, Elaina, and Penny looking on, curious as to what the private meeting would be about, Will and Gid followed Nigel to his office.

"Do have a seat, gentlemen," Nigel offered, taking in two chairs with a wave of his arm.

"Thank you," Will said as he and Gid accepted Nigel's offer.

"What can I do for you?" Nigel asked.

Will set the sack on Nigel's desk. "Would you keep this for us until tomorrow?"

"Yes, of course," Nigel replied. He opened the sack. "What's in here? Oh, my goodness, is this dynamite?"

"Yes, we're using it in the mine, but we won't be going back out until tomorrow, and I'd just as soon we not take it to the hotel."

"All right, I'll store it for you." Nigel put the sack under his desk. "As I said, I thought you had already returned to the mine. What brings you back so quickly?"

Will told of their confrontation on the road as they were on their way to the mine.

"Bloody hell! Someone offered a thousand dollars to have you two killed?"

"Not just someone, we know damn well it was Sandos," Will said, as he completed telling the story.

"We confronted the son of a bitch, but he denied having anything to do with it," Gid added.

"I'm sure you are right. Sandos is the only one with the motive and the means to pay to have this done," Nigel said. "But I would expect him to lie about it. Have you spoken with the constable about it?"

"With who?" Gid asked.

"With the sheriff," Nigel explained.

"We've spoken to Bower, but there's nothing he can do. The man who attacked us is dead, so there's no way to prove that he was the one that was paid to do it, let alone who paid him," Will said.

"I don't suppose he had the thousand dollars on him?" Nigel asked.

"No, he didn't have any money on him," Gid added, "except for three dollars and a nickel."

"Which you kept," Will said.

"By the way, you might want to see the governor," Gid suggested.

"Why would I want to see the governor?" Will asked.

"Because you might need another pardon for killing that guy," Gid said.

"What do you mean, *I* might need another pardon?"

"Well, hell, Will, you're the one who killed the guy. I'm just your little brother who happened to be there." Gid laughed.

"I can see right now, I threw that stick of dynamite behind the wrong rock."

"Heavens," Nigel said. "You killed the poor chap with dynamite?"

"It seemed the thing to do at the time," Will said.

Chapter Twenty - Five

Ivan LaGrange, manager of the Jersey Lily Mine, had come to town to speak with Sol Lewis, the president of the Bank of Arizona.

"I need forty thousand dollars in cash," Ivan said.

Sol stared at him. "Forty thousand dollars? The Jersey Lily doesn't have that much money in the local account. Maybe I could go out to Fort Whipple and send a telegram to Mr. Dabney, but even if there was a transfer, I wouldn't have enough cash on hand to cover that large of a withdrawal."

"All right," LaGrange said, "but I have to have cash. I hired all these extra men and they haven't been paid for two months. If I don't get cash money to them, and get it quick, they're going to walk out on me, and then where will the Jersey Lily be?"

"I recognize your dilemma, Ivan, but I'm afraid I

can't help you."

"Well, thank you. I'll see what I can do."

Ivan LaGrange rode out to Fort Whipple where he called on James Hunlet, the telegraph operator. He quickly wrote out a telegram and had it sent to Morris Dabney, located in Newark, New Jersey. Within an hour there was a return telegram.

CONTACTING ROCKY MT BANK DENVER
STOP WILL SEND ARRANGEMENTS WAIT
STOP M DABNEY

"Here you are, Mr. LaGrange," Hunlet said as he handed Ivan the telegram. "That one came back fast."

Ivan read the message. "Doesn't say much does it? The boss says 'wait' as if I didn't have a mine to run. What am I goin' do?"

Hunlet smiled. "If I was you, I'd go have me a high old time. With what you've asked this man, Dabney, to do, I don't expect an answer 'til tomorrow."

"I think you're right about that," LaGrange said. "If you hear before tomorrow, I expect you could find me at the Union Saloon, or else sleepin' somewhere close by."

"I know that's where I'd be," Hunlet said. "If you happen to see a gal named Gertie, tell her I'll be expectin' to call on her Saturday night."

"Gertie you say," Ivan said. "I'll call on her first, but it's been a month of Sundays since I've had time to be with a woman. I expect I'll be callin' on quite a few."

"No you won't," Hunlet said. "Once you been with Gertie, you won't want anybody else."

The next afternoon, there was a loud banging on the door of Gertie's crib. When she opened the door, it was James Hunlet.

"Hi, Babe," he said as he gave her a big kiss.

"Jamey, you can't come in. I'm with somebody."

"I know—he's the guy I'm looking for," Hunlet said. "LaGrange, are you in here? I brought your telegram."

Ivan rose up from the bed where he had spent the night. His head was pounding as he saw two empty whiskey bottles on the table beside him.

"Telegram? What telegram?"

"The one you were waiting for. The one from the owner of the Jersey Lily."

"Oh," Ivan said as he stumbled out of the bed, not at all concerned that he was naked. Grabbing the telegram he began to read:

MONEY ENROUTE STOP SEND COURIER & ESCORT TO MEET TRAIN ASH FORK 8:00 AM FRIDAY STOP I WILL ARRIVE END OF MONTH STOP

EXPECT PERSONNEL CHANGE STOP M DABNEY

"Damn, the son of a bitch is going to fire me," Ivan said. "That's just fine and dandy."

After arranging for a light coach and driver along with two guards to meet the train on Friday, LaGrange knew what he was going to do. He headed for the headquarters of the Prescott Defenders.

"Yes, Mr. LaGrange?" Sandos asked. "What can I do for you?"

"On Friday, a transfer of forty thousand dollars in cash will be on the 8:00 train coming into Ash Fork," LaGrange said. "The cash is to be brought to the Jersey Lily for payroll."

"I see. And you want to hire the Defenders to provide escort service for the shipment, do you?"

"Not exactly. Actually, I have something else in mind."

Sandos smiled. "I believe I know what that might be, if my guess is correct."

"My cut will be ten percent," LaGrange said. "That's four thousand dollars."

"All right. Come back in an hour. I'll make arrangement to have someone here for you to talk to. He'll be the only one here, so you can talk without fear of being overheard."

Ivan LaGrange went to the coffee shop at the Reed Hotel and even though it was well past breakfast, he ordered a cup of coffee and a plate of ham, eggs, and fried potatoes. As his head began to clear, he thought about what he was about to do. He had worked for Morris Dabney for seven years, being one of the first employees at the Jersey Lily, and now that was about to end.

For the past year, Dabney had pushed and pushed to have the miners work longer and longer hours, going deeper into the ground. It was he, Ivan LaGrange, who had been the one to enforce what Dabney wanted, and the men resented what he had to do, making his job unbearable.

The Jersey Lily would recover. Nobody would be hurt, the mine would survive, and he would be four thousand dollars richer, which would be enough money for him to go back home to Wisconsin. He had been raised on a dairy farm, and the thought of him having a few head of cows around, maybe making some cheese, was a pleasant one. Such thoughts were reward enough for him to be able to assuage any guilt he may have.

When he returned to the Defenders headquarters office, there was only one man there.

"Are you LaGrange?" the man asked.

"I am."

"The name's Dawes, but most folks call me Muley." Muley made no effort to shake hands with LaGrange, so LaGrange kept his own hands by his sides.

Muley Dawes was a big man with a protruding brow, and a puffy scar that ran from the eye it had disfigured, to the corner of his mouth. It was a frightening countenance, but Ivan didn't let it intimidate him. It was a necessary part of doing this business.

"It'll be forty thousand dollars, cash," LaGrange said. "It's coming by train to Ash Fork, at about eight o'clock this Friday morning, and I expect it would get to the Jersey Lily by late afternoon the same day."

"How's it gonna be handled?" Muley asked

"I've hired a coach to be escorted by two guards."

"I have to ask you, why are you telling us this? You work for the Jersey Lily don't you?"

"At this moment, I do, but I expect my employment is coming to an end," LaGrange said, "and when it does, I intend to be four thousand dollars richer."

Muley nodded his head. "I'll be right back."

Within five minutes, Muley returned with Jubal Sandos, making Ivan think that Sandos had been somewhere close by where he actually overheard the conversation.

"Two thousand dollars," Sandos said when he came into his office and sat down behind the desk.

"What do you mean, two thousand dollars?" LaGrange was surprised and irritated by the response. "You agreed to ten percent, which is four thousand dollars."

"Four thousand dollars is too much money to pay for information alone," Sandos said.

"But you agreed."

Sandos smiled. "Yes, but you've already told us all we need to know, and there's no way you can take it back is there? I'm afraid you have no choice but to be satisfied with what I'll give you."

LaGrange knew better than to anger Sandos because Sandos was right. He had already given him all the information he needed to rob the money shipment, and if he complained too much, Sandos could very well hold back the two thousand dollars, or worse.

"All right, two thousand dollars," he agreed, reluctantly. "When will I get my money?"

"When the job's done," Sandos said. "I suggest you go back to the mine and act like you don't know a thing. And whatever you do, don't let anybody see you coming or going from this office. Muley will meet you on the road somewhere and give you your money."

"This will be the biggest job we've had in a long time," Sandos said the next morning, as he was telling the others what LaGrange had said. "But we don't have much time to plan. First of all, we need some diversion so that nobody suspects the Prescott Defenders are the ones pulling this off. We need something where the whole town could be involved and they would know for sure that we are here."

"I have a suggestion," Ike Snow said.

"I'm listening," Sandos said.

"What if Chapman and I had a horse race? Folks know we're always doing that, but what if we held a real contest, with bets and all?"

Sandos nodded. "Sounds good. I'll go see Lieutenant Booth and see if we can use the Whipple Park course. Who wants to go see that bastard Weaver and see if he can print up flyers so we can put them up all over town?"

"I'll do it," Snow said, "and just so folks will know it's a real competition, the winner should get three hundred dollars."

"I don't think so," Sandos said. "If there's any prize money to be handed out it should go to Muley, Newman, Evans, and Crawford."

"Why? They won't be doin' the ridin'," Chapman said.

"No, but they'll be doing the robbing," Sandos said.

"Amos Chapman 'n Ike Snow is goin' to have 'em a horse race," Dan Coates announced as he tacked a flyer up at the Plaza Bit Saloon. "It's goin' to take place out at the horse park at 10:00 a. m. Friday mornin' 'n anyone as wants to bet on it, why, Colonel Sandos allows as to how he'll be takin' bets."

"What's this here race for?" someone asked.

"You've seen Snow 'n Chapman runnin' their ponies," Coates said. "The Colonel's done got tired of them a braggin' all the time. He says it's time to put 'em to the test."

Word was posted through all forty saloons along Whiskey Row so that by the time of the horse race, more than a hundred people were gathered around the track at Fort Whipple.

"There's more 'n a thousand dollars that's been bet," someone in the crowd commented.

"Well, I reckon so, I got twenty dollars on it myself," another answered.

"All right, boys," Sandos called out. "In order to be fair, this race will be the best three out of five half-mile heats. Are you ready?"

Chapman and Snow brought their horses to the starting line.

"When you hear the starter's gun, the race is on."

Snow's horse began acting up, turning in circles.

"You better get that horse straightened out, Ike," someone shouted. "Lessin' you're a' plannin' on runnin' 'im backwards for the whole race."

The others laughed, and Sandos waited until Snow's horse was under control, then, he pulled the trigger.

Chapman's horse got away first, but Snow's horse caught up and passed him, winning the first heat by a half-neck. The cheers from the crowd were explosive and quickly another five hundred dollars was bet on Snow's horse.

The second heat was run in fifty-eight seconds, this one won by Chapman's horse. Again, the betting was vigorous.

"Damn, this was a good idea," Chapman said to Snow as once more they headed for the starting line.

"Yeah, I think we were asking for too little, when we said three hundred dollars."

The third heat was a clean get away for both horses, but Chapman's horse won by fifteen feet.

"What happened, Snow?" someone called. "Has your horse done give out?"

"Not yet," Ike called out. "I was just holdin' him back."

"Sure, you were."

On the fourth heat, Chapman did hold his horse back, allowing Snow's horse to win easily. Up to this point the betting had been two to one on Snow's horse, but after the fourth heat, the odds evened out.

On the fifth and last heat, Chapman put the quirt to his horse, and he bested Snow's horse with a time of fifty-six seconds.

"Now that was exciting," Sandos said as the two

horses were slowly walking around the track. "Meet me in front of the Defenders Headquarters and I'll be happy to pay out your bets."

It was a smaller and lighter coach than the commercial coaches that maintained scheduled routes. And because it was lighter, it was pulled by a team of only two horses. Barney Caruthers was driving, and Abe Yancy and Myles Horst were riding as guards.

"My kid wants to go to college to be a lawyer," Caruthers said. "Can you imagine that?"

"Yeah, I can imagine that. Lawyers are smart and Kenny's smart," Yancy said.

"Ha, he's only twelve years old, 'n he's already a hell of a lot smarter than his old man," Horst added.

As they rounded a curve, they saw four mounted men just ahead in the middle of the road.

"What's goin' on here?" Yancy asked, with a worried expression on his face.

"I don't know it's . . ." Caruthers started, then he stopped. "Ah, there ain't nothin' to worry about. Them's all Prescott Defenders."

"They ain't wearin' no uniforms," Yancy said.

"Yeah, they don't hardly do that no more, but I recognize all four of 'em. That's Dawes, Crawford, Evans and Newman. LaGrange prob'ly hired 'em to come escort us on back to the mine."

"Hello, boys," Caruthers said with a welcoming grin. "It's good to see you come here to meet us. LaGrange sent you out to ride with us, did he?"

"No, Sandos did," Muley replied.

"No matter, it's the same thing."

"Not hardly, it ain't," Muley said and then to the shock of Caruthers, Yancy and Horst, Muley and the three men with him, drew their pistols and began shooting.

After several shots were fired, the driver was slumped in his seat, and the two guards lay dead on the road, their shirts spattered with blood.

"Stop your shootin'!" Muley called out.

The gunfire stopped.

"They're all three more 'n likely dead anyhow, 'n we don't need some rancher showin' up wonderin' what the shootin' is all about."

"Yeah, let's get the money and get out of here," Crawford said.

"Not yet. Pick that one up 'n drape 'im over his horse," Muley said.

"What for?"

"We're goin' to take his body off some'rs else 'n hide it."

"What for?"

"It's somethin' me' the colonel has got all figured out," Muley said. "Ain't nothin' you got to worry about."

When the coach hadn't reached the Jersey Lily by four o'clock that afternoon, La Grange put his plan in action.

"Duncan, how about you and McCoy ride up toward Ash Fork and see if you can meet the coach. They haven't gotten back yet, and they should have been here by now."

A few minutes later, as the two men were saddling their horses, LaGrange came out to talk to them.

"I think you boys better wear your guns," he said.

"What for?" Duncan asked. "We're just goin' out to look for 'em, ain't we?"

"I don't know," La Grange said. "But I've just got a bad feeling about this."

Duncan and McCoy, now armed, had ridden more than five miles up the road toward Ash Fork.

"Duncan, have you ever shot at anyone before?" McCoy asked.

"Except for the war, I ain't," Duncan said.

"Me neither, 'n I ain't never been shot at, even in the war," McCoy said. "Don't know why Ivan's sendin' us out here like this. Seems to me like that ought to be the job of Yancy and Horst. They're the ones that's s'posed to be guards 'n all."

"They are, but they ain't here, 'cause they's the ones that went with Barney Caruthers," Duncan said.

"I wonder how much money they're bringin' back this time."

"It better be enough to pay us our back pay," Duncan said.

"They's a bringin' a hell of a lot more than that," McCoy said. "Do you ever wonder what you could do with that much money?"

"No, I ain't never goin' to have that much, so I don't worry none about it," Duncan said.

"Yeah, well it's sure enough to make a feller start in 'a wonderin', I mean like what all you'd do 'n . . . there, that looks like the coach on up ahead," McCoy said, pointing. "Hey, it ain't movin'. I wonder why not?"

"This ain't good," Duncan said.

The two men urged their horses into a gallop, but even before they reached the coach, they could see that one of the four horses was down.

"Oh damn, Duncan, look at that," McCoy said.

Barney Caruthers was slumped forward in the coach seat, covered with blood. Horst was on the ground, like Caruthers, covered with blood. Yancy was nowhere to be seen.

"Son of a bitch," Duncan said. "You know what happened here?"

"Well, yeah, they was robbed 'n kilt."

"Yeah, they was, 'n Yancy's the one that done it,"

Duncan said.

"What? Why do you say that?"

"Barney 'n Horst are both dead. Yancy's gone, 'n I bet if we check the coach, the money's gone too."

"Damn, I've know'd Yancy for more 'n a year. I never thought he'd do nothin' like this," McCoy said.

"What's this? Who's this comin'?" Duncan asked.

Duncan's question referred to four riders who were coming toward them.

"I don't know, but it don't look good."

"Oh, no, wait. I recognize two of 'em. Evans and Crawford are a couple of them Defenders," Duncan said.

"Yeah, 'n them other two is Dawes 'n Newman. I've run into 'em in the Plaza Bit. They're a couple of loud mouths," McCoy said.

The four riders stopped, then looked at the bodies of Caruthers and Horst.

"Did you two men do this?" Crawford asked, pointing at the two dead men.

"Hell no, we didn't do this," Duncan said. "You think if we done this, we'd still be here?"

"Beside which, Barney and Myles was our friends," McCoy added.

"I don't think they had nothin' to do with it, Crawford," Newman said.

"Yeah, you're right. If they did, they wouldn't still

be here, they would a' took the money 'n gone. You boys mind if we take 'em into town?" Crawford asked.

"No, why should we mind?" McCoy replied.

"Yeah, I'd just as soon not have anything to do with it," Duncan added.

"How we goin' to get 'em in town?" Dawes asked.

"We'll take a couple of horses from the team," Crawford said.

Duncan and McCoy watched as the four Defenders took two horses from the team that had been pulling the coach, draped Horst and Caruthers over the horses, then started back to town with them.

"You think one horse can pull this coach by hisself?" McCoy asked, looking at the one remaining horse.

"I reckon if we get him free from the dead horse, he can. We can connect mine, and I'll drive."

The two men worked to separate the remaining horse, connected Duncan's horse, and started back toward the mine.

Chapter Twenty - Six

While Sandos and Addie were having lunch in the coffee shop, several of the diners came over to say something about the race Sandos had put on.

"It was very exciting," Addie said. "But why didn't you put something in the paper about it?"

Sandos chuckled. "It wasn't something that was a long time in planning. Chapman and Snow got to bragging about which one of them had the fastest horse, so I thought this would be a good way to settle the argument."

"It was a good way," Addie replied with a broad smile. "The whole town has been talking about it. Oh, there's the winner now." She pointed toward the door through which Chapman had just passed. Addie saw him talking to the waitress who pointed to their table.

"He's coming to our table," Addie said. "I wonder what's up."

"Ha, he's probably wanting us to brag on him for a bit," Sandos said.

"No, I don't think so. He's got a rather strange expression on his face."

"Amos, what is it?" Sandos asked.

"Colonel, I thought you maybe should know."

"Know what?"

"You know the coach Ivan LaGrange hired to meet the train in Ash Fork. The one that was supposed to be goin' out to the Jersey Lily?"

"Yes, what about it?"

"Two men from the mine just brought in Caruthers 'n Horst—both of 'em shot dead."

"Mr. Caruthers? Oh, my, he has a wife and child," Addie said, shocked and saddened by the news.

"'N that ain't the all of it neither. They're sayin' it was Abe Yancy what done it."

"Are you sure it was Mr. Yancy?" Addie asked. "Why would you say that? Mr. Yancy has been coming into this coffee shop with his family every Sunday morning as soon as he leaves the church service. He's always been such a nice person."

"It's the nice ones you have to look out for," Sandos said.

"What does that mean?" Addie asked.

"I don't mean to be flippant, my dear," Sandos said. "It's

just that a lot of deceptive people hide their evil intent behind the façade of being nice. Apparently, Abe Yancy was just such a person."

"It's still hard to believe," Addie said. "I suppose there was money on the coach."

"I'm sure there was, but there's nothing we can do about it," Sandos said. "That's going to have to be handled by the law. Does Sheriff Bower know?"

"I don't know if he does or not," Chapman said.

"It might be a good idea for you to tell him," Sandos suggested.

"Sheriff Bower just has one deputy," Addie said. "Don't you think you ought to offer him help from the Defenders?"

"My dear, Sheriff Bower and Governor Fremont have both made it very clear that they are not interested in our help. You may remember that the governor revoked our status as deputies."

"But surely you can do something?" Addie pleaded.

"I'm sorry sweetheart, but our hands are tied. There's absolutely nothing we can do," Sandos said.

"Well, there's something I can do," Addie said. "I think I'll call on Mrs. Caruthers."

"Yes, do that, I'm sure she would appreciate it. Chapman, why don't you join me for a piece of pie? I see they have what looks like apricot over there in the pie safe."

Addie stood there looking at the two men at the table for a moment longer, feeling a disquieting sense of helplessness. How could they think about eating a piece of pie when two good men's lives had been lost?

There were half a dozen women with Emma Caruthers when Addie got there. Kenny, their twelve-year-old son, was sitting on the sofa, next to his mother, trying hard not to cry.

"Emma, I'm so sorry," Addie said. "If there's anything I can do for you, please let me know."

"I, I don't know what anyone can do for me now," Emma said. "Oh, what am I going to do without Barney?"

"Did you hear who did it?" one of the other women whispered. "It was Abe Yancy."

"That makes it even harder," Emma said. "Abe always sat next to us in church. He's always been a friend to Barney and me, and even to Kenny. To think that he would do something like this." Emma dabbed at her eyes with her handkerchief.

"Mama, I don't believe Mr. Yancy did it," Kenny said, speaking for the first time.

"I know, honey, we don't want to believe it," Emma replied. "But they found your papa and Mr. Horst with the coach. Abe Yancy and his horse were gone. And to make matters worse, the money is gone. It only stands to reason that if he's missing, and the money's gone, then Mr. Yancy was the one who took it."

"But he's always been so nice to us," Kenny said, not wanting to believe it.

Emma reached over to pat her son's hand. "Sweetheart, I know it's hard to believe, but nobody knew about the money except for your father and the two guards. And of course, Mr. LaGrange. No one would have tried to rob a stage that was just coming down from meeting the train."

TERRIBLE TRAGEDY

The Advocate has just received intelligence that a money shipment bound for the Jersey Lily Mine has been robbed. Myles Horst and Barney Caruthers, two of the three involved in transporting the money, were murdered. The third man charged with the task of delivering the money, Abe Yancy, is missing. All who are acquainted with Yancy think it is unlikely that he committed a deed so foul, but irrefutable evidence seems to point to him as the perpetrator.

The amount of money stolen is forty thousand dollars, an amount so great that Ivan LaGrange, foreman of the Jersey Lily Mine, says the work at the mine will be hard pressed to continue until more operating funds are received.

Out at the Axis mine, Will and Gid, unaware of the robbery and killings, had just emerged each with a wheelbarrow. They were about to dump them for their routine check for color, when they saw a rider approaching.

"Looks like we're getting company," Will said as he instinctively moved toward his rifle.

"No need for that, Big Brother. That's Nigel Housewright," Gid said with a broad smile. "He must want to see what a real gold mine looks like."

"No, I don't think so. Something has happened. Look at the expression on his face."

"Don't tell me he's going to say The Beatrice was burned down, or worse yet, something has happened to either Penny or Elaina," Gid said, now reflecting Will's worry.

Leaving the unemptied wheelbarrows behind them, Will and Gid walked out to meet Nigel.

"Hello, Nigel," Will said. His greeting was cordial, because he hoped he was misreading the expression on Nigel's face.

"The governor would like you two to get into town," Nigel said.

"The governor wants to see us? Do you know why?"

"I have an idea, yes," Nigel said. "Friday morning, there was a shipment of cash money coming down from Ash Fork that was going to the Jersey Lily. The coach was robbed and the driver and one of the two guards were killed."

"You say one of the two. What about the other guard? What happened to him?"

"His name is Abe Yancy, and nobody has seen him. The suspicion is that Yancy is the one who did it."

"I don't recognize that name. Would I have ever met him?" Gid asked.

"Probably not," Nigel said. "I don't think he was ever in The Beatrice. They say he was a good man who was a pillar of the church."

"Hmmm," Will said, "that seems a bit odd."

When Will, Gid, and Nigel, approached the governor's office, Will and Gid dismounted to tie off their horses, but Nigel remained in his saddle.

"Aren't you coming in with us?" Gid asked.

"No," Nigel replied. "When the governor asked me to summon you, he didn't give me a reason why he wanted to meet with you. I gathered from that, that he wished to keep his own council, so I will return to The Beatrice, and leave the three of you for a private visit."

"All right," Will said. "I understand."

Nigel smiled. "However, I do hope you will come to The Beatrice afterward, and share what you can of the meeting. I confess, it has aroused my curiosity."

"I think it goes without saying, that we will be at The Beatrice," Will said, returning Nigel's smile.

The two brothers watched Nigel ride away, then they started up the walk toward the large brick building.

"What do you think this is all about?" Gid asked.

"I don't know, Little Brother, but I'm sure we're about to find out. If I had to guess, I'd say it has something to do with the Jersey Lily missing money."

"Yes, gentlemen, may I . . ." the governor's secretary started, but he was interrupted by Fremont himself, who had stepped out from his office.

"That's all right, Jerome, I saw them coming. Will, Gid, please, come on into my office," Fremont said. "Would you like a cup of coffee?" He pointed to a coffee pot sitting over a small, kerosene burner.

"Yes, thank you," Will replied, as the governor poured three cups.

"Please, let's talk over here," Fremont said, pointing to a seating area in the corner of the room.

The area the governor pointed to had a round table and four chairs. The governor chose the chair opposite the door, while Will and Gid each chose a flanking chair.

"Gentlemen, I know you are wondering why I have asked you here, so I'll get right to the point. I also know that you have found good color out at the Axis, and my proposal will take you away from that for a while,"

Fremont said.

"Governor, after what you did for us, we'll do whatever you ask," Will said.

"That's good to hear." Fremont paused for a moment, then took a deep breath before he continued. "Do you remember when I asked you to be special territorial deputies? Well, now I would like to activate that request. I will issue a formal proclamation saying that I have commissioned you both as officers of the law for the Territory of Arizona. That means any part of the territory is within your jurisdiction, and your commission means that your authority will supersede all city marshals, all county sheriffs . . ."

"And the Prescott Defenders?" Will asked.

"Especially the Prescott Defenders," Fremont said. "Of course, this deputy position does not include authority over a United States Marshal, but how often do we see one in Yavapai County?"

"I think I can answer for the both of us, when I say we'll be glad to do it," Will said.

"Yes, that goes for me as well," Gid added. "And I say it'll be good to stop pushing a wheelbarrow for a while."

Fremont laughed. "That doesn't sound like a man who may have hit a bonanza."

"Governor, back to the Defenders. Are you asking us to do what we can to stop them? Will asked.

"That is exactly what I am asking—not so much as the governor, but as a private citizen of Prescott. That bunch of hoodlums has been tormenting this town long enough, and I say it has to stop."

"I know that since they aren't considered deputies anymore, they're calling themselves private detectives," Will said.

"That's right," Fremont said. "They tell people they provide insurance, but when they go after perpetrators, I would say they become private detectives. I believe they compare themselves to the Pinkertons."

"I think there needs to be an adjustment to their operation," Will said.

"What are you suggesting?"

"If you could in some way stop them from collecting their protection insurance from the merchants, that would cut off their source of income."

"I believe I could do that. An executive order prohibiting anyone from acting as a private detective agency without a license would stop them." Fremont smiled. "Then when they apply, I can refuse to grant them the license."

"That would work," Gid said.

"Then I shall do it this very day."

"What about the Jersey Lily money shipment?" Will said. "I expect you'll want us to look into that as well, won't you?"

"Yes, but I'm going to ask you to work with Sheriff Bower on that."

"All right, if you're ready for us, we'll start today."

"Yes, by all means start today," Governor Fremont said. "Your commission is effective immediately. Oh, and I feel I must be honest with you. Your commission will be without compensation. I'm afraid there are no funds in the territorial budget to cover your appointment."

"You gave us our lives, Governor. That's compensation enough," Will said.

Fremont rose from his chair and walked over to his desk to pick up two sheets of paper.

CERTIFICATE OF APPOINTMENT

Know all men by these Present

That the appointment of Territorial Marshal

Has been given to

William Crockett

Whose authority will encompass all cities, towns, and counties

Within the Borders of the Territory of Arizona

Given by authority of

John C. Fremont

Governor of the Territory of Arizona

Gideon Crockett received an identical license.

Fremont handed them their certificates, then picked up a couple of tin-stars. "I'm sorry, I intended to have special badges made, but Sheriff Bower willingly supplied these two deputy badges which, with your certificate of appointment, will provide all the validation you need." He then asked Will and Gid to raise their right hand.

"Repeat after me."

As Governor Fremont mouthed the words of the oath of office, Will and Gid repeated them.

"I do solemnly swear that I will perform with fidelity the duties of Territorial Marshal for the Territory of Arizona, and that I will faithfully discharge the duties of the office to the best of my skill and ability."

Fremont handed each of them a badge, then shook their hands.

"Gentlemen, I would tell you that you are now on the payroll of the Territory of Arizona." He chuckled. "That is, if we had a payroll."

***

When Will and Gid stepped into The Beatrice later, they were greeted with a round of applause from Nigel, Sheriff Bower, Ben Weaver, Ki, Penny, Elaina, and half a dozen of the regular customers.

"How did you know about this?" Gid asked. "We haven't told anyone yet."

"Who do you think printed your certificates?" Ben Weaver asked. "I couldn't keep that to myself."

"Are you all right with this, Sheriff?" Will asked.

Bower chuckled. "How do you think Fremont got the idea? I'm the one who asked him to do this. Have a drink on me, then come on down to the office so we can talk about some things you need to know."

"Sheriff, you will do no such thing," Nigel said. Then he smiled. "They will have a drink on me, then they will go to your office with you."

Chapter Twenty - Seven

"I'm sure you've been told that a money shipment coming to the Jersey Lily was robbed," Sheriff Bower said.

"Yes, we've heard that," Gid said. "In fact, Governor Fremont suggested that we might work with you on that."

"Good, I can use your help," Bower said. "I know before you came to Prescott, you were known as bounty hunters."

"That's not exactly true," Will said. "We did go after men who were wanted, and we did collect bounties, but to say that's all we did was wrong."

"Well, whatever you call it, I want you to find Abe Yancy if you can."

"Yancy is the missing courier who took the money," Gid said.

Sheriff Bower was quiet for a long moment.

"Wait a minute, you don't think he did take the

money, do you?" Will asked.

"It doesn't fit with anything I, or anyone else, knows about Abe Yancy. Abe and I came here from Colorado together. I'd been a sheriff up there, and Abe was one of my deputies. When I got hired on as sheriff down here, I tried to hire him too, but the Jersey Lily offered him more money to be a guard, and he took it. I don't blame him for it, either.

Abe was a good church goin' man; there was absolutely nothing about him that would ever make you think he'd do such a thing."

"Forty thousand dollars is quite a temptation," Will said.

"Let me ask you this. If either one of you had been hired to ride guard for that money shipment, would you murder two of your good friends and steal the money?"

"No."

"Neither would Abe Yancy."

"Sheriff . . ."

"Call me Ed. We're both in the law-keepin' business now."

"All right, Ed, you said you told Fremont to hire us. It was because you don't think Yancy did this, isn't it?"

"I know damn well, he didn't."

"Do you have an idea who might have done it?"

"Yeah, I've got an idea."

"Who?"

"I'd rather not say, yet. I want you two to sniff around for a while and see if you come up with the same idea."

"I think we may already have the same idea," Will said.

"All right, who do you think it was?"

"It has all the markings of a Sandos operation."

"That's what I think, too," Bower said. "Well, not him personally. On the day the money was taken, Sandos was seen all over the place, so it couldn't have been him."

"What do you mean, seen all over the place?"

Sheriff Bower told Will and Gid about the race out at Whipple Park that Sandos had organized. He also explained that more than a hundred people had watched the race and could provide witness that Sandos and his men were in town, while the robbery was being committed.

"So that gives him an air-tight alibi, doesn't it," Will said. "That's convenient."

"Yeah, a little too convenient if you ask me," Sheriff Bower said.

"Two of the three money shipment couriers were found. Who found them?"

"The bodies were brought in by Dawes, Newman, Evans, and Crawford," Bower said.

"Let me guess, they're Sandos' men."

"Good guess."

"I wonder how it was that those four got away from

the race so quick," Gid said.

"I think we need to have a visit with Mr. Sandos," Will said.

When Will and Gid stepped into the headquarters building of the Prescott Defenders, they heard laughter coming from another room.

"How much money did we make off the bettin'?" someone asked.

"Two hundred and ten dollars." Will recognized the second voice as Jubal Sandos.

"So, me 'n Snow get a hunnert 'n five dollars each?"

"You and Snow get five dollars apiece. The rest of the money will stay with the group for operating expenses."

"As much money as we've done took in, seems to me like there's already enough for operatin' expenses."

"Sandos?" Will called out.

"What the hell? Who's out there?"

"Sandos, my brother and I want to talk to you," Will replied.

Sandos and three others came into the room at the front of the building.

"If it isn't the Crocketts," Sandos said. "Now that you've found gold, I'll just bet you're here to take out our insurance."

"We want to talk to you about the money shipment

robbery."

"Why the hell should I talk to you about that?"

"Because this says so," Will said as he pointed to the badge he was wearing. "We've been appointed territorial deputies, and we have an interest in that robbery."

"You know you're wasting your time coming here. On the day of the robbery, I was putting on a horse race—that was attended by at least a hundred people. Any one of those men or women will testify in a court of law that they saw me and my men out at the Whipple track at the same time the robbery would have taken place. So, I think you're barking up the wrong tree," Sandos said as he turned to go back to the room where he had been.

"And yet, Dawes, Newman, Evans, and Crawford are the ones who found the bodies. Aren't they your men?"

"They are," Sandos said as he stopped and turned around. "Are you accusing them? Most people, especially Emma Caruthers and Myles Horst's mama, are glad they found the bodies and brought them in for a decent burial. If those four had anything to do with the robbery, do you really think they would've brought the bodies back to town? No, they would have taken the money and run. Even you aren't too stupid to see that."

"As we understand it, there were the driver and two men escorting the money shipment, but only two bodies were brought in."

"Yeah, Abe Yancy wasn't brought in. To a thinking man, the fact that his body wasn't found should be enough evidence to prove that he's the guilty party. It's quite obvious he killed the other two, took the money, and by now, has left the territory."

"On the other hand, if Yancy isn't guilty, that's exactly what the actual robbers would want you to think, isn't it?"

"Crockett, if you've got something on me or my men, then make your charge. Otherwise, get out of my office," Sandos said, harshly.

"Oh, we're going to," Will said, as he and Gid started toward the door. Just before he left, he turned and flashed a sarcastic smile toward Sandos. "Make our charge, I mean."

They found Newman and Crawford in the Plaza Bit Saloon. They had two of the girls at their table, and everyone was laughing.

"Those two seem to be having a good time," Gid said, as he and Will stepped up to the bar.

"They ain't the only ones havin' a good time," one of the others at the bar said. "They've done bought a round of drinks for ever' one of us."

Will nodded, then he and Gid stepped over to the table.

"Ladies, I wonder if you'd excuse us," Will said. "We need to talk to these two men."

"What the hell?" Newman said. "You can't just come

up here 'n send our women away."

"Like I said, my brother and I want to have a conversation with you two. Now, we can talk here, or we can arrest you, and talk to you in jail."

"What do mean arrest us? You ain't got no authority to arrest us," Crawford said.

"Yeah, we do," Will replied, tapping his deputy's badge.

"Come on, Sally," one the girls said to the other one. "Let's let these gentlemen talk."

"Damnit," Crawford said. "You done run our women off. So, what the hell is it you want to talk about?"

"We understand that you and your buddies are the ones who brought back the bodies of Barney Caruthers and Myles Horst."

"Yeah, we did," Newman said. Suddenly the frown on his face was replaced with a smile. "Hey, are we gettin' a reward for that?"

"Well, I'm sure you can understand that we'll have to investigate it thoroughly before we can authorize a reward," Will said, seizing on the opportunity.

"All right, what do you want to know?"

"Tell us how you found them?"

"Me 'n him, 'n Dawes 'n Evans was just out for a ride when we seen the Jersey Lily coach just 'a standin' there on the road, 'n Caruthers was slumped in the seat, 'n Horst's body was lyin' on the road right along side 'im."

"You only saw two bodies?" Will asked.

"Yeah, that's all we seen."

"Where was this?"

"It was about half-way betwixt where Granite crick ends, 'n the south bow of the Juniper Mountains."

"Thank you, you've been very helpful," Will said.

"Does that mean we'll be gettin' our reward?"

"I'm afraid we'll need to do a little more investigating," Will said. "But we'll let you know."

"What do you mean, you're going to get a reward?" Sandos asked, his aggravation shown by the harshness of his voice.

"It's what the Crocketts said. They say they got to do a little more investigatin', then they can pay me 'n Crawford, 'n them a reward for findin' the bodies." Newman laughed. "It's kind 'a funny when you think about it, ain't it? I mean we're the ones that kilt 'em, 'n now we're goin' to get a reward for findin' their bodies."

"There is nothing at all funny about it, you ignorant fool," Sandos said.

"You ain't got no call to be mad at me," Newman said.

"Get out of my sight."

Newman, still confused as to why Sandos was angry with him, left the headquarters office with a hurt expression on his face.

"Chapman," Sandos said after Newman left.

"Yes, sir?"

"Take care of Newman. Take care of all four of those idiots."

"Take care of 'em?" Chapman asked, not sure what Sandos meant.

"Kill them. Kill all four of them. Get Snow to go with you. You and Snow can split up their share of the money."

Chapman smiled broadly. "Yes, sir," he said emphatically.

* * *

"Look up there," Will said, pointing. "I wonder what's causing those vultures to gather like that."

"I'll bet it's something bigger than a fox or a wolf. Let's check it out."

When they followed the vultures into the trees, they found a body, half out of a shallow grave. The vultures and other wild creatures had been active enough so there wasn't enough of the body remaining to be recognized.

"Damn, Will, look at that," Gid said, pointing.

Will looked where Gid directed him, and when he did, he saw what Gid saw. The body was wearing a leather belt, and on the belt was the name:

ABE YANCY

"What are we going to do with him?" Gid asked.

"We're going to borrow a wagon and a tarpaulin from the nearest rancher that's around here. Then we'll take this body into town," Will said.

"There are going to be some surprised people."

"Yes, I'm sure there will be. But we need to think about how we're going to let the others know."

"We're going to let the sheriff know, aren't we?" Gid asked.

"Yes. I figure we can discuss the best way to go about this with him."

Three hours later Will and Gid reappeared in Prescott, driving the borrowed wagon with their horses trailing along behind. Because the body was under a tarpaulin, nobody noticed, nor even paid any attention to them.

They parked the wagon in front of the sheriff's office, then went inside where they were greeted by Deputy Burns.

"Howdy, fellas," he said.

"Is Ed in?"

"Yeah, I think he just stepped out to the privy, he'll be back in . . . oh, there he is now."

"You're back earlier than I thought you would be," Sheriff Bower said.

"Come out to the wagon, Ed. We found something you

should see," Will said.

Sheriff Bower followed the two men out to the wagon, where Gid pulled back the tarpaulin.

"Son of a bitch!" Sheriff Bower said. "That's Abe."

"I'm surprised there's enough of him left for you to be able to tell," Will said.

"I told you, Abe and I were friends, and had served together. There doesn't have to be all that much of him left for me to know who it is. But here's the clincher." Bower pointed to his left hand. "Notice that he has only half of his little finger."

"I thought some critter got it," Gid said.

Bower shook his head. "He cut it off while he was skinning a deer. Bled like a stuck pig too, I'll tell you."

"Yes, well, we already knew it was Yancy," Will said. He lifted the canvas to show the belt.

"Oh, yeah, Abe was really proud of that belt. Where did you find 'im?"

"He wasn't more than a quarter mile from where the robbery took place."

"That's proof he didn't do it," Bower said. "But I didn't need proof. I knew damn well Abe didn't do it."

"Whoever did do it, wanted the blame to fall on Yancy," Will said. "They killed him and then buried him, hoping everyone would think he ran away. But they didn't bury him deep enough, and wolves, or a coyote, or maybe a cougar, dug away enough dirt that the top half of him was exposed."

"I'll be glad to tell his friends that Abe had nothing to do with this whole thing."

"Yes, but let's do it in such a way that the people who did do it, are going to worry about it," Will proposed.

"You got 'ny idea how to do that?" Bower asked.

"Yeah," Will answered with a smile. "I think I do."

Chapter Twenty – Eight

"And you want me to say nothing of this?" Ben Weaver asked.

"We do want you to write the story," Will said. "But we don't want you to speak of it, until the paper comes out."

"But the proof of Abe's innocence is wonderful news that will be appreciated by all of his friends. Why shouldn't I speak of it?"

"We want not only to establish Yancy's innocence, we also want to determine who the real guilty party or parties may be," Will said. "And we believe that the unexpected impact of seeing the article in the paper could be so startling that it might lead the guilty ones into making a mistake, a mistake that we can use to get to the bottom of this."

Weaver smiled, broadly.

"It will be the most significant issue of anything I've done since I've begun publishing in Prescott."

"How soon will the paper be on the street?" Will asked.

"People will be reading it over their breakfast coffee tomorrow morning," Weaver said.

ABE YANCY INNOCENT

In the recent, tragic robbery of the Jersey Lily Mine's money shipment, family, friends, and even the citizens of our community lamented the death, by murder, of Barney Caruthers and Myles Horst. But to add insult to injury, the third member of the trio of couriers, Abe Yancy, was missing.

The immediate belief, of course, was that Yancy was the guilty party. It was posited by all that it was Yancy who murdered the men who trusted him and, after that treachery, stole the money and made good his escape.

But that speculation has now been proven false. Abe Yancy's partially buried body was discovered near where the robbery occurred. His hasty grave was so shallow that his remains were easily exposed by carrion. It is now obvious that he was murdered, just as were his two friends. Those who perpetrated the foul deed of murder and robbery chose to bury Abe Yancy as a means of misleading the investigation, and for a short while the ruse worked. The disappearance of Yancy led all to believe that he was the guilty party, but the subsequent discovery of his body proves that he was innocent of the crime. Abe Yancy's many friends, while saddened that he, like Caruthers and Horst, was murdered, will also be relieved to know that the terrible stain of guilt has been lifted from him.

Yancy's body was discovered, and the renewed investigation of the robbery has been undertaken by Will and Gid Crockett. It should be noted that the Crockett brothers hold Governor Fremont's commission as Territorial Marshals. This newspaper is well aware of the exploits of these two men, and we predict an early resolution of the crime.

"Oh, my, Papa, look at this!" Addie said as she was reading the newspaper the next morning. "Mr. Yancy is innocent."

"What do you mean innocent?" Biff asked. "You mean he didn't run away with the money?"

"He didn't run away anywhere. Will and Gid found his body. Apparently, he was killed at the same time Mr. Caruthers and Mr. Horst were."

"I'm sorry that he was killed, but happy that his innocence has been established," Biff said.

"Yes, that's right isn't it? Here I was celebrating that Mr. Yancy is innocent, and I can only celebrate that because he was found dead."

"You say Will and Gid found his body?"

"Yes, that's what it says here."

"I wonder how Jubal Sandos will take that news."

"Why, why should you even have to ask such a thing? I'm sure he will receive the news just as everyone else will—sadness because Mr. Yancy was killed, but a sense of appreciation that the accusation against him has been proven false."

"You're sure he'll be glad to hear of Abe's innocence?" Biff asked.

"Of course I'm sure. Why wouldn't he be?"

"Why indeed?"

"Did you take care of Newman?" Sandos asked.

"Just like you said, Colonel. I took care of all of 'em, Newman, Dawes, Evans, and Crawford," Chapman said.

"Good. Newman couldn't keep his mouth shut, and that's how the Crocketts found Yancy."

"Hell, they would've never found his body if the dumb bastards had buried him deep enough," Chapman said.

"What did you do with their bodies?"

Chapman laughed. "Ha! Me 'n Snow dumped 'em down in one of them abandoned mines out west of town. I wish they was some way we could make it look like the Crocketts done it."

"It wouldn't make any difference. They're such close friends with Sheriff Bower now, he probably wouldn't arrest them, and if he did the governor would cut them loose again."

"Not necessarily," Judge Briggs said, speaking for the first time.

"What do you mean, not necessarily?" Sandos asked.

"Do you like it that the governor took away your ability to collect insurance money?"

"Of course not," Sandos said.

"There's a way to remedy that," Briggs said.

"How?"

"By making you governor."

"Ha!" Chapman said. "How you goin' to make Jubal governor?"

"Arizona does not have the office of lieutenant governor," Briggs said. "If something were to happen to Fremont so that he was no longer able to serve, a new governor would have to be appointed. As a judge with territorial authority, I could appoint Jubal as temporary governor, until it was made official by President Hayes."

"President Hayes, yes!" Sandos said. "I served with him during the war."

"And I was his judge advocate," Briggs said. "We would have no trouble getting you appointed."

"We're goin' to have to get us some more people," Chapman said. "They's only four of us left now, me 'n you, Snow 'n Coates."

"Once we take out the Crocketts, we won't need any more than four," Sandos said. "And look at this way. There's that much more money for each of us."

"Gentlemen," Briggs said with a little chuckle, "as soon as you kill the Crocketts and take care of Fremont, you'll be looking at Governor Sandos of Arizona."

Addie couldn't breathe. She had come to the Prescott Defenders headquarters to tell Jubal, what she thought was good news that Abe Yancy wasn't the one who robbed and killed the others, but as soon as she entered the reception area, she could overhear the conversation taking place in Jubal's office.

They had just confessed to murdering Yancy and the other Jersey Lily couriers; they had also killed Newman, Dawes, Evans, and Crawford, and now they were planning to kill, not only the Crocketts, but the governor as well. How could she have misjudged Jubal so? And here, all this time, she had thought she was in love with him.

She was about to confront Jubal with what she had just heard, but she realized that if she did that, she would be in great danger. She turned to leave and opening and closing the door as quietly as she could, she walked around beside the building, then ran down the alley. When she pushed into the sheriff's office a moment later, she was gasping for breath.

"For heaven's sake, Addie, what's wrong?" Deputy Burns asked.

"They're going to kill him! Jubal and the Defenders are going to kill the governor!"

"How do you know?"

Before Addie could answer, Chapman and Snow came into the room with drawn pistols.

"See there, Amos, I told you I seen her sneakin' away from the headquarters building," Ike Snow said.

"I guess you did. Come along, Missy. You'll be comin' with us," Chapman said.

"And just why would I do such a thing?"

"Because, if you don't, we're goin' to kill you," Chapman said.

"Look here, you can't just come in here and . . ." Deputy Burns started to say, but his challenge was interrupted by a gunshot, and Burns went down with his hand clasped over the wound in his stomach.

* * *

It was Elaina who found him. She had stopped by to bring him a biscuit and bacon for his breakfast.

"Jimmie, guess what? Have you seen Mr. Weaver's . . ." Elaina stopped in mid-sentence when she saw Burns lying on the floor. He was holding a bloody hand over a wound in his stomach. "Oh, my God, Jimmie!" she shouted.

Elaina hurried to him, then knelt beside him.

"Elaina, tell Ed that the Prescott Defenders took Addie Reed, and they're going to kill the governor."

"I don't care. You're hurt and I'm going after the

doctor," Elaina insisted.

"No, you can't, Elaina. Find the sheriff and tell him what I told you. Then you go get the doc. Now, hurry!"

Nigel and Penny, Sheriff Bower, and Will and Gid, were sharing biscuits and bacon that Penny had made for all of them. Someone must have said something funny, because they were all laughing when Elaina pushed through the swinging doors into The Beatrice.

"Elaina, what are you . . ."

"They shot Jimmie!" Elaina shouted.

"Who shot him? Where is he?"

"The Prescott Defenders shot him. He's lying on the floor in the sheriff's office," Elaina gasped out. "They've got Miss Reed, and they're going to kill the governor!"

"Ed, you do what you must do," Nigel said. "Elaina, you summon the doctor. I'll see to Jimmie."

"Nigel, I'm coming with you," Penny said.

Chapman and Snow hurried Addie from the sheriff's office to the Prescott Defenders headquarters building. They shoved her inside.

"What is this?" Sandos asked. "What is she doing here?"

"She heard us talking," Chapman said.

"And then she went down to the sheriff's office to tell him what she heard," Snow added.

"Did you take care of the sheriff?"

"He wasn't there," Chapman said. "Burns was, and we killed him."

"Addie, you would betray me like that?"

"Betray you? What do you mean betray you? I had no idea I had fallen in love with a . . . a murderer. And you say you want to kill the governor? You are insane."

"What do you want to do with her, Colonel?" Chapman asked.

"Leave her here, with me. I'll deal with her. You take care of your business and be damn quick about it."

Sheriff Bower had gone to the governor's office to protect him, while Will and Gid decided they were going to meet the issue head on. They started toward the Defenders headquarters.

"If you're going to kill a snake, you cut off its head," Will said. "And Sandos is the head."

"Yeah, but it looks like we're going to have to take care of the snake before we get to its head."

"I see what you mean," Will said, noticing the men Gid was talking about.

"There they are!" Chapman shouted, and he snapped a shot off toward Will and Gid.

Will returned fire and saw a little spray of blood and brain matter as Chapman went down. Gid's shot took down Snow, and Will finished off Dan Coates, who had fired a wild shot toward him. Now the only threat remaining would be from inside the headquarters building.

Sandos was holding his gun, looking out through the window. Addie was standing behind him.

"Damn! The Crocketts killed Chapman, Coates and Snow."

"That means you're all alone now," Addie said. "Why don't you give yourself up?"

"And hang? No thank you."

"Then what are you going to do? Will and Gid took care of your men. You don't stand a chance against them."

"Oh, yes I do," Sandos said. "They won't want you to die, and if I come out with you, they'll drop their guns, or else I'll kill you."

"Or I will kill you," Addie said, quietly.

"What?" Surprised by Addie's comment, Sandos turned around to see Addie standing behind him, holding a Derringer, six inches from his head.

She pulled the trigger.

For the rest of the summer, Will and Gid worked diligently at the Axis, recovering more than three thousand dollars in gold. After one particularly long and arduous day, they were resting in front of their hut when two riders approached them.

"Who do you think that is," Will asked as he poured out the coffee grounds that were left in the now empty pot.

"They both look sort of familiar, but I can't recall either of their names," Gid said. He pulled the skin back that led into the hut and grabbed his gun that was nearby. "We'll be ready for whoever it is."

When the two men got within a hundred yards of the hut, they dismounted and walked up the narrow path, leaving their horses ground tethered.

One man was very much out of breath.

"Whew, I had no idea how isolated you are up here," he said as he took off his hat and wiped his brow.

"That's the way we like it," Gid said. "Keeps away anybody who might want to steal something."

"You don't recall meeting me do you? I'm Joseph Reynolds and Governor Fremont introduced us at the miners' ball."

"And I'm Frank Bugbee."

"You're Diamond Jo," Gid said. "Yes, I do remember meeting you—and you're Frank . . .?"

"Bugbee. I had just bought the Hidden Treasure claim when we met. It's on the back side of the mountain a little closer to the Jersey Lily."

"Have you met with any success?" Will asked.

"Not to the degree that you boys have," Frank said, "but that brings us to why Diamond Jo and I are here."

"Yes, I believe when we met, I was on my way to a new mining district that is showing very positive results," Reynolds said. "I intend to invest in a property in the Date Creek Mountains, but in the meantime, I would like to have a stake on Lynx Creek."

"And . . .?" Gid urged.

"I was wondering if you would consider selling the Axis. Frank has agreed to sell the Hidden Treasure, but to make the investment worthwhile, I need a bigger stake, and I would like to purchase your claim if you'd be willing to accept my offer."

"It depends on what your offer is," Will said.

"Would thirty thousand dollars be to your liking?" Reynolds asked.

"Yes!" Gid said not waiting to confer with Will. "We'll take it!"

Frank smiled. "One Crockett has agreed. What about the other one?"

"I was going to say let us sleep on it, but I guess my brother's already put his two cents in, so what can I do but go along with him?"

"Thank you, thank you," Frank said as he hurried to shake their hands.

"I think he's happy," Will said.

"And so am I," Gid said. "I wasn't cut out to be a miner."

It took only a couple of days for Will and Gid to clear out their belongings at the mine. After trying to explain to Woman what was going to happen and saying goodbye to the placer miners on Lynx Creek, they headed into Prescott. It took less than a week for the completion of the paperwork for the transfer of title to the Axis, and for the delivery of the bank draft finalizing the transaction. It was with both joy and sadness that they headed for The Beatrice to tell their friends goodbye. There, they learned that Nigel and Penny were going to be married.

"Well, congratulations," Will said.

"We're going to be married in London," Penny said, happily.

"Is that right? Well, it'll be good to visit where Nigel grew up," Gid said.

"It isn't a visit, we're moving there," Nigel said.

"Oh? You don't think there'll be a problem?" Will asked.

"Queen Victoria has given me the title of Baron, and I'm going to be able to resume my musical career," Nigel said. He chuckled. "Apparently, the Secretary to the Sovereign is no longer concerned that I might make an attempt to claim the crown."

"What about The Beatrice?" Gid asked.

"I've given it to my loyal and faithful friend, Ki."

"Perfect," Gid said. "That's really good of you, Nigel. Uh, Baron. Uh, what do I call you now?"

Nigel chuckled. "I would hope that you would call me your friend. And as a friend, you would call me Nigel."

"Then Nigel it is," Gid said, with a wide smile.

Sheriff Bower came into the saloon then. "I saw you two going this way so I figured you'd be here," he said. "I didn't want to let you get away without saying goodbye."

"We were going to stop by before we left. How's Burns doing?"

"Just fine. Dr. McCandless said he's a very lucky man, but he should be back on the job before winter."

"I think it's because he's had such a good nurse," Ki said. "Elaina ain't been worth a damn since Jimmie got shot. All she wants to do is tend to him."

"She's tending to her future husband," Penny said as she smiled at Nigel.

"I'm glad everything is working out for everyone," Will said. "The town should be in good shape now that there aren't any Defenders around."

"Speaking of which, there's something you might want to hear," the sheriff said.

"Oh?" Will asked.

"It turns out that our late friend kept a meticulous ledger. Jubal wrote down every penny that he took in, and a quick look at those books turned up a couple of interesting things. One, as we already suspected, was that Judge Briggs was on Sandos' payroll. While you've been up on the mountain, he was tried, convicted and sentenced to twenty years in a federal prison. No doubt some of the people he sent up will be happy to see him."

Will laughed. "No doubt."

"Oh, and the robbery of the money shipment that was coming to the Jersey Lily mine. . ."

"Yes, what happened to it?" Gid asked.

"We found it in a safe in Sandos' office," Bower said. "But there's even more. Sandos' ledger told how Ivan LaGrange was supposed to get two thousand for setting up the whole robbery. He was also indicted and is looking at twenty years in prison."

Will smiled. "Well that pretty much ends the reign of the Prescott Defenders."

"It does, but we couldn't have done it without you two," Sheriff Bower said. "Is there any way we could get you to stay? The territory needs good men."

"No, it's time to move on," Will said.

"Where will you go?" Penny asked.

"We don't really know," Gid said. "For the first time in our lives we have a piece of real money, so it might be good to think about some way to hang on to it."

"Does that mean you'll be settling down somewhere?" Nigel asked.

"It's hard to say," Will said. "We need to do a lot of thinking."

If You Liked This, You Might Like: Lou Prophet: The Complete Series, Volume 1

Lou Prophet's life as a bounty hunter has taught him one rule: You don't stop riding till the job is finished. Prophet is repeatedly caught in bloody crossfires and he is determined to show the outlaws that justice doesn't always wear a badge.

Join the bounty hunter as he searches for a gorgeous showgirl, chases down a brutal gang, protects his partner at all costs, escorts a Russian noblewoman on an Arizona trail and captures stage-robbers!

"A storyteller who knows the West."—Bill Brooks

Lou Prophet: The Complete Series, Volume 1 includes – The Devil and Lou Prophet, Riding With the Devil's Mistress, The Devil Gets His Due, Staring Down the Devil, and The Devil's Lair.

AVAILABLE NOW ON AMAZON

About the Author

Robert Vaughan sold his first book when he was 19. That was 57 years and nearly 500 books ago. He wrote the novelization for the mini-series Andersonville. Vaughan wrote, produced, and appeared in the History Channel documentary Vietnam Homecoming.

His books have hit the NYT bestseller list seven times. He has won the Spur Award, the PORGIE Award (Best Paperback Original), the Western Fictioneers Lifetime Achievement Award, received the Readwest President's Award for Excellence in Western Fiction, is a member of the American Writers Hall of Fame and is a Pulitzer Prize nominee.

Vaughan is also a retired army officer, helicopter pilot with three tours in Vietnam. And received the Distinguished Flying Cross, the Purple Heart, The Bronze Star with three oak leaf clusters, the Air Medal for valor with 35 oak leaf clusters, the Army Commendation Medal, the Meritorious Service Medal, and the Vietnamese Cross of Gallantry.

CPSIA information can be obtained
at www.ICGtesting.com
Printed in the USA
LVHW041031241121
704328LV00010B/1136